David's finger stroked down her back, following the arc of her spine

Ashley smiled, but kept firmly to her side of the bed.

"You make me feel cheap," he finally said, no trace of hurt, only humor in his voice. David continued to talk, his finger trying to coax her closer. "I know you're only here to use and abuse me, but I have needs, too."

At that, Ashley stared at him suspiciously.

"You think of me as just a fast-action pump and drill, variable speed settings and excellent torque, but I have feelings, and when you turn away from me…" He looked at her, hazel eyes dancing, and sniffed.

"What do you want?" she asked cautiously, not quite trusting appearances, but willing to go with it, because he made her take chances she didn't want to take.

He grinned. "I don't know. But I need to feel you respect me."

Ashley scooched close to him. "I respect you."

He sniffed again. "I need you to like me for my mind, not just the awesome sex."

Dear Reader,

When I started this story, I knew it would be a long-distance-relationship book, and I needed something to keep Ashley grounded in Chicago. It needed to be something more than business, something more than love for the city.

A family who needs her?

Families are a sticky and messy business, the rubber cement that can stretch and pull but never seems to let go. And even later, when you think it's gone, you find the stray piece of glue tacked to a finger, or stuck to the kitchen table, and you realize that glue will always be a part of you no matter how hard you try to wash it off. In many ways, that's exactly what a family is—the good and the bad all rolled into one congealed, rubbery ball.

The world seems to idealize the family unit, yet the reality is often so much more elastic—and interesting.

I hope you enjoy the read.

Best,

Kathleen O'Reilly

Hot Under Pressure

KATHLEEN O'REILLY

TORONTO • NEW YORK • LONDON
AMSTERDAM • PARIS • SYDNEY • HAMBURG
STOCKHOLM • ATHENS • TOKYO • MILAN • MADRID
PRAGUE • WARSAW • BUDAPEST • AUCKLAND

If you purchased this book without a cover you should be aware that this book is stolen property. It was reported as "unsold and destroyed" to the publisher, and neither the author nor the publisher has received any payment for this "stripped book."

Recycling programs
for this product may
not exist in your area.

ISBN-13: 978-0-373-79489-8

HOT UNDER PRESSURE

Copyright © 2009 by Kathleen Panov.

All rights reserved. Except for use in any review, the reproduction or utilization of this work in whole or in part in any form by any electronic, mechanical or other means, now known or hereafter invented, including xerography, photocopying and recording, or in any information storage or retrieval system, is forbidden without the written permission of the publisher, Harlequin Enterprises Limited, 225 Duncan Mill Road, Don Mills, Ontario M3B 3K9, Canada.

This is a work of fiction. Names, characters, places and incidents are either the product of the author's imagination or are used fictitiously, and any resemblance to actual persons, living or dead, business establishments, events or locales is entirely coincidental.

This edition published by arrangement with Harlequin Books S.A.

® and TM are trademarks of the publisher. Trademarks indicated with ® are registered in the United States Patent and Trademark Office, the Canadian Trade Marks Office and in other countries.

www.eHarlequin.com

Printed in U.S.A.

ABOUT THE AUTHOR

First published in 2001, Kathleen O'Reilly is an award-winning author of more than twenty romances, with more books on the way. Reviewers have been lavish in their praise, applauding her "biting humor," "amazing storytelling" and "sparkling characters." She lives in New York with her husband, two children and one indestructible goldfish. Please contact the author at kathleenoreilly@earthlink.net or by mail at P.O. Box 312, Nyack, NY 10960.

Books by Kathleen O'Reilly

HARLEQUIN BLAZE
297—BEYOND BREATHLESS*
309—BEYOND DARING*
321—BEYOND SEDUCTION*
382—SHAKEN AND STIRRED**
388—SEX, STRAIGHT UP**
394—NIGHTCAP**

*The Red Choo Diaries
**Those Sexy O'Sullivans

Don't miss any of our special offers. Write to us at the following address for information on our newest releases.

Harlequin Reader Service
U.S.: 3010 Walden Ave., P.O. Box 1325, Buffalo, NY 14269
Canadian: P.O. Box 609, Fort Erie, Ont. L2A 5X3

For booksellers everywhere.
Stacey, Anne, Elsie,
I'm looking at you.

1

ASHLEY LARSEN climbed over the family of three, mumbling "excuse me," but honestly, in the wide-bodied jet, there was no elegant way to get to her seat with her dignity intact—especially since darling little Junior kept poking her in the rear and laughing maniacally. All the while Mom tried to pretend that nothing was amiss.

Little booger.

With a tight smile plastered on her face, Ashley climbed over the skanky-handed hellion, and then plopped into her seat with a relieved sigh. She hated the five seats in the center aisle. What designer thought *that* was a good idea? Especially on a day like today, when the direct route to her seat was blocked by the sweet little old lady who wanted to stuff the three-foot antique lamp into the overhead compartment. Patiently, the flight attendant was explaining how honestly, truly, cross her heart, the baggage handlers would treat the fragile piece with care. Stubbornly, the little old lady wasn't buying it for a minute, and Ashley wished her all the luck in the world. Thank God that was over; now on to the real death-defying feat— preparing for takeoff. After a slow count to three hundred— twice—she pulled the plastic bag from her carry-on and then pushed the suitcase back under the seat in front of her. Furiously she kicked off her travel shoes with some previously unleashed aggression, and then donned fluffy pink bunny slippers. If she was going to die in the air, she wanted to be with at least one thing close to her heart.

Ashley hated flying. Her sister Valerie called it her Erica Jong moment, but it wasn't sex that Ashley was afraid of, only moving through the skies at supersonic speeds, a gazillion feet off the ground. Physics had never been her best subject, and besides, she knew there was something seriously wrong with the concept. However, she hated the idea of being a slave to her fears, so, as a survival mechanism she had created her flying ritual. Every month, when she took off from O'Hare airport on her latest buying trip, she meticulously followed the same pattern to maintain sanity. Whatever worked.

Soon everyone was seated, the antique lamp was stored below and the flight attendant droned the standard disclaimers about pulling away from the gate in ten minutes. Just as Ashley had properly prepared herself for takeoff, another passenger made his way down the aisle, claiming the one remaining empty seat in the airplane. The one between Ashley and Mr. and Mrs. American Family, who were futilely trying to keep Junior amused. *Now* they decided to resume their parental responsibility. Couldn't they have done it earlier, when he was playing pin-the-sippy-cup on Ashley's butt? *No.*

Pointedly, Ashley stared out the window because she wasn't normally a rude person, but air travel brought out one hundred and one demons in her, none of them Emily Post-like. Valerie said that the buying trips were good for her. That the only way to conquer a fear was to tackle it head-on. Valerie could be a total pain, and one day Ashley was going to stop listening to her sister's advice. But not today. Today she needed the ritual.

A hard thigh brushed against hers, and she jumped.

"Sorry." The voice was deep, husky and appropriately apologetic. Okay, there was another reasonable, sane human being on this flight. Ashley turned and the polite smile froze.

Hello, hot man.

His trousers were an off-the-shelf-khaki, his shirt, a nicely mussed crisp white, which, on most men would scream copier repairman, but here…it was like newsprint veiling a diamond.

Yes, sometimes clothes made the man, but sometimes, the man made the clothes.

After logging thousands of air miles, she'd traveled next to perfumed matrons decked in crystal-encrusted fleece, overly large seat huggers, squeegee businessmen who thought she looked lonely and, yes, a veritable cornucopia of families from hell, but never, *never*, had she actually sat next to a man with a nice smile, wonderfully wicked hazel eyes and a lovely, lovely body that begged to be unwrapped.

Ashley swallowed.

"Not a problem," she said, and then promptly looked away.

Come on, Ashley. Flirt a little. Pep up your game. Give him the goofy smile. Guys like that.

It was Valerie's voice. The first time in three years that Ashley had felt heat between her legs and she was listening to an imaginary lecture from her younger sister. *Not anymore, no way, no how.*

"I didn't think I was going to make it," said hot man, continuing to converse with her.

Ashley was torn between wanting to converse with hot man and sinking farther down into her seat and hiding her bunny slippers, but alas, it was impossible in the sardine-like conditions. "And you made it," she said, giving him the goofy smile until she realized what she was doing and promptly stopped.

"After running the four-forty through Terminal two. The next flight to L.A. isn't until tomorrow at six, and I just want to get this over with. You ever feel like that?"

"Always."

He smiled, then immediately frowned, the wicked hazel eyes glancing politely to the aisle.

Married. Must be. Or attached.

Subtly—unconsciously—Ashley's eyes drifted, which she hated, to his left hand. She wasn't on the make, she wasn't interested, she didn't need a man. She wasn't even thinking about being on the make, no matter how much Valerie nagged her.

But that didn't explain the little heart-thud when she noticed there was no ring.

You're a wimp, Ashley.

As she contemplated her own human needfulness, the stewardess pulled out the life vest to demonstrate the life-saving effects of the floatation device. Ashley imagined the floatation device bobbling alone in the ocean, her hands aching with cold from the water of the Great Lakes, her face dimming to a pale blue, her lungs weakening ever so slightly. Her hand locked onto the armrest because she knew that Lake Michigan had an ambient temperature of fifty-nine degrees Fahrenheit in April, which didn't sound too bad, but she'd seen that damn Titanic movie. She didn't want to live it.

"First flight?" asked hot man, the nice smile returning, which did have the unexpected effect of calming her fears…somewhat.

"No, sadly, I became a platinum passenger last year. I'm merely a coward at heart."

"I'm sorry," he said, the hazel eyes flickering more toward green—a warm, earthy green that did more to distract her than a muscle relaxant ever could, and reminded her that she hadn't had sex in a long time.

"Don't be. It's a family trait. Yellow-bellied, lily-livered Larsens, that's us."

He smiled again, and she felt the tell-tale heart-thud again. She unlocked her gaze from the captivating green of his eyes, and drifted to where Junior was most likely planning his latest nihilistic techniques.

Ask his name.

No.

It's only a name, a polite introduction. Not an invitation to the mile-high club.

I don't care. Shut up, Valerie.

I'm not even here.

I know. I swear when I get back on land, I'm going to see a therapist. It's the only answer.

Don't be a wimp, Ashley.

I'm very self-aware. I'm a wimp.

Why do I even try?

Because you're sadistic, and you revel in my pain. It makes you feel superior.

I'm not even here.

"Don't talk to me," muttered Ashley, wondering if hearing her sister's nagging meant that she was a woman on the verge of a nervous breakdown. The wind was certainly blowing in that direction.

"I'm sorry?" asked hot-guy.

"Oh, not you. I hear voices."

His brows rose—charmingly, of course. He really had a great smile. It wasn't a full-bodied smile, just a quick rise on the right side of his mouth where his mouth smashed headlong into a tiny dimple. "Part of the phobia?"

"No, my psychotic sister. Do you have a psychotic sister?" she asked, firmly believing that everyone should have a psychotic sister.

"No."

"You are *so* lucky. I always thought a brother would be cool. As long as he doesn't nag."

"Your sister nags?"

Ashley nodded. "Like a mother."

"I'm sorry," he said, apologizing again, and she noted how rare it was to hear a man apologize. Jacob had never apologized. Not once.

Right at that precise moment, Junior stabbed hot man in the hand with a particularly lethal twisty straw, and he yelped, his hand diving toward the armrest, trapping hers in a death grip of pain.

Ashley yelped, too, Junior laughed hysterically and Mom politely looked in the opposite direction, as if all were right with her world. Muscle relaxants could do that to a person.

Hot man's hand lifted from hers, and Ashley's normal blood flow resumed. He looked at her, the hazel eyes no longer wicked—now they showed true fear. About time he appreciated the seriousness of their situation. Four hours next to the toddling terror of the skies, who was now demanding macaroni and cheese, obviously oblivious to the plebian limitations of airplane food.

"He just broke out from the pen," Ashley whispered confidentially. "Wanted in four states. I saw his mug on the post office wall."

Hot man leaned in close and she could feel the whisper of his breath.

Ah, yearning loins, aching to be filled. Thy name is lust.
Shut up, Valerie.

"Stabbed you, too?" he asked.

"Nope. Butt-fondling in the third degree."

"Really?" He grinned. "A mastermind of crime with discriminating taste."

He's flirting with you, Ashley. That's definitely flirting.
Shut up, Valerie.

"So, why're you going to L.A.?" asked Ashley, flirting in return. "Vacation. Business. The fresh air?"

"Business," he answered, kicking his feet toward the computer case in front of him. "I'm a business analyst. You?"

"Buying trip. Clothes."

His eyes raked over her, noting the bunny slippers, and she felt the twinge again. The loins were definitely starting to yearn. "You like to shop that much?"

"I own some boutiques," she spoke, the words stumbling out of her mouth like pebbles. She'd bought the stores as a post-divorce present to herself, but what had been an impulsive plan to reinvent her life, hadn't quite blossomed as she'd hoped. As a kid, she loved to shop for clothes, loved to put together outfits that seemingly didn't belong, but then somehow worked. Unfortunately owning four disjointed clothing boutiques required more than stylish élan. Ashley's business sense hadn't magically appeared as Valerie had believed, and a good eye for color and style couldn't compete with designing ads and balancing the budget. In fact, in the past few months, usually when she was paying the bills, she thought about selling the stores, worried that she couldn't cut it. It was when the rent got raised for the second time in as many years that she worried she was like some people on those television reality shows. Thinking they could sing, but when their mouths opened the world's worst sounds emerged, and the home audience is sitting there wondering why the heck these types ever, *ever* had the wonky idea that they belonged in the limelight.

There were certain similarities.

Ashley's smile fell, the plane moved slowly back from the gate and she felt the familiar lurch in her stomach.

"Scared?"

"I'll be fine," replied Ashley, and she would. Business problems, personal problems, fashion problems, in the big scheme of things, they didn't amount to much that couldn't be overcome. In the end, Ashley was a survivor. When she was working on a new store window—surrounded by encouraging mannequins draped in subtly fitted, beautifully crafted, casual couture—the dream returned. She could do it. All she needed was to keep the faith.

She gave hot man a weak smile, and he covered her hand, a grip that was supposed to be comforting.

If you'd only twitch the thumb, a tiny caress....

Shut up, Valerie.

He had large hands, warm hands, with long, long fingers that looked so full of possibilities.

"Everything all right?"

"Peachy." The engines start to roar.

Quickly she took out the air-sickness bag.

Just in case.

DAVID MCLEAN hadn't been excited about a side-trip through Chicago to see his brother. Ex-brother. Chris had lost any claim to family bonding after he'd slept with David's wife. Yeah, nothing like a little wife-sharing between brothers. Four years, and it still pissed him off.

Still, in the face of pink bunny slippers and shoved in close quarters with a young psycho in training, David felt something unfamiliar tug at his face. A grin. Yes, that was definitely a grin.

The woman was just nervous enough to be unthreatening. He liked her. Her hair was dark, nearly black, and she had soft brown eyes and a nose that was too big to be called pert. But it gave her a little something extra—character. And she had a nice mouth, plump lips that were always held slightly parted, like a kid viewing the world for the first time, or a woman in the beginning throes of climax.

There was something stirring in his khakis—trouble. Sex held the whip hand, and turned men into stupid dogs. Like, for instance, Chris. And Christine. When he first introduced his future wife to his brother, all three of them had laughed about their matching names. The day he had found them in bed together, the laughter had stopped.

He shot a furtive look at the bunny slippers.

"I'm David," he said, carefully displacing thoughts of Chris and Christine.

"Ashley."

"Are you from Chicago?"

"Born, bred and will most likely die here as well."

"Cubbies fan, aren't you?" It was there in her eyes, that sort of lost hope, winning seasons long denied. Idealistic dreamers—a rarely seen species that was going to naturally select itself into extinction.

She winced. "I know, it's pathetic, isn't it? Are you from Chicago?"

"New York."

"Ah, home of the Yankees."

"What can I say? I live in New York. We always back the money team."

"Sad to be bought so easily."

He shrugged, and looked out the window. The plane had stopped moving toward the runway. They were returning to the gate.

Immediately Ashley noticed. "Something's wrong, isn't it?" Her finger jammed at the call button, just as the captain came on the speaker, his voice Prozac calm and soothing, which only made her more nervous.

"Ladies and gentlemen, we've had a slight mechanical issue. Nothing to worry about. I'm going to pull us back to the gate and have the mechanics check things out. We'll have a short stop where you can disembark, if you choose. However, you will need your boarding pass to reboard."

"We're not flying?" she said, and he noticed the relief in her voice.

"We're going to fly," answered David, wanting to reassure her, but more importantly, he needed to get to L.A. The sooner he left Chicago the better.

"I'm not taking off my slippers," she answered. "They can't do that to me."

"It's okay, I'm sure it won't be long," he told her, not his usual brutal honestly, but he suspected there was normally more color in her face, and if bunny slippers made her happy, who was he to take them away?

"What sort of mechanical problems do you think we're stuck with? I was on a flight to Miami when they thought the landing gear was hosed, but it turned out fine."

"Let me tell you about the time that I was flying to Houston. The engine blew…." Her eyes shot up four sizes, the pale color bleached to a ghostly hue, and he clamped down on his tongue. Hard. *Okay, David, great going here.* "Sorry. We landed fine. They have back-up engines, so if anything fails…" He realized he wasn't helping, so wisely he decided to shut up.

Damn. He liked talking to her. Normally he pulled out his computer and worked through flights, but this afternoon had left him feeling unsettled. Two weeks ago he had told his ex-wife that he would be in Chicago for a meeting. He would finally see them. But then he'd arrived at O'Hare and the city of big shoulders closed in on him.

He shouldn't have called them. Christine had said she was pregnant—*oh, joy!*—but in the end, David lied, leaving a message saying that his meeting had been canceled and he wouldn't be stopping in Chicago after all.

David didn't like being a coward. He never did—except for this.

The pregnancy had stung. Not that he wanted Christine back, but it irked him that she preferred his brother, that fidelity wasn't part of her vocabulary, and that he, a man who evaluated million-dollar business opportunities on a daily basis, could do so poorly when picking out wife material.

"I know of a little knockwurst place in Terminal One," he blurted out, because he didn't want to sit here sulking over the social implications of having a nephew birthed by his ex-wife. Bratwurst and sausage were so much more appealing. Then he glanced down at her feet. "Oops. Never mind."

"Down by Gate B12, between the ATM and the security check?"

"Yeah, you know the place?"

"Heh. I eat there all the time." Her mouth parted even more, drawing his eyes. Trouble stirred once more. "There are few things to get me out of my bunny slippers, but knockwurst and blown engines will do it. Let's go before junior scarfs down another chocolate bar."

2

HIS NAME WAS David McLean. His hair was a rich brown, cut conservatively short, but it suited him, suited the all-American, man-most-likely-to-know-how-to-fix-a-car-engine allure. Yes, he'd never model like one of those designer-wearing scruffy-jawed man-boys, but there was something about him that fascinated her. He was curious and intelligent, asking questions about everything, yet not so willing to talk about himself. Eventually she discovered why.

He was divorced and his jaw clenched like a vise when he'd mentioned it, so it wasn't one of those "parting as good friends" situations.

The restaurant was quiet and dark, the wait staff moving efficiently and effortless, and the large, overstuffed booths were conducive to divulging confidences to perfect strangers.

"It's not easy, is it?" she asked, thinking of her own divorce. Two weeks of wounded pride, several weeks of sorting out the finances and understanding what was whose and five months of awkward questions and well-meaning advice from friends. But then Ashley woke up one cold December morning and she knew she would be okay. Not fine, not great, but she was going to live. It was while in that fragile state that Valerie convinced her that she should do something radical with her life, live out her dream and buy a chain of four small Chicago boutiques. Start fresh.

"Not going that well?" asked David, when she told him what she did.

"Why would you think that?"

"I don't know. You don't have the joie de vivre that a lot of small business owners get when things are breezing along."

"You see a lot of small business owners?"

"Oh, yeah. From Omaha to Oahu. Kalamazoo to Klondike. I've seen a lot."

"Oh."

"Owning your own business is a lot of work. I sit on the sidelines and tell people how much their business is worth, how much it's not worth, what they are doing wrong, and recommend whether our investors should go all in or not. My job is the easy part. After I look over the operation, talk to a few customers and suppliers, I go plug some numbers into a spreadsheet, and then I'm on to the next business, the next opportunity."

"I used to be an insurance claims appraiser."

His mouth quirked, amused, and she cut in.

"Don't say it. I know. I have the insurance adjuster look."

"Nah, not an insurance adjuster. Maybe bookstore owner or candy maker. Something more personal."

"I think that's a compliment."

"It is. You're too cute for the insurance business. So why fashion?"

Cute. He thinks you're cute.
He's from New York.
Who cares? Take a chance, Ash.

For a second she met his eyes—a little more bold than usual. "I want to prove something. I want to take a plant and nurture it, care for it, water it and watch it bloom."

He snapped his fingers. "Florist. I can definitely see that in you."

She began to laugh because if he ever saw her plant shelf, he would be rolling on the floor, too. "No florist, sorry. I wanted to do something that I could master. Something challenging. I was stuck, and I needed to prove that I could do something different." It was nearly Valerie's post-divorce speech verbatim, but Val had been right. Ashley had just neglected to tell her sister that last key point.

"And fashion is challenging?"

Ashley nodded. Men really had no idea. It had taken her two hours to decide on the yellow gypsy skirt, the perfect pale green cotton T-shirt and a kaleidoscopic glass-bead necklace. The outfit had vague Easter-egg overtones, but worked nicely with her hair, and best of all...no wrinkles when traveling.

"Good luck."

"Thanks."

He sat back from the table, his eyes tracking to the bank of departure monitors nearby. "We better go back to the tarmac of terror."

"You're anxious to get out of here?" she asked, noticing the slight jaw-clench again. That, and the disappearing smile.

"No. It's fine."

Yeah, she'd seen that movie, too. Knew the ending. "Denial, much? Don't worry. It'll get better."

His gaze met hers, and the warm green was analytical hazel once again. "Has yours?"

"Oh, yeah," she lied. It hadn't gotten worse, but it hadn't gotten better. Instead she was stuck in this post-divorce limbo where she had no knowledge of how to proceed, and no inclination to leave the comfort of her own solitude.

"So when's the last time you went out?"

"Not too long ago."

"How long?" he probed, and she didn't like the awareness in his eyes. It was that same probing look that her sister got before she would launch into a lecture. Ashley shifted in her seat.

"I don't know," she answered vaguely. The divorce had been three years and eight months ago, but she didn't like the idea of dating again. It felt too wrong. She was a thirty-two-year-old woman, not a twentysomething college kid. She couldn't go sit in a bar. If she signed up for a matchmaking service, she was afraid no one would pick her. And most of the blind dates she'd had had been with total losers. People had good intentions, but their judgment left a lot to be desired.

"Has it been longer than a year?"

"Maybe. But I've been busy," she said, dodging the question.

He stayed silent for a second before nodding. "Understand that. I'm not one of those men who has to be married. I cook. I do my own laundry. There's a whole group of guys who get together to watch the games in a bar. I'm independent. I like my independence." It was the battle cry for the walking wounded. Ashley knew it well.

"Then it sounds like you're in a good place." She gave him the fake smile. The one that says, "whatever you say is fine."

"I think I am. You?"

"Oh, yeah." Abruptly, she decided to stop the charade. Here was a comrade in arms. Someone who knew exactly how it felt. Why not tell the truth? She missed cooking for two. She missed waking up on a Sunday morning and not having to plan out the day. She missed being able to come home from work and laugh about her coworkers—not all of them, but there were a few who were laugh-worthy. Ashley and Jacob had been married for seven years, and it was never the world's greatest marriage, but still… "Sometimes it is, but sometimes it's not. Well, you know, there are things I miss."

"Gawd, yes."

"At night. It's lonely."

"Exactly."

"I mean, I know I can get Valerie to watch…." He shot her a shocked look and then recovered quickly, but not before she noticed. Oh, man, he thought she was talking about sex, which she wasn't, but now, okay, her mind was going there, she was thinking the sex thoughts… *No, don't think about it, Ash.* Quickly she fumbled back into the conversation. "I like watching horror movies at night and my sister is a total wimp. All we get are historical dramas. Television is something best done with another person." *Okay, Ashley, got over that one.* Not too shabby.

David, however, still looked mildly shell-shocked. "Totally," he answered in a tight voice.

"You like horror movies, too?" she asked, getting a little cocky and daring to tease.

"We should get back to the plane," he answered, not taking the whole teasing thing well. She knew that men got a lot more wired than women about sex, but he seemed more laid-back than that. Wrong, Ashley. Quickly she changed to a safer topic.

"Get back to Junior? You're as sadistic as Valerie."

"Maybe he's asleep."

THEY HAD NO SUCH luck once they got back on board. Junior was riding a sugar high, judging by the chocolate smeared across his face and the way he kept bouncing on his seat. But at least all weapons were out of his possession.

David watched as Ashley changed shoes again, noticing how nice her feet were. Smooth, compact, lots of well-turned curves. His cock stirred and he turned away. Turned on by a foot? Weak...very, very weak. It'd been a long time since he had spent several confined hours in the company of a single woman. After the divorce, he'd thrown himself into work, mainly because he liked it, he was good at it, and if he couldn't have a family life, at least he could build up his retirement account. Today had been like a cold dunk in a deep ocean, the familiar patterns coming back to him, the jittery nerves coming back to him, and the hard-on coming back to him as well.

It was because there wasn't anything they could do about it. That's what this was. Economics. Supply and demand. Decrease the availability of supply, and boom, demand shoots out from every pore, zipping in his brain. Ergo, the hard-on.

If she hadn't mentioned sex. Well, honestly, she hadn't mentioned sex, she just mentioned the word *night* and his imagination took off from there, wishing they weren't at an airport, wondering if that skirt was as easy to slip off as it looked so he could feel her skin under his hands. Tawny skin, creamy skin, soft, touchable skin rubbing up against him...

David studiously avoided looking at her skin, his eyes moving upward, touching on her chest. Lots of well-turned curves there, too. After that, he looked away, met Junior's knowing eyes and glared. Heading to an altitude of thirty thousand feet, it wasn't going to get any easier, so better to concentrate on other, less arousing things. Junior launched a Lego piece in his direction.

Like survival.

TWO HOURS LATER they were still at the gate. They were waiting on either a part, or a new plane, the pilots weren't sure which would arrive first, but they had high—ludicrously delusional—hopes for getting away tonight. In the face of such facts, Ashley had long abandoned her fear of flying. It was obvious they weren't going anywhere anytime soon.

Instead she was thigh-locked with David, who had very nice thighs, too. Hard. His arms were fab as well. Thirty minutes ago, he'd pushed up his sleeves, and her gaze kept stalling out on the biceps, which were bigger than most, an odd incongruity for khakis and a button-down, and she wondered why. He wasn't bulky enough to be a weight lifter, but his arms were too big for a swimmer or a runner, and definitely too big for a tiny airplane seat. They kept brushing against hers, casually, which didn't explain the electric shock to her system.

Not that he was making it any easier. Conversation had ceased about half an hour ago when she caught him staring at her chest, and they both looked politely away.

Damn.

She crossed her legs, uncrossed her legs, and had a hare-brained urge to ask him to join her in the bathroom. She'd pulled out *Vogue* and *Harper's* and *Lucky,* but even the lure of the sloe-eyed models in their daring designs hadn't dimmed the awareness that simmered in the air.

The bright spot in the tension was Junior, which said a lot about her feelings of desperation. Junior wrote on David's hand with a pen, and David laughed, sounding more relieved than amused. Junior ran up and down the aisle, and Ashley counted the number of times, choosing note to fixate on the discreetly covered ridge in David's khaki slacks.

Do not go there.

Go there, Ashley.

Oh, yeah, good of you to talk. You can't have sex on a plane, Valerie.

People do.

Not me.

There was a momentary pause in her thoughts, because right now, given readily available options, she could *so* have sex on this plane.

Another thirty minutes passed, and the flight attendants were passing out drinks. Yes, alcohol, the world's most potent aphrodisiac. When the flight attendant stopped at their row, David shook his head, Ashley shook her head, and Junior's mother and father opted for double vodka tonics.

Outside the window, the lights of the airport started to dim. If she lowered her hand one inch, just one tiny inch, she would be touching his thigh. If she were careful, it would look like an accident.

Junior spilled a glass of orange juice on those khakis that she was not looking at, and David shot sideways, and there was a momentary barrage of touches. His hand, her breast. Her hand, his thigh. She jumped back, arching toward the window, and he moved away, hugging his seat. Junior's mother apologized, and Ashley's nipples were powered by a thousand jet engines, ready for takeoff.

It was shortly after her breasts had recovered from the shock that the captain came on the speaker and announced that moment they all had been expecting.

"Ladies and gentleman, we tried. But there's bad weather

in New York, and we couldn't get the plane that we were hoping for, and they can't get the part here until the morning. So I'm sorry to say, we won't be going anywhere. If any of you need hotel accommodations at the airport, there's a flight attendant waiting to give you the details."

A hotel. Suddenly the word took on new connotations and images. A hotel implied a bed, privacy, something much more comfortable than a tiny bathroom designed by Boeing. A hotel implied *sex*.

The cabin lights went on, and people around them began to move. Everyone was moaning and complaining, and, in general, not in a very happy place. However, Ashley's happy place was getting happier by the second. She didn't want to look at him, didn't want to assume, most of all she didn't want to act as if she didn't know what she was doing. After all, she was mature, she was an adult, and after eight hours of sitting thigh-to-thigh with this man, she was primed to explode with only a touch.

He turned, a slight inclination of his head, and she met his eyes. It was ESP of the most carnal kind. She licked her lips, his gaze tracked her tongue and she knew that he knew.

He leaned down, his mouth near her ear. "You should know that right now, I'm a very happy man." Ashley felt the touch in her ear, down to the soles of her feet, and every single inch in between, especially the happy place. She tried to smile, but that involved mind-body cooperation, and right now there was none. Slowly she regained the capability to speak and she did manage to smile, although she wasn't sure how it looked.

"Happy is good," she told him.

She was going to have sex with David. She was going to peel off his shirt, feel the muscles of his bare chest crushing her breasts. She would rip off his briefs, since she instinctively knew he wore briefs—tight, white briefs, with his sex jutting out from the band— and then finally, finally, he would push up inside her, filling her...

She felt her muscles contract once, contract twice.

Her mouth tightened and her eyes opened and spied David, who was watching her with eyes that were nearly black.

Ashley nodded once. "I think we need to go. Now." He grabbed the carry-ons and then they both took off running through the airport, Ashley's bunny slippers cooperating nicely.

3

THE FIRST STOP was at the newsstand for condoms.

Condoms!

I can't believe you're sitting here watching a man buy condoms. I mean, I'm glad and all, but Ash, he's not a serial killer, is he? This is not smart. How much do you know about this man?

I know enough that I want to sleep with him. No, not sleep. I want to have sex. I want to kiss him, I like watching his eyes get all dark and sexy. You'd be surprised what you get to know about a guy when you're trapped on a grounded plane for eight hours. He's not a serial killer.

It's your funeral.

Shut up, Val. You're not here, and he is.

She pulled out her flats from the carry-on and switched out of the bunny slippers. Not going to need those until tomorrow.

After an eternal four minutes, David walked back from the newsstand wearing a slight flush, his eyes dodgy, not like a guy who was an old hand at buying condoms at the airport—and not like a serial killer, either.

"I don't carry them," he apologized.

"I understand," she said, and decided it was best not to talk about this anymore.

The shuttle to the hotel was fast and silent, and it glided through the darkness, getting them there way too fast. David didn't touch her. He didn't need to. She could feel him, feel his eyes, feel his thoughts.

When the shuttle arrived at the hotel, David took her bag,

his arm brushing against hers, and she jumped. It was like a scene in some of her favorite horror movies, but not in the "someone's going to get hacked up" sort of way, but more "someone's going to get laid," and it was going to be good. Really, really good. Her loins started to ache, her blood pounding.

At the front desk was a seventeen-year-old who didn't need to be up this late. As David handled the registration, Ashley held back because she didn't know hotel registration protocol for this arrangement. Did they need two names? If so, should she use her real name? It was a whole new world, and honestly, she didn't need to know about it. There were much more important things to think about, so she and her aching loins were going to hang back and wait it out.

Three seconds later, and then David was back. It was time. *It wasn't enough time.*

"You don't look so good. You need a drink? We can chat more," he told her, because obviously eight hours stranded on a plane wasn't enough for Ashley. Oh, no, she needed more chat time.

"We should get a drink," she said, her brain furiously stalling for chat time, while her other parts were yelling at her to get the heck upstairs.

To the right of the front desk was the hotel bar. It was dark, sleek, a place with low lights, big comfortable chairs, and an IMAX-sized mirror on the wall. Ashley leaned up to the bar. "I'll take a double shot of tequila," she told the bartender.

"Make it two," added David.

While he waited for the drinks, she picked out two chairs, far from the bartender, but not far from the mirror. David set the shot glasses on the low table and settled in the chair next to her. "You should know that I have taken defensive driving, been married only once, have no contagious, nor sexually transmitted diseases and I never pick up strange women in airports."

For some reason, that made her feel a lot better. "Me, neither.

I mean, men. I never pick up strange men." And after that mangled confession, she licked the salt from the rim of her glass.

David leaned over, and kissed the corner of her mouth.

"Salt," he murmured.

"Mouth," she responded automatically, staring at his mouth. It was a good mouth. It was hard, stubborn and looked liked it knew what it was doing.

"Tongue," he replied.

"Oh, God," she whispered, and then poured a sharp splash of tequila down her throat. "You would tell me if you think this is slutty, right?"

Ash, that's a stupid question. He's not going to tell you that. Men like slutty. When it comes to sex, men have no scruples, no morals, no ethics.

"Absolutely," he lied.

"Okay. That was stupid."

"We can get two rooms," he told here, doing a great impersonation of an ethical man who still wanted sex.

Is this what you want, Ash? If it's really and truly what you want, then Do It.

She looked at David McLean, the once-divorced, defensive driver with eyes currently tending to brown rather than green. Eyes that said he wanted her. And Ashley made up her mind. It was no contest. Not even a minor dilemma.

"I want to have sex with you. I want to do something new and exciting, at least once before I die, most likely in a plane crash. Stranger sex is exciting." As she said the words, she caught her reflection in the mirror. Her eyes were the same, yet different. She was…glowing, which could have been the warm-toned lighting, but she didn't think so.

"Stranger sex?" he asked, his mouth quirking up at one side. She liked that about him, the way he didn't fully smile, but only partly committed to it. Like a man who wants to laugh, but isn't quite sure it's the correct thing to do.

"Yeah, you know, stranger sex. The unknown, the forbidden, the lady and the tiger."

Now she was fully staring at the mirror in front of her. Her, the wild-eyed seductress—slight overstatement—with him, the harried businessman, which was probably true.

Kiss him, Ash. Plant a big smoochie right there.

Throwing caution to the wind, Ashley leaned over and kissed him. Once, on the side of the mouth.

"Salt," she murmured.

Then she boldly moved her mouth to his.

"Mouth," he whispered against her lips.

It was nearly a kiss. A press of skin, an exchanging of breaths. It wasn't enough.

"Tongue," she said, and magically, it was a kiss. Mouth, tongues, and oh, yes, that was passion. David McLean was a most excellent kisser. He was earnest, sincere, unafraid. Best of all, he made Ashley feel earnest, sincere and unafraid. She forgot about the mirror, and the hotel room, and only focused on one thing— his mouth. The way his tongue mated perfectly with hers.

He tasted like lime and salt and hot, sweaty, body-smashing sex. Maybe that was only her subconscious talking or the humming moisture between her legs, but she didn't think so. Ashley moved closer, wild-eyed seductress that she was, and then his hand was at her jaw, holding her while that magic tongue moved in and out, intensifying the hum between her legs.

When he lifted his head, those hazel eyes were dark, sleepy and irresistible. Ashley could only stare.

"Two rooms?" he asked.

She shook her head, not wavering or worrying even once.

They walked to the bank of elevators without touching, because Ashley didn't want to touch him at the moment. Touching implied combustion, and neither a hotel hallway nor a hotel elevator was the place for combustion.

Not for Ashley, and apparently not for David.

This is it, Ash. We're sure he's not a serial killer, right? What if you get strangled or something?

David looked at her, his hungry gaze falling to her mouth.

Ashley told the voices to shut up.

DAVID'S HAND SHOOK as he inserted the keycard in the lock, but honestly, he was too primed to try and be smooth about this. He opened the door, told himself to go slow, then immediately ignored all his normally responsible, conventional wisdom and grabbed Ashley, kicking the door shut behind them.

Her arms curled into his hair, pulling him closer, and they stumbled toward the bed. He wasn't like this. He wasn't ever like this, so who was that man fumbling her shirt over her head, lifting her skirts, or dive-bombing for her mouth?

That mouth.

She kissed like she dressed. Not completely stylish, but there was an understated flashiness, and a zing. Definitely a zing.

David heard a moan. Hers. Oh, definitely a zing. Now he was moaning, too.

He tumbled on top of her, completely without finesse, but thankfully, she didn't seem to mind. Her legs wrapped about him, pelvis surging toward him, and his hands went to his fly. Her breasts pressed against him, soft peaks in white cotton. If his zipper would ever get unstuck, he'd shove the bra aside, because he wanted to see…

The room began to shake. What was that? He could hear the roar of a jet engine. The airport. They were at the airport. That wasn't his cock. Calm. Remain calm.

Condom. Oh, shit. He needed a condom.

"Wait," he nearly yelled. He needed to get control. He needed to breathe. In the dim light of the single bedside lamp, she looked up at him, clothes ransacked into parts, exposing more skin than covering. Great skin. Gold and rose mixed together like mother-of-pearl. She wore white cotton panties. With a sun-yellow gypsy skirt, she wore white cotton panties, and did she even *know* he had a thing for white cotton? He definitely had a thing for white cotton. It was sexy as hell. She was sexy as hell.

His hands were still shaking as he shoved her bra aside. Like a total amateur.

Dude, get a hold of yourself. She's going to think you haven't done this in like, months.

She'd be right, but he didn't want to advertise the fact.

The foil packet tore exactly as it was supposed to, and then...

"Let me," she whispered in a husky voice that sent every drop of his blood out of his head. Into his head. There was courage in her eyes. The bunny-slipper woman, who was a trembling coward at ten thousand feet, now seemed mightier than any warrior queen with her clothes askew.

Oh, no. Her capable hands got busy on his cock, sending ten thousand volts to his system. *Concentrate on something else. The breasts, for instance.*

Didn't work.

David wasn't going to last, he was going to explode and this was going to be over. No way.

He pushed her into the bank of pillows, roughly, again with the no-finesse thing, and then...

Then...

Yes.

She was tight, perfectly tight, and wet.

He opened his eyes, looked down at those dark, dancing eyes and swallowed.

Had he truly forgotten that sex could be this awesome? Yes, yes, he had.

"Oh," he managed to say.

Ashley smiled at him, and it was a marvelous smile. A smile for a hot summer's day, and he was so glad the airplane had had a mechanical failure. He was even glad for Hellboy Junior. Being like this, surrounded by her, was worth it, so worth it. He rocked his hips, going deeper inside her, and her smile turned serious. Again he thrust, just to see if it was as good as the first.

Yes, yes, it was.

Then his mind began to shut down, and biology, desire and sex took over.

Greedily he drove inside her, plunging into that moist heat. Her pupils were wide, dilated, and her mouth...it was exactly as he'd imagined. No, it was better than he'd imagined. This was so much better than he imagined. Ashley tried to talk. Couldn't. Her nails scraped down his back, down his butt, and it was the best pain ever. *Ever.*

He should be doing more for her, pushing buttons somewhere, but his body was running on autopilot, pumping hard and fast, and she didn't seem to mind. Her hands locked on his shoulders, pulling him, pushing him, and there was no finesse there, either. And he'd never had such great, mindless sex in his entire life.

Another plane took off, and the bed shook, only this time it wasn't a plane, it was David and Ashley. It was nearly an hour later, after all the planes had been grounded for the night that the room stopped spinning, the bed stopped moving, and David's heart landed back on the ground.

Stranger sex? Is that what that meant? Shit. They were going to have to do that again.

ASHLEY SLID OVER to the far side of the bed. You didn't cuddle with a man you'd known less than one day. Actually, you normally didn't share a hotel room with a man you'd known less than one day, but in this case, after the last two hours, her standards could be relaxed. There was a moment as she listened to the ever-efficient sounds of used condom removal. Too much information, oh, man, she was not cut out for this.

"Are you okay?" he asked, rolling over, and they were so close, so naked, actually not completely naked, there were clothes still attached to both of them...barely.

"I'm good," she answered, a total understatement if there ever was one, and Ashley didn't usually understate. Honestly, she had to say that David McLean had the best bed head ever. Brown strands falling into his eyes, a cowlick in the back, and she wanted to reach over, smooth it back into place. She kept her hands still. They were strangers. You couldn't go around fixing a stranger's hair. Sex? Yes. Hair-fixing? No. Again with the rigid standards.

"How good?" he asked, not seeming to be needy, but still curious.

"Really good."

"Oh, good," he sighed, and fell back on his back. "That was freaking nuts. You were right."

"I was?"

And what did "nuts" mean? He sounded happy, beyond happy even, but nuts? What sort of word was that? No, she was getting all paranoid again. She would not get paranoid. This had been awesome, and she had been an active part of that awesomeness.

He cleared his throat. "I've never done something like this before, and it's…I don't know, it's just…great."

Now, see, "great" is so much better than "nuts."

"It was, wasn't it?" she said, sounding like she did this all the time.

He nodded, and she grinned, completely ruining the confident, sophisticated image.

"Why isn't it always like that?" she asked, studying her past sexual behavior pattern to figure out why this was different. Why here, why him, why now? She hadn't had sex in a year…two? Maybe it was the long dry spell that made things so…stimulating?

"It isn't always like that because not every man is me," he answered, sounding exactly like every man. He started to laugh. "Whatever it is, it's not ambience, that's for sure." He cast a long look around the all-American airport hotel decor.

She followed his gaze. He was right. A single torchère light stood in the corner, the bedcovers were orange—*orange!*—but the drapes were a nice touch. A garden green with large tropical flowers. Cheery.

Ashley pulled up the sheet and blanket to cover her chest discreetly. David McLean, on the other hand, was certainly not shy. His legs, half in half out of bed, exposed lean thighs. The legs were tan, with an indentation where his ass joined the thighs. It was a fine ass, smooth, firm…exactly like his… *No, Ashley focus on the conversation.*

What were they talking about? Oh, yeah. "That…bam," she began, searching for a better word, failing, and no, it wasn't because of his fine ass. "I mean, what's that about? If I knew you better, would it disappear?" Her eyes kept stealing lower. Conversation with a naked hot man was harder than it looked.

"The zing? That never lasts. I've had some great first dates before, and then, you get to the third date, and you're thinking, who is this person?"

"Exactly," she said, curling up next to hot man with the fine ass, because miracles did not happen often. "Familiarity. And then it all goes down the drain."

"Too bad they can't market that. That bam, that zing. Advertisers would go crazy."

"I know absolutely nothing about advertising, but you're right."

"Thank you," he told her.

"For what?" she asked, because honestly it was no big deal to agree with him. He was right. She knew he was right.

He cocked his head toward the bed. "For doing this. For staying with me tonight. I feel good. Normal. Better than normal. Like I could run a marathon. Alive. Not so dead."

Don't look, Ash.

Not looking, not looking, not…looking. Nope, she looked. Not dead yet. Getting livelier by the second.

He turned, studying her. "I didn't know I could have sex with a stranger in a hotel without guilt. Without trying to analyze everything."

"You're analyzing everything."

"Occupational hazard." He leaned back into the pillows and sighed. Not a restful man, David McLean. "It shouldn't be so hard to start over. Just a date. That's the Holy Grail for me. I want to find a woman to go out with, and have a nice evening. A good conversation, a little fun."

"There would be tons of women wanting to go out with you," Ashley told him.

Good God, what was wrong with the women in New York?

Nothing wrong with him. He's a serial killer.

Right, Val.

"It seems like all the women I meet are weird, neurotic, or needy. Or eighteen. I have standards."

Speaking as a weird, neurotic woman, neither needy, nor eighteen, Ashley knew he was doomed and felt it her duty to speak the truth. "Sorry, you're out of luck. All that comes with the estrogen…except the eighteen part." His eyes looked nervous and she laughed. "Have you tried online services? A friend of mine met her husband online."

"Normal people don't do that, do they? It doesn't seem like, I don't know, there's something wrong with me?"

Ashley waved a hand. "Not anymore. Everybody's too busy to go and hang out somewhere on the off chance they'll meet—" she held up quote fingers "—the One."

David still didn't look convinced. "A dating service. It sounds painful."

For women, yes, for men, ha. "Go for it. Women would jump all over you."

Like you did, Ash.

"You really think it'd be okay?"

Ashley nodded.

"And you swear that normal people sign up?"

"On my honor as a fashion professional."

"I don't know."

"Try it," she urged, because he needed to find that perfect

petite blond, black-dressed New Yorker who would appreciate a man who was simply…nice. That, and a pile driver in bed, which made for a nifty combination.

After a moment of consideration, he sighed, but then nodded. "I'll do it. Just a test. You've given me courage."

That out of the way, his eyes skimmed over her, and she felt the tingles again. That wasn't courage. No siree, that was lust. She gave him courage. He gave her lust. There was something wrong with that equation. "You should do it, too," he added.

"Oh, no. It's not for me."

Ashley didn't want to date. She didn't need the hassles, the aggravation, or the neurosis. Nope. Everything she longed for was right there. Long, lean, stranger man, naked in her bed. She hadn't known she could do this. "I don't want a date. I want an affair. An exotic, femme-fatalish affair. Doesn't that sound perfect?"

"You should live in New York," he said, possibly reading her mind. "If you lived in New York, I'd give you an affair."

"No, thank you, Yankee man. I'm staying right here in the Windy City. Well, actually, I'm leaving in the morning for L.A., but I'm coming home here. To Chicago."

There was a momentary silence as she contemplated that statement. They were complete strangers, didn't even share the same state. One more plane ride to L.A., and then she'd never see him again. It made the night seem…alluring, adventurous. The lady and the tiger, and tonight she wasn't the lady.

Become the tiger, Ash.

David propped up on one elbow. "You want to get dinner in L.A.?"

"Aren't you tempting fate?" she asked, tempted to tempt fate herself.

"By eating?"

"By having a date. What if that destroys the bam, the zing? What if the only way we can have this is by meeting in hotel rooms and losing our exterior selves in a moment of wild abandonment?"

David looked at her, slightly awed. "You came up with all this from one shot of tequila and sex?"

"No. I've been thinking."

"You could think?" he asked, his eyes narrowed. "I couldn't think. Why could you think?"

"Not then. Now."

He rapped a hand against his heart. "Good." Then he looked at her in that way she was learning to recognize. "Do you honestly believe all that?" he asked seriously. There were two David McLeans. One, resident goofball, but the other was hardcore analyst. He was probably excellent at his job.

"I think it deserves some consideration," she replied, but honestly, she did believe it. It explained everything.

And he didn't look at her like a crazy person, which made her like him more. "Okay, meet me in L.A. In a hotel room. Chateau Marmont. We can be Mr. and Mrs. Jones. We'll test your theory."

"We'd just…exchange a room number and then I knock three times on the door, and…?"

"Yeah, or we could just meet up in the lobby," he explained in a practical voice.

Ashley sighed. "It's easy to tell you're Mr. Bottom Line. No sense of adventure at all."

"This from a woman in bunny slippers?"

She held up a naked foot. "Not a pink floppy ear in sight."

His eyes crinkled. "Bare flesh. Seductress."

"You think?" She held up her foot again, watching one of his long, lean thighs dig itself into the covers until it was buried completely. She was going to miss that naked thigh, that firm flank, *that stellar ass.*

"You have very sexy feet. I was watching them on the plane."

Feet? No. It would have been better if he were a serial killer.

"You think my feet are sexy? You're not gonna get weird and suck toes, are you?"

He must have some flaw. This one would explain it.

Thankfully, he looked horrified. "No. But I could, you

know, start at the arch, work my way up, see where I land..."
And she could see the gears turning in his head...all because of a foot. Her foot.

Ashley stared at the appendage of interest, considering the possibilities. "That sounds...decadent."

"Bam?" he asked, raising a brow.

"Definitely."

"Good. I didn't push any buttons before, and I'm sorry about that, but you felt so good. I got carried away, and I feel like I have shirked my manly duties."

She wiggled her toes. "Go forth, and unshirk, my devoted slave of pleasure."

He pushed down her body, and his mouth pressed against her arch, and the first time it tickled, causing her to giggle. But then he moved up her calf, and it still tickled, but a different tickle. A warm tickle, a tickle between her thighs.

"Oh," murmured Ashley, then she shot upright, horrified by a new thought. "You have more condoms?"

"A whole box. Now let me get back to my unshirking."

Ashley fell back against the pillows, and his mouth touched the inside of her thigh, and there were no more giggles. Only the sighs and ragged breathing of a woman having her buttons pushed. Every single one of them. Sometimes twice.

"I'm very glad you went for the box, rather than the travel size," she told him.

"Bam?" he whispered, his mouth unshirking behind her knee, and moving north at a steady, yet wholly orgasm-inducing speed.

Ash, you're way too easy.

Shut up, Val.

4

THEY HAD GONE through four more condoms, and the 5:00 a.m. wake-up call hadn't even been necessary.

Ashley was dog tired. She hadn't been this tired in years. Thirty-two-year-old women did not stay up all night having sex with strange men in airport hotel rooms.

Or at least not every day of the year.

"We can't do this again," she told him, her face buried in the pillow.

He chuckled, an exhausted chuckle, but a chuckle nonetheless. "Eighteen was a long time ago. You can sleep on the plane. I can sleep on the plane. I need to sleep on the plane."

She lifted her head from the pillow. "We shouldn't do this again."

Comprehension dawned. "Oh." He waited for more of an explanation. Ashley gathered her meager, yet dog-tired courage.

"Tonight was fun. Like being somebody whose life I've secretly always envied. But if we go out to dinner, or meet in a hotel, I'm afraid I'll lose this fantasy, get embroiled in the completely weary minutia of my life, and I'd rather end on the high note."

"That's a very defeatist attitude."

"No, sometimes things are just too good to take a chance and possibly ruin," she told him bluntly.

"Do you ever get to New York?" he asked, a totally unfair question, because fashion, New York? *Hello?* Did he honestly think she was *that* bad at what she did?

"Sometimes. A bit. You ever come to Chicago?"

"Not if I can help it," he answered, a defeatist attitude if she ever heard one.

"This was fun," she repeated, rising from the ashes of the bed. Outside, the windows started to rattle again. The airport was waking up. She walked to the shower, femme fatale of the friendly skies, and she felt muscles that she didn't know she had.

He watched her closely, and she gave her hips an extra wiggle.

"I could help you," he offered gallantly.

"In the shower?"

He lay there naked, on his back, head pillowed on his hands. Long, lean, and ready to go. Dog tired? Who said she was dog tired?

You did.

"Come on, Yankee-man," she ordered in a husky voice she didn't even know she possessed.

And she didn't have to ask twice.

LATER ON, they didn't talk to each other on the plane. The 6:00 a.m. flight to L.A. was crowded, but thankfully, Junior and the doting parents from hell were absent. Ashley was stuffed next to a plumbing salesman from Portland who wanted to chat. She pulled out her magazines and pretended to be interested in the latest fall forecast, but instead, her sandpaper eyes kept tracking to the front of the plane. Seat 16A to be exact, where she could see the back of his head. A perfect bed-head, neatly combed into place.

It had taken her two hours to dare to stroke his hair, smooth it the way it longed to be smoothed, and she could still feel it, the fine strands tickling her fingers, still smell the shampoo and soap. Still smell the sex.

Don't get there, Ash. Not with you-know-who sitting next to you.

Ashley stopped gawking at Seat 16A and instead focused on the magazine spreads in front of her, but her eyelids drifted shut.

She woke up three hours later, having slept through the flight. In her lap was a small white piece of paper. A business card.

David McLean.
Brooks Capital.
Analyst.

On the back, in firm, decisive, indelible black ink was scrawled a cell number and one word.

Anytime.

It was enough to make her not-quite-jaded-enough divorcée's heart sigh.

Carefully she put the card in her wallet, hidden right behind her driver's license. It was her memento, a souvenir she would never forget. Some moments were best not to be repeated... except while dreaming.

CHICAGO WAS WARM, windy, and loud. Ashley took a cab back to the Larsen house in Naperville, which was equally warm, not so windy and not nearly so loud. Their street was lined with towering elm trees, hand-painted mailboxes and well-used bicycles. It wasn't New York, certainly not Los Angeles, but it was home.

Already Ashley began to feel revived.

After the divorce, she'd moved in with Val, their mother, Joyce, and Val's daughter, Brianna. Three generations of Larsen women sharing one roof. A scary thought, all those hormonal fluctuations duking it out with the inherent uncertainty of the family genes. Frank Larsen, the ne'er-do-well who had sired Ashley and Valerie, was now on his fourth marriage, electing to spend his golden years with his twentysomething secretary in Malibu.

Ashley threw her carry-on in the general direction of the couch, and walked into the kitchen. Val was talking on the phone, stirring dinner over the stove and watching the news. Multitasking, thy name is Valerie.

Val punched a button on the phone, and waved a wet spoon as a way of greeting. "How was the trip?"

"Productive. Very productive," Ashley answered, focusing

on the business aspects of the trip rather than the pleasure aspects, because Val might be her sister, but there were secrets that would never be divulged. Doing David McLean in the O'Hare airport hotel was one.

"Can you watch the monster while I go to a meeting?"

"Mom not home from work yet?"

"No. Inventory."

"I can watch her. You don't need to ask." Val was thirty, a single mom with a fondness for things that weren't good for her and a hard line in her eyes that Ashley didn't think would ever disappear. Ashley liked to blame it on Marcus, the drummer who'd dropped into Val's life, left her pregnant and alone, and then moved on to a bigger gig in St. Paul, never to be heard from again.

Sensing her guilt, Val gave her a long, searching look. "Why are you so jumpy?"

"I'm always jumpy. Flying. Slays me every time." To further illustrate her point, she held up a suitably unsteady hand.

"Ash, you are one weird sis, but you're the only one I've got."

A small tornado ran into the room before skidding to a halt. "Ashley, Washly, Bo Bashley, Me Mi Mo Mashly. Ashley." At eight, Brianna Larsen possessed the trademark Larsen nose, which all plastic surgeons yearned to compress, and more energy than Val and Ash combined.

Brianna shook back her hair in a completely eight-year-old diva manner. "I learned a new word from *South Park*. Douche bag. As in, Kenny is a world-class douche bag."

Ashley looked at Val, fascinated yet delighted by the sparkle of humanity in her sister's too-hard, too-black eyes. "And did your mommy tell you what douche bag meant?"

Brianna nodded. "It's a soap bottle filled with water and it gets you springtime fresh."

Ashley knocked fists with her sis. "Creative and honest. Excellent, my friend. Her vocabulary is improving by leaps and bounds. Her teacher will love you."

At that simple yet comforting discourse, Val's eyes narrowed, and Ashley realized her mistake. Ashley was acting too relaxed, too confident, too pleased for a woman with a deathly fear of flying and a business that wasn't getting off the ground. Immediately she wiped the satisfied smile off her face.

"You sure you're okay?" Val asked, because she was the blustering bull. Ashley was the worrier. After living together for four years, everyone had their assigned roles. Ashley knew hers, Val knew hers, their mother knew hers, and even Brianna was very aware.

"I'm fine," replied Ashley, giving her voice an extra quiver. "Go on. I'll take over the supper. What's on the menu tonight?"

All doubts appeased, the world back in order, Val continued to stir, her eyes focused on the stove, rather than her sister. "My specialty."

"Mac and cheese it is."

Val glared. "With spinach, darling child, because we all love green food."

Brianna, being one-hundred-percent Larsen and knowing a con job when she heard it, promptly rolled her eyes. "Douche bag."

Val ruffled her daughter's hair. "Brat. Listen to Aunt Ash. I'll be back in a couple of hours, and Ash, do not forget the green food."

Brianna fought with every inch of her small being, but in the end, responsible parenting prevailed, and Ashley shamed her niece into eating an extra helping of green food. Val came home from her meeting, Mom came home from work and four Larsen women sat on the couch watching *Pride and Prejudice*—the Colin Firth version.

Truly, there was no place like home.

Every time there was a crisis, home was always there. Every time she felt alone, home was always there. No, they weren't the typical American family, but in a lot of ways, the typical American family had nothing on the Larsen women of Chicago.

Ashley had never imagined herself divorced. She thought her marriage to Jacob would be forever. He was comfortable. They were comfortable. Why would anyone want to leave that? But Jacob had, and Ashley had no place to go but home. Home was good.

By the time the grandfather clock struck eleven, Mom was sacked out in the recliner and Brianna was curled up with her head in Ashley's lap, fast asleep.

Val picked up her daughter in her arms, sagging a little from the weight. "I think you're overdoing the mac and cheese."

"She's only eight once. It's too early for her to start dieting," Ashley replied, as would any overindulgent aunt who thought her niece was perfect.

"You're not her mother, only the auntie." Val looked down at her daughter and shook her head. "How did I get this kid?"

"The old-fashioned way."

Val's laugh was harsh and self-directed. "What if you screw her up with all your spoilage and worrying?"

"I won't," assured Ashley automatically, not insulted at all. It was a conversation they'd had many times, and usually late at night, when doubts were prone to wander in on creeping shadows. They weren't talking about Ashley. Deep down, Val had the same paranoid Larsen heart they all did, certain that when anything good happened in her life, it was going to disappear, just like the mac and cheese. Golden and gooey and warm, and then poof, you look down and the pot is empty, and your stomach curdles with an angry hunger.

"Swear you won't screw her up?" Val asked.

"Swear."

Val looked at Ashley, still doubting, but hopefully not quite so much. "Okay, but I only believe you because secretly we know you're the smart one. And because you're here."

"You're smarter than you think, Val," said Ash softly.

Accustomed to performing feats of unimaginable flexibility, Val used one knee to power off the television remote. "A 'searching and fearless moral inventory' Ash. That means you don't lie to yourself. You don't tell yourself you're smart when you're on your third job in five months. You don't tell yourself you're smart when your bank account is DOA."

As it always did when the doubts grew larger, Val's voice also got louder, a little bit brassier. Brianna stirred in her mother's arms. "Hey, loud people, I'm trying to sleep here."

Val swore, completely unacceptable to eight-year-old ears. Nobody minded. "Wake Mom, will you?" she asked Ashley.

Ashley fought back a yawn, uncurled from the couch and rubbed her mother on her shoulder. "Mom. You need to get to bed. You have to work in the morning."

Joyce Larsen blinked her eyes and came awake abruptly. "Did I miss the news?"

"Yes, Mom, you slept through the news."

"Darn. I wanted to hear the weather. I bet it rains tomorrow. You should have woke me up."

"I'm waking you up now. Go to bed, Mom."

"I'm glad you're back, Ashley. I always worry about you flying. You're going to crash someday and die."

"I know, Mom. Get some sleep."

And people wondered where she got it from.

Thirty minutes later, Val dragged herself into the kitchen, obviously knowing where Ashley would be. When faced with the complications of life, some people turned to the church, others turned to sports. Ashley turned to the kitchen. To be more precise—cheese. "What should I do?" she asked, slicing up a wedge of swiss into small bite-sized nibbles.

"About what?" Val asked. "Your pathetic excuse for a love life?"

At that, Ashley almost told her. The words nearly slipped from her lips, but even with Val, she couldn't share. How could she talk about something she didn't even understand, and still didn't quite believe? "I'm talking about the stores."

"You're going to figure out what's wrong and fix it."

Fix it. *Yeah, just fix it, Ash.*

It sounded so easy, so completely staring-her-in-the-face easy. So why couldn't she figure it out? Forcefully Ashley hacked off another square before handing the cheese to her sister. "Why don't the women of Chicago realize that not only am I providing non-cookie-cutter clothes at a decent price, but by shopping at Ashley's Closet, they are contributing to the livelihood of struggling fashion designers everywhere?"

Val shrugged. "You could have a sale. A big sample sale thing."

"Sales, schmales," mocked Ashley, sawing furiously again.

"Tell me how you really feel."

"I need something pizzazzy, jazzy."

"You'll find it. You've got jazz."

I need jazz.

Ashley watched as Val popped a cube of swiss into her mouth, glad to see her sister's confidence level back to normal.

Val was a fast-spinning top that could fall off with only a word, a look, or a doubt. Unlike most people, when Val tipped over, it wasn't minutes or hours before she got up, it was weeks and months. It was Ashley's job to make sure she didn't tip.

"What's your schedule tomorrow?" Ashley asked.

"Seven to three. Why?"

"I've got a lot of catch-up to do at the stores. The Lakeview manager isn't returning messages, so God only knows what disaster will befall when I walk in the door. You won't see much of me. You and Mom have Brianna covered?"

"Yeah. We're good."

"Night, sis," said Ashley.

"Night." Quietly she took the last bit of cheese, then flicked off the light. Ashley could hear the soft sounds of Val padding down the carpeted hall behind her, and she ended the night the same way she always did.

"Val, I'm proud of you."

"As you should be."

Ashley smiled.

ONCE IN BED, Ashley pulled out The Card. She should have slipped him hers as well. But no, she didn't, she'd been cowardly, and because of that, if she wanted to ever see him again, it was all up to her

Ash, you go to Manhattan lots of times. Go see that new designer on the Lower East Side. You've been dying to see his work. This is your chance.

And what was the polite time frame to call up a man, whom you expressly told that it would be a mistake to see again?

There was no statute of limitations on a booty call.

He truly did have a fine booty.

Her hands curled and uncurled like a happy kitten because she could remember the feel of that firm piece of flesh under her fingertips, remembered the pleasuring fill of his thick sex. Now that was jazz. And no, she wasn't completely cheap and shallow. She liked him. He made her comfortable with herself. With everything, really.

That was the pull of one David McLean. He wasn't exotic, or vain, or some slutty billionaire.

He was, quite simply, the man she wanted.

Ashley stared at the card, recalling how his voice whispered against her ear, and she knew. That was it. Decision made. She'd set up an appointment in New York. Then she would call him, and if things were meant to proceed, he'd be ready, willing and available.

A long-distance affair.

Decadent.

Her mouth curved up at the corner, and all that night she dreamed of David.

THE LAKEVIEW STORE was a wreck. Her manager had quit, one salesgirl was late and the strapless smocked sundresses were priced twenty percent lower than what she paid for them. It was enough to make a weaker woman cry. But not

Ashley, not this time. She was still flying high on the aftershocks of great sex.

For the next week, Ashley worked eighteen-hour days to get the store back in order. Her first instinct was to promote the lead sales associate to manager, but honestly, that wasn't smart and she knew it, so she caved and put a Help Wanted sign in the window. Forty-eight hours later, she'd hired a new manager, a gum-popping twentysomething named Sophie, who didn't meet her eyes all the time, but her resumé was good, and she wore a great vintage Halston to the interview. That alone was enough to get her the job.

By the middle of the week, the Lakeview store was in better shape, and the Naperville, State Street and Wicker Park stores were holding their own. She was ready to make the call. It was late on a Wednesday that she decided to do it because she worried about whether he'd be alone on a Friday, or whether a Monday morning call seemed too needy. And what if he slept in late on Sundays?

Thankfully, he picked up on the first ring.

"Hello."

"David? It's Ashley," she told him, praying that he wouldn't ask, "Ashley-who?"

"Hi," he said, completely the perfect response.

"I'm going to be in New York."

"When?"

"Two weeks. If you're not busy..."

Don't be busy. If you're busy, I'm never going to call a man again in my life. Ever.

Don't be dramatic, Ash.

Shut up, Val.

"Not busy. We'll get dinner. Or a show. Or does that sound too normal? We don't have to do normal. You can stay here if you want. I've got space."

"No. I'm booking a room," she answered firmly, not the frugal answer, which was part of her problem, but hotels were dim, mysterious, sinful. Apartments were warm, homey and mundane. And if she found herself settling into his warm, homey and mundane, what would happen to all that smoking-hot passion? Would it disappear, as if it had never existed?

Not going to happen. She liked this smoking-hot passion. She was going to keep it.

"Is your hotel near the airport?"

Ashley tried not to laugh, but failed. "No."

"Good. How's work?"

"Not so good. But I'm optimistic."

"Much better than defeatist."

"Probably."

She thought about all the other things she could say, but they sounded neither exciting, nor affairish, so she elected to hold her tongue. "I should go now," she told him.

"Call me when you get in. Have a good flight, don't forget to pack your bunny slippers, and Ashley—"

"Yeah?"

"Thanks for calling."

"Anytime," she answered, before quickly hanging up.

5

THE FRIENDLY SKIES were extinct, along with dinosaurs, cheap interest rates and the commitment to customer service. The next week David flew fifteen thousand pain-filled miles to Portland, Houston, Seattle and two trips to DC. In the process, he discovered that the plastics company in Portland was running dangerously low on working capital, the oil services company in Houston was ripe for a friendly buyout and the people who worked in government had zero people skills. As he was waiting on the tarmac to head back to New York, Christine called.

"I'm sorry about your meeting. I debated a long time to call, kept hoping that you would call, but you didn't, so I decided I should. It would mean a lot to me, and Chris, too, if you could come and visit."

David eyed the air-sickness bag, felt the aftertaste of hard feelings rise in his throat and in the end politely opted to spare his fellow passengers excessive hurling noises. He was thirty-four, not four. "I'll try," he lied.

"Maybe you can reschedule the meeting. He misses you. He's your only brother."

Sucks, dude. I feel your pain.

"They're telling us to shut off all electronic devices, Christine. I need to hang up."

"David, you don't have to be like this."

Because he was exactly like that, David hung up.

IT WAS A WEDNESDAY afternoon at the start of earnings season, and the offices of Brooks Capital were humming with closing-bell guesses and bets and gossip and shadow numbers that were most likely pulled from someone's ass. David's office was on the forty-seventh floor, one below the executive floor, but he wasn't worried. His boss liked him. He liked his boss. Things were proceeding nicely. And nowhere else but Brooks Capital could he learn from the best of the best, Andrew and Jamie Brooks.

There were three monitors on his desk, one green screen to monitor the markets, one open to e-mail and the last was his latest work in progress, Portland Plastics. Market recommendation: Hold.

The door opened, and his boss, Jamie Brooks, walked in, perching herself on the desk, high heels swinging to an unknown beat.

"You have the latest on Houston Field Works?" she asked coolly.

Without missing a step, David handed over the folder. It was a test. She liked to test him, see if he was ever at a loss. He hadn't failed yet. "Anything else?" he asked confidently.

Jamie opened it, skimming over the introductory fluff, jumping right to the bottom line. "You're going to Omaha on Friday?" she asked, not looking up from the words, her expression an unreadable blank. David still wasn't worried.

"I'll be there." Nebraska was the home to an alternative energy company that was close to going public. On paper, they looked good. But David's job was to visit, kick the tires, peek under the hood and in general, see if the hype was worth it.

"Good," she said, and then closed the folder with a snap. "You're in for the pool on the Mercantile Financials report?"

David pulled a crisp c-note from his pocket. "Down ten-point-one percent."

She stared at him with appraising eyes. "Gutsy."

He shrugged modestly.

"Andrew says up three-point-four," she remarked. Andrew was Jamie's husband. The Man. Capital *T,* capital *M*.

In the last seven years, David had followed Andrew's every

move. When Andrew opened his own fund, David jumped at the chance to follow. When the market had put most hedge fund managers out on the street dancing for nickels, Brooks Capital had not only survived, but they were also still turning the same solid returns year after year. Andrew was as thorough and methodical as David, and he was usually right. Andrew Brooks made his reputation on being right. This time, however, Andrew Brooks was wrong.

"He's too high," David told her, perhaps more confidently than he should, but he'd done his homework, and he had a feeling. You always did your research, always gleaned over every piece of data available, but when push came to shove, bet on your instincts.

Not taking her eyes off David, Jamie slid the bill back and forth through her fingertips, thinking, considering, wondering if David could beat the master. Eventually she broke down and laughed. "Breaking from the crowd. I like it."

During his first days on the job at Brooks Capital, Jamie had intimidated David, but then one afternoon he had brought her a report on a waste management company in Dallas, and she'd pointed out the one tiny, yet deal-breaking detail that he'd missed. At first, he'd been all pissed and thought there was no way that she could be right, until that night, when his cooler head prevailed, and he went over his numbers, and holy shit, she was correct. Since then, she'd earned his respect in spades.

"We'll see who knows better," she said, still doubting him, but he didn't mind. Jamie provided a novel perspective in the male-dominated world of finance. And currently, that was exactly what he needed. A novel female perspective.

"Can I ask you something?"

"Shoot."

"Do you know fashion, you know, the business side—what makes a company work, what makes it not work, what women like in clothes?"

The swinging high heel froze. "Broadening your horizons

into fashion?" she asked, coughing discreetly. "Brave and not afraid of the stereotypes. Definitely gutsy."

"What do you know?" he asked, battling forward, even though he was deathly afraid of stereotypes.

"Driven by trends at the high end. At the mid-level, it's more about the classics and originality, and at the low end of the spectrum, it's nothing but trendy knockoffs and bargain-basement prices. What are you interested in?"

David thought over Ashley's travel attire and took a guess. "Mid-level. So, classics and originality are the drivers?"

Jamie nodded. "It's the *America's Next Top Designer* mentality. Women don't like to wear something that someone else is wearing. We're very territorial about fashion."

"America's Next Top Designer?"

"Television show. Ratings up ten percent on an annual basis, three years running. They've launched four successful designers, one not-so-successful designer, but I think that's because of his crappy designs. The guy was a certified disaster area."

His face assumed the requisite manly look of horror. "A show about sewing?"

"You have to watch. It's a train wreck, but a fun one. Why the interest?" she asked.

"It's for a friend. She's got these clothing boutiques, and is having some issues. I thought I could give her some advice. Try and figure out what's going wrong." Next week Ashley would be in New York, and he wanted to understand the fashion industry, help her determine what problems could be fixed, and also have his wicked way with her eight ways to Sunday. It was a big assignment, but not impossible. It might mean watching reality TV. It might mean learning what was hot on the female clothing market. He would survive. Probably. Hopefully.

"This is all for a *she?*" asked Jamie, quirking one perfectly arched brow, just as David's e-mail window popped into sight, indicating an unread e-mail had arrived.

David, I would *love* to meet you. I'm nineteen, which is younger than what you requested in your profile, but it's a mature nineteen…

He inched his shoulders forward, blocking the view, blocking the view…not quite blocking the view from his boss.

Jamie glanced at the now-fading window, then glanced pointedly at David. He elected to stay silent. It seemed the prudent thing to do.

"Dating again?"

He shrugged in a completely noncommittal, I-don't-want-to-talk-about-my-private-life manner.

She didn't take the hint. "I think it's a good thing. You should have done this a long time ago. I have some friends—"

"No," he answered quickly.

His boss shook her head, then smiled. "All right. Have it your way. But if you change your mind, I swear, they're all nice women."

David pulled another hundred out of his pocket, mainly to divert her. "Give me another hundred on Mercantile Financial."

She took the bill, clearly not fooled by the diversionary tactic, but gave him a pass, because Jamie was nice like that. "More courage, sport. And Andrew's going to kick your ass, but you're brave. I like it."

Once Jamie left, David wiped the wayward sweat from his brow and opened the offending e-mail.

Dating. He could feel the perspiration pooling at his neck. After the night with Ashley, he'd thought he was ready for this, she'd told him he was ready for this, but…this was wrong. It felt wrong. It felt…idiotic. David never liked feeling like an idiot, but after he saw the picture, the idiot feelings got worse.

Oh, yes, there was a picture. It was a picture that men—cheap, goaty bastards that they all were—would jump all over. Totally not safe for work. She was pert, all right. Too pert. There was no meat in those breasts. No experience, no... Stop, he thought, stop now. He minimized the window, opting for a safer, more calming spreadsheet.

Right then, his cell phone rang, saving his cheap and goaty ass. Was it boneheaded to stare at a topless picture of a willing nineteen-year-old from Brooklyn while wishing his caller ID said Chicago? Probably.

"Yeah," he answered.

"David?"

"That's me."

"It's Martina. From I-Heart-You.com. They said you okayed the call."

David closed his eyes. Courage. He only needed courage. He could do this. "Yeah, I remember you," he mumbled, trying to remember. "Female...twenty-seven."

"Twenty-four."

"And a...lawyer?" he guessed.

"Editor."

"Oh, sure. Only a second ago I got off the phone with a lawyer. My mind can be like a black hole sometimes. Too many late nights," he rambled on, wincing.

"I wanted to call and chat. See what you sound like."

What he sounded like? What was that about? He had a voice. An average voice. And now what was he supposed to say? "Yeah. This is what I sound like."

And who was this Martina anyway?

"You work on Wall Street?"

"Yeah," he repeated, exactly as an idiot would.

"I like that. It must be very exciting."

David glanced at the green screen, then at his report, and frowned. "Thrilling." After a long, panicked moment, he realized he was supposed to add to the conversation. "So, why a dating service? Do you meet any...good guys this way?"

"They're all better than my ex. The man was a pig. Cheated on me once, but I stayed strong. Kicked him right out of my life."

And what could he say to that? His panicked eyes shot to the Dow, searching for some constant, some bit of normalcy.

The market was down three hundred for the day. It seemed only fitting. "Sorry. Want to have lunch?"

"Love to. I'm in midtown. Tomorrow?"

"Can't." David checked his calendar, looked at the open day next week and frowned. He didn't want to do this, he really didn't want to do this. But it was time to man up, move forward and get back on track. "Next Wednesday? April twenty-second. Noon?"

"Love to," she told him.

Good God. He had a date.

IN ALL THERE WERE four mindless dates. One Kim, one Pam and two Ashleys, who sadly, were nothing like the original. Oh, the women were all nice enough, hot enough, but there was no zing, no bam. Just a feeling that he was reading a magazine, looking at pretty pictures, and there were no articles with the pictures. Ashley had been wrong, telling him to try a dating service. He'd known she'd been wrong, but he felt a strong urge to go through with her suggestion, if for the sole purpose of being able to tell her she was wrong when he saw her again.

The only slightly enjoyable date was with Martina, who was nice, blond, the type who wore a lot of black. Not in the goth sense, but in the twiglike New York female sense who only know one color. Black.

They met at an outdoor café on 52nd, crowded with springtime traffic, and for forty-five minutes he listened to her talk about Barney, the ex, until David felt solely responsible for the sins of the entire male gender.

"You must hate listening to me like this," she told him over dessert.

"I don't mind. Honest," he said, because as long as she monopolized the chatter, he didn't have to say a word.

"Sometimes I think I still love him. He liked to flirt, and sometimes he carried it too far. That makes me stupid, doesn't it?"

David's first instincts were to agree, that infidelity could never be forgotten, but that wasn't the way to carry on normal human relations. Besides, he knew what love could do to people. "Not stupid. Love isn't easy. You think it should be perfect. That if two people are together, they stay loyal, they stay together. If you can't do that, is it really love?"

"I think it could be."

"Your ex was weak."

"Not true. He was very strong, but sometimes Barney..." Martina's voice trailed off with a sigh and David understood that an argument over her ex's flaws was pointless. She had her heart set to stupid and he wasn't going to talk her out of it.

"He works on Wall Street, too. Chase, in investment banking. I shouldn't have called you. I should be out looking at cops, or firemen, or cabbies. Some other type. Instead all I want to do is call him back, say I want to try again."

"Don't do that."

She looked at him confused, not getting the big picture. "Why not?"

"'Cause he's a pig. You told me he was a pig. You don't want to be in love with a pig."

"You're right."

"I know I'm right." When people got soft, they got stupid. Here was Martina, proving his theory and he'd only known her for an hour.

She twirled her fork on her plate, making circles in the raspberry sauce. "Do you know any guys from Chase?"

"You're thinking of hooking up with one of his colleagues? That's pretty cold. Clever, but still cold."

"And betray him? God, no. I wanted to see how he was doing."

David felt like banging his head on the table. She was turning soft. Martina would call this prick, take him back and get screwed all over again. Sad story. Why did people do this to themselves?

But who was he to judge? "If I hear anything, I'll let you know," he promised. Inside he told himself that she should be running from this clown, far and fast. She was a nice kid. Too bad he couldn't help her.

Hmm, maybe he could.

FOR DAVID, Ashley couldn't get to New York fast enough. Three days and counting, and already his nights were getting better. Two nights before, he'd dreamed about her e-mailing him a photo, not safe for work. And then last night, she'd been there in his private Lear jet, dressed in a flight attendant's uniform. She came toward him, then sat on his lap in the best sort of way. In between triple-X fantasies, he'd been researching the fashion biz, even reading the top magazines, not that it helped. David still hadn't developed a clear understanding of the business side of the industry, but he had developed a clear understanding that he didn't know shit about fashion.

Women were odd.

His ex had understood fashion. Christine was always meticulously dressed, down to the perfectly matching shoes and earrings, and David hadn't bothered with the details of what women wore. There were two states. Clothed and unclothed, and honestly, as a man, he preferred the latter.

But this time, he perused the pages of *Vogue* as a man on a mission. He could help Ashley. He didn't know how, but he knew he could, and he knew he would. He was an analyst. It was in his blood.

Eventually, Tuesday arrived. David told himself it was no big deal. Of course, he did so *after* he dug out a tie that he hadn't worn in seven years—not since his first lunch at Brooks Capital. In the back of his mind, after two weeks of dealing with samples of New York's single women—strange e-mails, stranger propositions, and more personal questions than he'd ever known existed—he'd been worried about seeing Ashley in person again. Wondering if the reality lived up to the Ashley-memory hype in his brain. After Brittany, Pam, Ashley and Ashley, he was now a lot more doubtful about his own judgment.

He was supposed to meet Ashley after she finished her meeting at a small studio in Brooklyn, because to pick her up at the airport would seem *ordinary*—her word, not his. However, a cab ride across the Brooklyn Bridge was no big deal, and with the late afternoon sun at his back, he now found himself on an artsy street that looked like Soho-cum-late '80s. Up and coming, trendy, yet not quite brain-exploding expensive.

The front of the building was a large plate-glass window with sleek black mannequins in the window. Some were dressed, some undressed, and he suspected that was intentional, although it did defeat the primary purpose of a large display window, which was to advertise one's wares. David wasn't interested in mannequins though, dressed or otherwise, instead his hungry gaze sought out Ashley, nearly buried beneath a rack of dresses.

She didn't see him; she was too engrossed in the clothes to notice. For a second, one greedy second, he stopped to stare, comparing reality to the hype. Three weeks vanished into nothing. His mouth grew dry.

He shook his head, his brain, lungs and libido all running amok.

Why her? What was it about her that drew his eye? Her hair? It wasn't long; it wasn't short. It hung right at her shoulders, curving under on the ends. She wore what seemed to be the requisite Ashley Larsen skirt and tank. Her curves weren't model-thin, nor Playboy-lush, just neat and cushiony, and exactly right for his hands…for his cock.

David told himself not to go there because he was *not* a randy dog. They had several hours of polite conversation before he could go there. No point in killing his self-control before he even started.

Then she pushed back the dark of her hair, starting a conversation with the designer, and he could feel that hair, remembered that hair brushing against his chest, and oh, yeah…

Hell.

There he was, killing his self-control, and there wasn't a damned thing he could do about it.

She turned, met his eyes. He couldn't look away. He wanted to take her right there. His cock pressed forward, exactly as if that was the plan. It wasn't memory or hype.

Sex. The great decider.

He focused on the concrete sidewalk, shaking off the lust that he knew was in his eyes, and when he walked through the door, he was completely in control once again.

6

CONTROL LASTED about seven minutes because it took David seven minutes to decide he hated Enrique's guts. The man-boy was stab-you-in-the-back ambitious, with a Latin glo-tan, and the biggest sin of all, he kept dismissing Ashley with his eyes, as if she were intruding on his personal space at this tiny, most probably rat-infested workshop.

"I like what you're doing with prints," she gushed, while David stood there, silently seething.

The little twit swept toward the green flower print in the window, his arms wide, as if he were about to burst into song. "People shy away from big, but if it wraps the body, captures the spirit in a sensual embrace of fabric, it's fantabulous. There is no other word."

"I'd like to sell some of your designs in Chicago," Ashley told him, nodding politely.

"My work belongs here in New York. Next to the latest Polly Sue's Fashions, my clothes cannot breathe." He took a deep breath, drawing circles of air with his hand. "They need to breathe."

"Ashley…" David started, but then she flashed him a nervous smile. No, he was not here to interfere, he was not here to smash a fist in Enrique's smarmy little face.

"Give me a second here," she told him, completely not understanding the dynamics of the room. People got one shot, and if they weren't in one hundred percent, you walked away, no mess, no fuss.

Ashley turned back to Enrique. "It's a very good opportunity. I don't carry a lot of stock. I'm more interested in quality than quantity. Ashley's Closet—the unique, exclusive, shopping experience."

Enrique smiled tightly. "No, Enrique does not think so."

David didn't think so, either. He stepped beside Ashley because now it was time to interfere. "If Enrique doesn't see the opportunity, he's not the visionary you want. You need designs that cry out above the masses." David looked around the store, hiding his anger, his eyes carefully bored. "This isn't it."

Enrique turned four shades of red, and Ashley punched him in the arm.

"My designs are miles above the masses," the designer snapped. "Who are you?"

Now, there were certain times when Wall Street had a cachet, when David knew he'd picked a job in high finance for a reason. This was one of those times. He pulled out his card and handed it to Enrique. "We're backing Miss Larsen on this. A retail play on *America's Next Top Designer*. Finding only the best designs, letting judges and her clientele see who is most deserving of Chicago's Next Big Look."

Ashley's mouth gaped, only slightly. David kept his features carefully schooled in arrogant boredom.

"You're going to create a reality show?" asked Enrique, his eyes now resting on Ashley with the appropriate amount of respect. *Yeah, buddy, don't mess with my girl.*

No. Ashley mouthed the word to David. He ignored her, and waved what he hoped was an artistic hand. Now that the words were out of his mouth, honestly, it was a brilliant idea.

"Oh, no," he said. "Not at all. We're going to create exclusivity. As you said, above the masses, not mingling with the masses. There will be exposure, of course. The press, possibly some morning-show type coverage, but we want the experience to focus on the designs themselves, rather than a three-ring circus surrounding the designers."

Ashley only stared.

"Why not New York?" Enrique asked, dollar signs now reflected in his eyes.

"Why not New York?" repeated Ashley, and there were no dollar signs in her eyes, but now she was curious, and he could see her working through the details.

David nearly smiled.

"New York has been done. L.A. has been done. This is a very boutique experience, not something for the tabloids. We felt Ashley's Closet had the right mix of both fresh and élan. Image is all."

"Can I think about it?" asked Enrique, and Ashley nodded her head.

David clenched his hands, not happy to be working with Enrique. The dimwit would have to learn to treat Ashley with respect, but that would come eventually. "You have twelve hours to decide. We have other designers to look at. There is no time to waste."

Enrique looked at the clock on the wall. "I'll do it," he said.

David nodded once. He'd never had a doubt. "We'll messenger the contracts."

Ashley turned to David, her smile nervous. "Contracts? What contracts?"

DAVID SLUNG HER carry-on over his shoulder and Ashley scurried out the door after him onto the busy Brooklyn sidewalk.

"You are in so much trouble," she started, as soon as Enrique was out of visual range. "I can't believe you just made all that up."

He stopped, and looked at her with complete seriousness, no twinkle of mischief at all. "No. I think you can do it. Do you?"

He'd been serious? *Seriously serious?*

"Of course I think I can do it," she lied. Her mind flipped through all the pros, and the cons, and then more cons, and then the biggest con of all, that she could actually get anyone in the fashion universe to care.

"You shouldn't doubt yourself, Ashley," he told her, because she'd never been a good liar. A double-barreled baby carriage zoomed past, and Ashley moved aside, only after the mother glared meaningfully.

Hesitantly she took a step closer to the safety of the brick wall behind her. "David, I was looking to get some interesting designs in the stores, to sell more stock, not make the evening news."

The light turned, cars began to move and David moved dangerously close to the curb, signaling for a cab, handling her luggage and still managing to carry on a conversation at the same time.

"You won't make the evening news. It's the morning show circuit you're after. *Good Morning, Chicago*. Maybe Oprah. Nothing too much because you want people to come into the stores to see the designs. Just a taste. That's all you need."

Oprah—oh, God, he was tossing out Oprah like they were discussing last season's overstocks. Ashley watched as the line of cabs moved past, and there was no one stopping. "Are there no empty cabs in Brooklyn?"

"It's a bad time of day. Everybody is leaving Manhattan, not going in," he explained, his arm still patiently outstretched.

"How long are we going to have to wait?"

"Not that long."

Ashley took a hard look at the line of unlighted cabs, took a harder look at the weight of her carry-on and then took a hard, hard, hard look at the bridge. The choices were narrowing exponentially. Again, she glanced toward David, so capable, so confident, so sure.

He actually thought she could do this. He actually thought that she could bribe/blackmail/arm-twist almost-famous designers to bring their newest and best looks into her boutiques.

Maybe she could. Maybe it wasn't a big deal. So why did it feel like a big, big deal? She looked at the bridge, looked at her heels.

No, Ash, don't be a fruitcake. You'll only embarrass yourself.

David doesn't think I'll be embarrassed.

He doesn't know you're thinking of hoofing it across a huge-ass bridge in heels. Do you know what those little rebars do to heels?

I can do this.

Go ahead, don't listen to me. But if you get stuck...I'll be laughing.

Ashley lifted her chin, grabbed her carry-on from David. "Let's walk."

"There will be cabs, Ashley. We can wait."

He didn't think she could do it.

"No," she said, taking off for the span as if it were Everest.

She was about to walk to Manhattan. Frankly, it didn't seem that far. And they had a nice walkway specifically for pedestrians to walk safely across, high above the traffic. Of course, the walkway was very high. Very, very high. Very, very above-the-clouds high.

Okay, Ash. One step at a time. Not hard at all.

"Ashley!"

She turned and looked, hefted her bag an inch higher. "Are you going to come, or not?"

"This is not a good idea," he told her, but he was walking. Progress.

"And yours is?" she drawled with more than a little sarcasm. Yes, it was sarcasm because he was probably right, and she didn't want to admit it; however, he didn't think she could do this, she didn't think she could do this, but the only way to overcome a fear was to do it. So, while there might not be intelligence in this decision, there was value, and sometimes that made it smart.

David tugged the carry-on from her hand and continued onward. She didn't fight much. Any. "The show is a great idea."

Sadly, he was right, and she took two steps to catch up. "Are you actually considering backing this?"

David shook his head—that was a big no—and she was

both relieved and disappointed. Relieved because with money came lots of responsibility. Disappointed because, well, it would have been heady to know that David was behind her, and with money, she could do wondrous things.

"You don't need any capital, Ashley. That's the beauty of the idea. Maybe a few ads if you want. You should have some receptions for the showings, but mainly, it's the idea. Do you like the idea?"

"Maybe," she replied, trying to keep pace with him. He was fast, his legs a mile longer than hers, but she managed and now they were up on the span, climbing higher and higher in the center lane, the going-home pedestrian traffic flowing against them. Still David kept on walking, not looking in her direction. On the level below them, the cars zoomed back and forth, and below that—far, far below that—lurked the black waters of the East River. She didn't know how cold the East River was in May, probably not as cold as Lake Michigan, but it looked dangerous nonetheless. Ashley looked down, slowed down.

"If you don't like it, don't do it," he stated, his voice laced with frustration.

"It's brilliant," she admitted. "What if no one cares?"

"Of course they'll care," he answered, starting up again, overtaking her, passing her, until she was nearly running to keep up.

"Can you stop for a minute?" she yelled, causing a biker to nearly tip over. She didn't even care. Damn Yankees. Thought they owned everything.

"What?" He stopped and turned. His dark eyes focused on her, without a trace of comfortable green. His face looked pinched, flushed, and not from the heat. At ten thousand feet in the air, there was no heat, or at least, not that sort of heat.

He was aroused.

Oh. My. God.

Well, maybe mad and aroused, a strange combination that piqued both her curiosity and her nipples. Why was he mad?

She was the one who should be mad. What right did he have to steal her hard-earned anger?

"I'm talking here," she said, determined not to be intimidated—or seduced—out of her own self-righteous indignation. "Couldn't you have discussed this with me first, instead of throwing it out there?"

"It just came to me, Ashley. If I had thought of it earlier, I would have discussed it with you, but honestly, it's the perfect solution, and you got Enrique—the prick—but okay, you got him locked in, so what's the problem?"

It would have helped if they weren't standing on a bridge with a gazillion New Yorkers walking home from work. It would have helped if there wasn't a large body of water way too close beneath her. It would help if he didn't look so Davidly. He stood there, feet wide, her carry-on slung on his shoulder, letting the sea of people wash around him, ignoring the cabbies a thousand miles below them, cars honking, bikes whizzing past, the barges schlubbing through the water, all the noises, the bigness of the city, and simply stood there, staring at *her*.

And your boutiques, Ash. Let's not lose sight of the boutiques.

Some of the hardness, some of that arrogance, left his eyes, and immediately she felt her body release the tension, and her breathing return to normal.

"If you don't want to do it, you don't have to," he offered again, watching her carefully. "I'll go back, tell Enrique that the whole thing is a sham, give him an earnest and sincere apology. Then you can get back on your trail of finding more clothes for the store. Is that what you want?"

Oh, undermining her own undermining. Sneaky. Very, very sneaky.

She peered out across the bridge, through the webbing of steel cables toward the booming skyline of Manhattan. Why the hell not?

"I'm going to make this work," she announced, completely

without fear, or mostly without fear. There wasn't a lot of fear. Honestly. "Do you think I can pull this off?"

He nodded once.

"Really?" she probed, looking carefully to see if there was even a speck of doubt in his eyes.

He nodded again. No doubts.

"Thank you," she said, smiling. A man who evaluated million-dollar deals for a living believed she could pull off the most out-of-left-field idea she'd ever heard.

Whoa. Awesome stuff.

David started walking again. "And it's about time you thanked me. Now, tell me where we're going. I have no idea where we're going."

"Hotel Wilde. I thought it was unboring."

"You're not boring."

"I could be more exotic though, more flashy, more élan-ful." She checked her skirt, and immediately thought she should have accessorized better. Maybe a clunky bracelet...or gold. Gold was good.

He stopped, put down the carry-on and leaned against the metal railing. Then he took her hand, laid it hard against the thick ridge behind his fly.

The man has no need for accessories.
Do not say another word, Val.
S'all right. I like him.

"You don't need more élan. Trust me."

The oxygen was getting thin up here, causing a throbbing void between her thighs. It had been three weeks since she had felt—or filled—that void. In Chicago, Ashley had tried not to dwell on the void because it seemed pointless and unsatisfying. Although in that moment, with the feel of all that, Davidness still hot in her hand, Ashley realized the void was about to get filled.

Hello, New York.

With the breeze whipping through the steel girders and deadly water a meager thousand miles below, Ashley tugged at his tie, drew David close and touched his mouth with hers. It was intended to be a hello kiss, a thank-you kiss, but it wasn't any of those. Instead, it was two very overheated people exploding. In less than a heartbeat, she was locked to him, his hands knotted in her shirt, pulling and twisting. His hard mouth worked over hers, and she could feel the anger firing under the surface, his heart pounding against her breasts. Mad...and aroused.

Bliss.

She dug her hands in his hair, his hard ridge firmly pressing between her thighs, and her wanton thighs quivered again.

Below them came the sound of a siren winding down, and then a bullhorn. "I know it's a tourist thing, but you guys really need to get a room."

David lifted his head, his breathing labored, and Ashley felt the sea of traffic wash over her, and it didn't seem scary. It felt exciting. Her gaze met his eyes, and she could read his mind. They were going to have sex again...soon. And it was going to be even better. She was going to be naked. He was going to be naked.

Eighteen naked hours before her flight home.

Eighteen hours wasn't going to be enough.

The siren wound up again. "Hello! Earth to Romeo and Juliet. Get a room, will ya?"

Ashley smiled, as any good tourist would. "That's where we're headed."

THE HOTEL ROOM had red walls. Scarlet walls that were the color of hell. Behind the bed hung a modern painting of a woman's open mouth, or at least David hoped that was a mouth. Red, wet. He twisted his head.

No, that wasn't a mouth.

Whoa.

Ashley was in the bathroom freshening up. He shouldn't have walked her across the bridge, but he needed to work off some of his excess energy. He hadn't been ready to sit in a cab with her, not without mauling her. David wasn't a mauler. He was an analyst.

The extra poundage in his shorts seemed to dispute that fact.

"The bathroom is great. You should see this," Ashley yelled, and then she emerged from the bathroom, wearing a blue striped tank, blue skirt and sandals, and it was sexier than black lace. There were no buttons, no hooks, no zippers, nothing but easy-access cloth.

"Are you still mad?" she asked, and it took him a second to realize she meant emotionally, not mentally. Madness. In a lot of ways, that's what it felt like. He was fevered and incoherent. It couldn't be healthy.

"I was never mad," he answered, fighting for what was left of his self-control.

She walked toward him, and then he could smell her—smell the quiet intensity that always hung in the air around her. He closed his eyes, absorbing her smell. For the past hour, all he could think about was touching her, burying himself inside her.

Nearly three weeks since he'd seen her; three weeks was a long time. A man could want a lot in three weeks. A man could hunger a lot in three weeks. It was the most logical explanation.

Except he had no logic. It was as if she twisted the wires until logic was impossible.

The madness started all over again. His eyes opened, and she was still there. Waiting for him to do something.

"David," she whispered urgently. Her eyes flared, and he snapped.

They fell to the bed, and he offed her skirt in mid-fall. The panties were not removed, merely pushed aside. Condom was hastily installed, this time his fly was thankfully unstuck, and then David was buried deep inside Ashley. It took a second to restart his lungs, restart his heart, but his cock needed no restarting. No, it had found heaven all on its own.

Once again, there was no finesse. Actually, after three weeks of waiting, it was more frenzied than before. He prayed she didn't mind. The blind hunger in her eyes said she didn't.

It was fast, it was furious. Way too fast and way too furious, and she came with a long, low moan that ripped through him. This was more death than sex. His orgasm nearly killed him. After he came, David collapsed against the pillows.

Once again, Ashley scooted over to the far side of the bed. Considering the size of this bed, that was halfway to Jersey. His arm raised toward her, his fingers stretched, but her back had that turtle-shell look going, and David admitted that he didn't know what to do.

They had a relationship defined by sex, hijacked by sex, and anything outside of sex—friendship, romance, business—now felt strained.

Was that really a bad thing?

He considered the smooth bare back in front of him, the golden rose hue of her skin, the sleek curve of her spine and decided that yes, yes, it was.

This was going to have to stop. He was going to have to make it stop.

He liked Ashley, he liked talking to her, he liked the almost-not-quite confidence in her. As a divorced man getting e-mails that flipped his stomach, he understood it.

The first time they'd had awesome sex, they had talked about it, laughed about it, because it was so extraordinary, a once-in-a-lifetime deal. But the second time? What do you say when you realize it's not once-in-a-lifetime, but every time?

No, he wasn't going to analyze this. Not now.

"Ashley," he said, and the turtle-shell relaxed…a little. She turned, and her hair brushed across her eyes. He wanted to see her eyes, but she kept them hidden.

"Are you okay?" he asked.

She nodded quickly.

"Are you mad?" he asked.

She shook her head.

"Are you ever going to talk to me again?"

She giggled. The face lifted, and he saw the spark back in her eyes. Something lifted in his chest.

"Are you hungry?" he asked, because he thought he should feed her. It seemed polite.

"No, thank you."

"How was the flight?" he asked, and she inched closer. That was good.

"Uneventful."

"Takeoff?"

"I took four Dramamine," she admitted.

"Landing?"

"I slept through it."

He gave her an attagirl smile. "Excellent."

"I think it was the medicine and the two glasses of wine that did it."

"I think it was you."

Divorce had done a number on him, but he could look at his career and feel good about his decisions. Ashley didn't have that luxury. Divorce and career were going after her, double-barreled. It didn't seem fair. He wanted to pull her to him, and hold her, but lying in a black-sheeted bed with a woman's sexual organs artistically laid out on the wall was not the place to hold someone in comfort.

His fingers opened and closed, and if a man wasn't an analyst, he wouldn't have noticed.

She sighed, and rolled onto her back, staring up at the red ceiling. David eyed the shadowy curves where the covers barely hid her nipples, and his cock pushed against the sheet. Oh, jeez, he was such a goat.

"I'm going to have to find more designers," she stated, her voice a little firmer now.

"You will."

"Can you help?"

It was a tempting idea, part of the reason—a lot of the

reason—he blurted everything out to Enrique like he did, and didn't give her a chance to say no. So, she was in Chicago, and he was in New York. It was the best of both worlds. All the excitement. None of the commitment. No worries.

"Is that what you want?" he asked.

Her worried gaze met his eyes. "It's what I want." After a minute she spoke again, not so worried this time. "Why the argument on the bridge?"

"Because the *USS Intrepid* was booked."

She didn't laugh.

He met her eyes again, and this time, he knew he was the worried one. "I thought you'd like it," he offered.

"No, you didn't," she told him, completely unfooled.

David sighed. "Okay, I didn't think you'd like it. You needed the distraction. You needed to walk across to know you could do anything you wanted."

"Like stranger sex?" she asked, an innocent question. The look on her face wasn't so innocent.

"Not exactly," he told her. Honestly, he didn't know why he kept pushing her like some cheese-dick asshole. It wasn't who he was. He was laid-back, carefree, except when consumed by raging lust. But when he'd watched her with that jerk of a designer, when he saw the beaten look in Ashley's eyes, it ate at his gut and pissed him off. Probably because it reminded him of a lot of things about his own life that pissed him off, too.

And wasn't that too much self-analysis for the day? His analytical eyes wandered back to the covers where he could ogle Ashley and analyze her naked flesh to his heart's content. No worries.

"I liked being on the bridge," she told him, and then she smiled.

"I did, too."

"Do you like the hotel?" she asked, and her voice was so full of enthusiasm, he wasn't heartless enough to tell the truth.

"Love it," he said, punching a pillow in a golly-gee sort of way. Frankly, it wasn't so bad. Actually, it was growing on him.

The red walls were growing on him. The sleek black sheets were growing on him. Nah, that was all bullshit. It was the idea of Ashley underneath him that was growing on him.

Perhaps sensing the direction of his thoughts, she sat upright, covers falling away, and she grinned. "It's sorta goth-vampire falls in love with George O'Keefe and they have a love child. It's very now."

He liked seeing her unassuming grin, seeing the way it belonged on her face. This was Ashley Larsen the way God had intended. "Yeah."

"And you should see the shower." She stood up, all bare and curves, and David felt his control slipping away. "It's delicious. You can fit like fourteen people in there."

All David needed was two.

7

AN HOUR HAD PASSED, her skin slightly pruned. Ashley stepped away from the three walls of jets and wrapped a toasty towel around her body.

David was otherwise occupied, studying the brass pipes and hardware that trailed down the tiled walls like a half-filled Scrabble board.

His hands were gentle, yet firm on the metal. "I like it. Brass Fittings. I'm going to have to remember that name. Easily customized, yet still well made."

Honestly, he was well made. Very subtle, very lean. Wide shoulders that would be best displayed in a straight-cut European style. Long legs that could wear white, a pant color that few men could carry off well, and then there was the derriere...

Ashley sighed.

He looked back at her. "I don't think they're public. Have you heard of them?"

She shook her head, totally bemused. "I don't think I ever have."

"I'm going to look it up."

He was so curious, so intent, so completely content with himself, whether he was sexy, jerky, analytical, or nice. She didn't understand him, didn't quite understand what they were doing, and she didn't think he did, either.

You're having great sex. Go with it, Ash. It's nothing more than that.

And what happens when it goes bad, or even worse, fizzles?
What happens if it doesn't?
Can you just relax and enjoy the moment?
No. Moments don't last, that's why they call them moments.
Right then, her cell rang, and Ashley ran to get it.
It was Val.
"Hey, what's up?" Ashley asked in a brisk, businessy, not-having-fun, not-getting-laid tone.
"I can't find the school form from Brianna's doctor. I looked everywhere, Ash. Where'd you hide it?"
A family crisis. They occurred often, usually on a daily basis. Ashley tucked the towel securely in place. "I didn't hide it anywhere, Val. Did you look in the desk?"
"I looked there. Mom took apart the kitchen. They need it tomorrow. You won't be back tomorrow. I need to find the form."
"Don't panic," Ashley told her in a calm, soothing voice.
"That's easy for you to say, she's not your kid."
"That's not fair."
"You're right. I'm panicked. I'm in bad-mother mode. I don't like bad-mother mode. It makes me surly. Tell me where the form is and I'll get off the phone and leave you to your clothes calls."
David padded into the room, completely naked, completely not shy, and her eyes were drawn...drawn...
Ashley swallowed, not used to overt male nudity. Jacob had been shy, never wandering around naked, never making her tongue grow too big for her mouth.
"Ash?"
She jumped and shifted her eyes away from the light. "Did you check the coffee table in the living room?"
"I did."
"Did you move Brianna's books out of the way? Things get hidden under there."
"I didn't move the books, but wait a minute, we're moving the books now, still moving, still moving, and yes, thank you, Jesus, that *is* a doctor's form. You are a lifesaver."

"I know," she said, feeling the bed shift under added weight. Ashley kept her eyes averted until she couldn't help herself and the eyes turned back to the light.

David was sacked out next to her on the bed, and was studying her with his analyst's look. Curious, assessing, trying to figure out the conversation from the one side that he was hearing.

"I should go, Val." And she should because she wasn't going to tell David about Val, and she wasn't going to tell Val about David.

"Why are you trying to brush me off here?" asked Val.

"Work to do," she lied, not liking the lie to Val, but it made things easier. There were dishonest lies, and then there were lies for the betterment of mankind. This was definitely the latter kind.

"Brianna wants to say hello. Say hello to Aunt Ash, will you?"

"Hi, Ashley, Bashley."

"Hi," whispered Ashley.

"We miss you, Ash. Valerie said that when you got back you'd take me shopping."

"I don't think she said that."

"She didn't, but she thought it."

"I don't think she thought it."

An impudent hand was tugging at her towel, threatening to remove it, and she clapped strong—pit-bull strong—fingers over the hand. She would not have this conversation with her niece without the sanctity of a towel. It seemed...well, way too debauched for her.

"I have to get back to work," Ashley said, since she sensed the towel would not be around for long.

"I love you, Aunt Ash. We all do. See you tomorrow. And don't be too scared on the flight."

"You're an angel," Ashley told her, then hung up the phone.

"Who was that?" asked David.

"My niece and sister. I told you."

"Oh, yeah, the bossy one."

"We should get dressed and go eat," she said, feeling intensely naked under his gaze even though she was still wearing a towel.

"Okay." So with an easy shrug, he got dressed just like that. As if everything was no big deal. For Ashley, everything was a big deal, worthy of consideration and internal debate because her first instincts usually weren't good.

She liked analyst-David. He was harmless, sometimes goofy and didn't make her think about things she didn't want to think about, and when he was like that, the David need wasn't so overwhelming. It felt warm and comfortable, like homemade chicken soup.

It was when he was hard and moody and decisive that she got nervous. Ashley was, or had been, a firm believer in considering all your options, make a plan—i.e., buy four boutiques—stick to the plan, and with enough hard work and perseverance, the plan paid off, or you hoped it would. But sometimes it didn't—i.e., expenses for said plan boutiques outweighed income—and you had to readjust. It was the readjustment that gave her grief because Ashley wasn't a good readjuster. She needed consistency. She needed routine. She needed time for the internal debate—in order to plan, of course.

Ashley took her clothes from the bed and got dressed, as if everything was no big deal. He watched her though, and the air started to heat up again. She kept her eyes on the mirror, but in some ways that was worse. She could see his eyes watching her, and feel the automatic pull in her body. She wondered if he could see what was happening to her—see the damp clench between her thighs, see the heavy swell in her breasts.

She thought he could because his eyes were hooded and shadowed, and there was a dark flush to his face.

Quickly she pulled on her skirt, tugged that tank over her head, and this time when she looked at him in the mirror, his eyes had returned to the same no-big-deal hazel, and the heat was nothing more than the lack of an open window.

Her smile was mostly relieved.

"Ready to go?" she asked.

"Anytime," he answered in a warm, comfortable voice, exactly like chicken soup.

That, she could handle.

DAVID TOOK HER to eat at a barbecue place on 125th street. It was a hole-in-the-wall with great ribs and fried green tomatoes. Over dinner they argued about baseball, politics and the irrational idiosyncrasies of the female fashion style. Actually, David threw Ashley that last one because he liked to hear her argue, liked to watch her cheeks smolder and her shoulders jerk when she got particularly fired up. It took a lot to fire up Ashley Larson, but when she was sparked, the whole world burned brighter. David liked the burn.

"Tell me about your family," he asked after their plates had been cleared from the table. He felt like he should know more about her. He knew the big stuff. Knew she was afraid of flying, knew she wanted to make her stores a success, but he didn't know all of the little stuff. Like her family, and why she didn't say much about her marriage. He wanted to understand how a female came by a fascination for horror films, and whether her ex-husband was somehow responsible. David made his name, and most of his decisions, by thorough research, and reviewing a problem from all angles, and although he'd reviewed Ashley from many physical angles, it was the stuff inside her head that made him curious.

"You don't want to know about my family," she commented, dodging his question, which of course, made him more curious.

"I do."

"I have a sister, a mother, and a niece."

"What was the call about?"

"Val lost a form. She needed help finding it."

At one time, David might have called Chris for exactly that, called him to talk about the hell that was now airline travel, might have even called him to bitch about the dating service.

It was one of the reasons that Chris' betrayal hurt. He wanted to cut his brother out of his heart, out of his life, but Chris was there, they shared DNA, they shared memories. For nearly ten hellish years, they'd shared a room. Amputating your brother wasn't as easy as someone might think.

"And they called you on a business trip to help find it?" he asked, watching her push back her hair, part avoidance, part nervousness, a lot sexy.

Quickly she shook her head, sending her hair back in her face. "My family's boring. Let's not talk about my family. Let's talk about exciting things. Like how you're going to revitalize Ashley's Closet." She propped her chin in her palm, waiting for David to spout forth some powerful bits of sage business acumen.

He shifted uncomfortably in the old wooden bench of a seat. "Not only me. We. You're a part of this team. You can do it. I have faith."

It wasn't that he was worried about his part. He'd given insightful advice to corporations valued in the billions, and he was always on target. Her four measly boutiques would be a walk in the park. However, if he went in, turned around her business and left, what would she do without him?

That question echoed over and over in his head like an annoying commercial.

Somewhere, buried beneath the sizeable ego—earned, not exaggerated—below the male pride, which wasn't his fault, beneath the canniness of his brain, David knew that Ashley Larson was a helluva lot braver than he was, and that she kept her wings clipped for some reason he didn't understand. He wasn't convinced it was the divorce, although that seemed the most likely culprit. It was important to him that she succeeded—even without him, especially without him, because David McLean was only a temporary fixture in Ashley Larson's life.

One of them would move on, settling into a permanent relationship first. Maybe David, maybe Ashley.

David frowned.

Ashley laughed at his face. "You don't need to look so worried. I'll help. These are my stores. My dream. What kind of slug would let somebody take over their dream? Stop looking so miserable, you're making me nervous. What are you thinking?"

David was still caught back at "temporary fixture." "Thinking about what?"

"How many designers do we need? It should be small enough to be manageable, but big enough to rate on the event-o-meter."

"Three," he answered without hesitation.

"Three is great. I thought about four, but that's a strange number, and there could be a tie. Seven's too many, and five feels too big. I couldn't handle five."

"You could handle five."

Ashley frowned, a long wrinkle of forehead and nose. "Do you think I should do five?"

"Yeah," he told her, just to see what she'd say.

She met his eyes, shook her head. "Nah. Too many."

"I think you're right."

"Me, too," she agreed. "We'll have Enrique, there's a girl in Miami who's great. Mariah D'Angelo. I saw her work online, and I'd love to see it in person."

"So you should go."

"I'll go." Then she paused to consider. "You'll meet me there, right? I mean, would you want to come—no, no." Finally she sighed, and there was that sad look of resigned self-awareness in her face, like when you overslept and you knew you shouldn't because there were eighty thousand things to get done. David never overslept, but sometimes he thought about it.

"I wasn't always like this," she told him.

"Like what?" he asked, knowing exactly what *this* was.

"I've never been the most decisive person. Actually, *thoughtful* is the word I like best. But after Jacob, I don't want to commit to anything. Do you have that problem?"

Of course not. David was decisive, able to leap tall judgments in a single bound, and once the decision was made he didn't look back and never had any regrets. "Not a problem for me."

"Then what happened to you? Because everybody knows, when you get divorced, you're marked for life. What's your mark?"

David bore the mark of Cain, or in this case, Chris. But that hadn't *marked* him. He wasn't indecisive or lacking in self-confidence as a result. No, compared to Ashley, David had come through his divorce fairly unscathed. "I don't think I have one."

She held up a hand to her ear. "Can you repeat that please? I missed it against all those throbbing molto-basso sounds of male denial."

"I'm not in denial."

"Lie, much?"

"Honestly, I'm fine."

She laid her chin on her palm. "Then why don't you talk about your marriage at all? Huh? Riddle me that one, Mr. I'm-So-Well-Adjusted."

That small puff of air was the sound of male ego being deflated by a woman who wears bunny slippers on a plane.

David gathered his courage, met her eyes and almost lied, but eventually the truth made its sorry way out of his mouth.

"My wife had an affair," he confessed.

Okay, it was a half-truth, and he hadn't even told her the worst part, but some things were not meant to be shared.

Instantly her face was awash with concern. "I'm sorry. You must have really loved her. You look like it still hurts."

He schooled his features, removing all looks of hurt. Hurt was not to be shown. Showing hurt belonged to the female of the species, not to men. "Wounded pride," he answered crisply, schooling his voice to remove all sounds of hurt as well.

Ashley still didn't look convinced. "I'm sorry, even if it is merely wounded pride."

"Thanks," he said, and quickly changed the subject from the details of his divorce. "I'll meet you in Miami."

She brushed one thoughtful finger over her lips. Lucky finger. "Why are you doing this? For the sex?"

David was frustrated. It wasn't the way she said it, she was thoughtful, strike that, pondering, and didn't seem insulted at all. No, it was what she said because it sounded so…wrong. David thought about defending himself, since it wasn't like that, he wasn't like that. Not completely.

"I signed up for an online dating service. It was miserable, thumb-screws, drawn-and-quartered sort of torture. I can't do that. This, I can do."

"This?"

"This." He pointed an accusing finger at her because he didn't like the snickering twinkle that was fast appearing in her eye. "And don't make it out to be sleazy. It's not. Not completely. If you lived in New York, it wouldn't even sound remotely sleazy. It'd be completely normal. But noooo, you don't, so if it's quasi-sleazy, it might sound that way, but it's not. I travel a lot. It's not a big deal to synchronize my schedule to match yours." David sighed. It still felt sleazy. Possibly because he wasn't an affair type of guy. He and Chris were raised to respect women, value honesty, work hard, and stand when "The Star Spangled Banner" was played. Apparently, David had been listening to their parents harder than Chris when the whole "value honesty" lectures were covered. No, not going there. This time he concentrated on Ashley, met her eyes squarely.

After a moment, a smile bloomed slowly. "Okay," she said.

He peered closer, checking to see if Inquisition Ashley was really finished. "Really?" It seemed too easy. "Okay? Just like that?"

"Yeah. Just like that."

David heaved a glorious sigh of relief. "I like you, Ashley Larsen."

I like you lots.

"I'm glad." She shot him a curious look. "You really signed up for an online dating service?"

"You said I should. I thought, it's time, I should, and then I did." He shook his head. "I knew I shouldn't have."

"What happened?"

"So, first there was Kim, then Pam and then…" Abruptly he stopped, frowning.

"And who was next?" she prodded.

"Jane." It sounded oddball to tell Ashley that he'd been out with another girl named Ashley. Actually two other girls named Ashley. The world was full of Ashleys, and it wasn't his fault. Now it sounded a little obsessed, and he wasn't. There was just a hell of a lot of Ashleys. Statistically, that did not make him obsessed.

Ashley leaned across the table. "Why does Jane make you guilty? I see guilt on your face. You slept with her, didn't you?"

"After one date? Do I look like a man whore?"

Her eyes said yes, thankfully her mouth stayed shut.

And now he was blushing. A thirty-four-year-old divorced man who'd been cuckolded by his brother did not deserve to be labeled a man whore. He shouldn't have to stoop so low as to blush. He told himself to stop, but she started laughing. The damned blush remained. "Only for you," he defended. "And that's only because I don't see you enough. I think you're right. It's the distance thing. It's like Spanish Fly."

"It's a good thing I don't live in New York," she told him, and he nearly disagreed with her, clamping down on his tongue just in time. That would be twice that he brought up her living in New York, which would suggest a pattern, a train of thought, a need, and that's not what their relationship was. It was not how they defined it. It was not what they both wanted.

"I think we're moving on," he said. "You know, getting past the whole black plague of divorceness." There. That sounded correctly ambivalent.

"I should sign up for a dating service, too," she said.

Instantly he knew that was a bad idea. An idea of disastrous proportions. She was vulnerable, easily swayed, ready to leap into bed with every Dick, Dick and Harry Dick that was out there.

"After all the horror I've endured, now you want to endure it, too?" he asked. It sounded logical, completely unlike the throbbing molto-basso sounds of male denial.

"It sounds interesting. I should broaden my horizons, don't you think?" There was a glint in her eyes, a spark of mischief and things that he knew were cock-twistingly bad.

"I think an intracontinental affair could broaden horizons," he told her, not wanting to think about his cock. Not thinking about his cock. Not thinking about his cock. "Jet-setting around the country, a hotel room in every port, a glass of champagne under every beach umbrella. That could seriously broaden your horizons."

And if that didn't work, there were some other positions they could think about. Light bondage, for instance. David had been a one-hundred-percent homogenized sex participant before, but scarlet nether lips for hotel wall art made a guy think about nether lips, and how his cock fit into said wall art.

Ashley lifted her hands, feigning innocence. "But that's only once a month."

"We could go bi-weekly. I'm not averse to the idea," he offered, a total understatement.

"But you thought that would get boring."

"No, you thought it would get boring," he corrected. "I never thought boring. Not once."

"But what about all that variety that I'll be missing out on…" Her voice trailed off wistfully.

"If you want variety…" And his voice trailed off wistfully, too.

"With other men," she finished.

David narrowed his eyes, sensing mischief afoot. "Are you toying with me? Me, Mr. Not-So-Well-Adjusted? Me, Mr. I'm-Heartbroken-After-the-Divorce? Me, Mr. Downtrodden-and-Depressed? Are you that cold?"

She nodded once, a smile playing on her face. "Miami."

"Miami in June. And now that that's decided, can I escort you back to your hotel room? You could toy with me some more," he coaxed in a low voice that was carefully designed not to sound carnally obsessed. But to be fair to himself, they didn't have a lot of time, and it'd be another month before he saw her again. Miami in June.

"It would be my pleasure."

"Yes, I think it will," he promised, and when David made a promise, he kept it.

It was lunchtime on Friday when he took her to JFK, and there was a particular moment when she was about to go through security. He was all charm and old-school proper, but the hazel eyes were darker than before. His hand stayed firm at her back, a polite touch, yet a little more. Around them, a thousand air travelers rushed through the terminal. Posted signs were explaining what the FAA allowed, what the TSA permitted, the proper procedure for taking off your shoes, but there was no protocol posted for saying goodbye to David.

He confused her, he fascinated her, he wanted her...yeah, she knew all that. Their relationship was all flash in the pan, big fireworks, little common sense. It was the leaving that made this relationship work. Instinctively she knew it, and she wasn't going to give him any more. Because that would be stupid.

Ashley put a hand on his arm, pulling him closer, ostensibly to be heard above the madding crowd, but actually because she needed to be closer, needed to share his personal space for just a bit longer. She liked it there with him. They fit.

David looked at her. Frustration clouded his eyes, which were even darker now, and a particularly vile suitcase jammed into her side.

He swore, pulled her against the wall and kissed her.

It was a lot more flash in the pan, big fireworks, and she lifted up on tiptoes because she loved the flashing lights behind her eyes, loved the way he kissed with such desperation.

He lifted his head, gave her a last glance and then walked away without looking back. Not once did he look back. It was a tiny thing, but it hurt. She watched him leave, wondering if he would turn around, but he didn't. Casual white shirt, well-worn blue jeans, but no regretful look back. Eventually he disappeared into the crowd, and the businessman behind Ashley prodded her. "You in line?"

She nodded once, went through the motions of pulling off her shoes and wondered why David hadn't looked, and why it should bug her. A no-look was better. It illustrated the casualness of their relationship, their twin desire to have a fling. Besides, airports were busy places, everyone fast and ready to go about their business. It wasn't the place for look-backs. It was the place to be processed and pressed forward.

After she handed her boarding pass to security, she passed through the metal detector. She was flying eight hundred miles back home, back to her family, back to her stores. Back where she belonged.

If this intensity didn't fade though, if this fling turned into something more, David would want her to move to New York. He even brought it up, and she had seen the worry in his eyes. David was the one who would demand things of her, doing a mock TV show with three up-and-coming designers was the least of what he'd expect her to do. He'd want her to leave Chicago, leave her stores, leave Val.

Ashley wasn't a leaver. Jacob might have left her, but Ashley was the port in the storm, the parked car, the unbudgeable rock. That was what her family needed, and that was who she was. Then she laughed at herself. She and David had seen each other twice. Three nights of great sex didn't a relationship make. No, relationships were built on things more solid and reliable.

Her bunny slippers came out of the bag and she rubbed the pink fur affectionately.

"Looks like it's just you and me, kid," she said to her good-luck charm, but she did look back, just once, and frowned.

8

DAVID DIDN'T STOP until he climbed inside the cab, and then he was forced to sit, forced to think. It wasn't supposed to be difficult to say goodbye when you're having a jet-setting intracontinental affair. It was supposed to be easy. The brain of a man last screwed by the female sex did not filter through a hundred excuses to get her to stay. The brain of said man, who really didn't need to be thinking like this right now, should not want to pull her close and whisper promises—unless they were promises of the sexual kind. David whapped his forehead with his palm, telling his half-wit brain to get it in gear.

And then came calm, rational reasoning to explain said half-wit thinking. Ashley was right. It was the distance. It made things seem better, more mysterious, more erotic. He kept telling himself in the cab all the way to his financial district apartment, skipping the afternoon at the office. When he got home, he sorted the mail, paid the bills, ordered groceries for the next week, skimmed through all the shows on TiVo, but by the time eight o'clock came around, he was still restless, still itchy in his own skin. So, ignoring the actually functioning part of his brain that said he was making a mistake, he called her.

"It's David," he said stupidly, racking his brain for something mundane to talk about that wasn't boring, and on the other hand, didn't indicate he was calling simply to hear her voice. Because he wasn't. He wasn't.

"Hey," she told him.

"Any problems on the plane?"

Scintillating, dude. Late night snooze-a-polooza.

"Miraculously, not a one."

"You're a regular Captain Kirk now, aren't you?"

"You watch *Star Trek?*" she asked, her voice dripping with amused scorn.

"Never," he defended.

"Liar," she told him softly, and the word wrapped around him, nearly as soft as her. Nearly as warm as her.

"Maybe," he answered truthfully because a weakness for *Star Trek* and the accompanying jokes was much safer than explaining a month was a really long time to wait. A freaking long time, and she'd been in Chicago for less than thirty minutes, and his apartment was way too lonely, and she'd never even been there. And why hadn't she been there? Was there something taboo about his apartment?

"What did you say those Miami dates are?" he asked

"I didn't. I've got to check in with Jenna, the designer, and then my store managers will have a collective hissy fit if I'm not around to hold their hands, and then there's Val…"

Ashley had responsibilities. She had ties. She had things that occupied her time, rather than sitting in an empty apartment with a great view of the South Street Seaport. When had his apartment gotten so empty? "Oh, yeah. Stupid me."

"You're not stupid. Why did you call?"

"It was good to see you," he started to say, but then switched channels before he could freeze up. "I wanted to make sure the plane didn't crash."

"No crashes."

"No crashes are good."

There was a long pause when he knew it was time to say goodbye and hang up, but he didn't. He sat there listening to her breathe.

"You could come to New York next weekend. I'd spring for the ticket. I know things are tight for you."

You're being stupid, you shouldn't say this. You really shouldn't say this.

"I can't do that. Work. I've been playing hooky too much already. Weekends are the busy times." She didn't even have to think about it. Not a second of hesitation.

"You're right. It was an idea. A stupid idea."

"You're not stupid."

"No, I guess not. Ashley..." David forcibly restrained himself from talking. He was a smart guy, but something about this whole situation was turning him stupid. He liked to think it was his Boy Scout personal ethics and sense of nobility—the idea that he wasn't a guy who would do anything for a quick lay. But it wasn't a sense of honor that had him pushing her for more. It was the simple fact that he couldn't stop thinking about her.

"Listen, I have to go," she told him, stopping him before he could get really carried away, which was only a good thing, and he should be grateful that one of them was seeing sense.

"I should go, too," he said, lying back on his pillow, wondering if he'd ever see her in his bed. On his pillow. Stupid.

"'Bye."

"'Bye."

"David?"

"Yeah."

"Thanks for calling," she whispered, and the hesitancy didn't sound as if she were being polite, didn't sound as if she were lying, and he told himself that maybe he wasn't being so stupid after all.

WHEN ALL ELSE FAILED to occupy his time, David threw himself into work. Every night, he was haunting the downtown offices of Brooks Capital, pouring over 10Ks and 10Qs and building models of company financials. If his instincts were starting to go on the fritz, there was always the hard truth of numbers. Numbers didn't lie, numbers didn't sleep with your brother and numbers were not afraid of flying.

It was the middle of a bustling Wednesday afternoon, and

he'd just spent two hours on a conference call with an adhesive supplier to a vinyl-composition-floor-covering manufacturer. By the end of the call, he was propping his eyes open with paper clips. Retail, yes, biomedical, yes, technology, yes, energy, not great, but okay, but vinyl flooring? God deliver him from vinyl flooring. He had just switched over to the warm comfort of his spreadsheets, when his cell rang. David checked the caller ID. New York. It was safe.

"David McLean."

"This is Robert Golden from Goldstein, Goldstein and Lowe. I'm calling to discuss the property at 357 East 39th Street."

His mother's old apartment. "Yeah?"

"I'm sorry to interrupt your workday, but I think you'll find this good news. The building's going condo. You've been making some tiny rental income up to now, but with a sale we believe we can make you and Christopher McLean a nice chunk of change. Is Christopher your father?"

"Brother. Mom gave the apartment to both of us before she passed away." Their mother had thought two names on a deed would mend fences. Their mother had been wrong. David managed the rental, and every month he wrote out a nice check to Chris. Look, Ma, no talking necessary.

The lawyer named a figure that caused David's blood pressure to spike. "That much?"

Money was a tricky thing in the McLean family. Pete McLean, David's father, had been raised on a cotton farm in Arkansas before moving to New York to make his mark as an electrician. Pete McLean hadn't trusted money or flash, he valued hard work and honesty. David valued hard work and honesty, too, but he knew what money meant. He knew what a college education meant—choosing a different path from Chris, who was now a practicing electrician in Illinois. Chris would never make the money that David had already made, but he had a three-bedroom house in the burbs and an SUV in the garage. Like his father before him, Chris never wanted to be anything more than solid middle-class. In a family of sturdy everymen, David was the ambitious outsider.

The lawyer droned on, explaining all the benefits of selling the apartment. "You'd be foolish to turn it down. We want the transition to be a win-win for everyone."

"And if we're not interested in selling?"

"That's what the court system is for."

Spoken like a true shyster. David interrupted him before he got too deep into his spiel. "Let me talk to Chris," David said and then hung up.

For the next seven hours David went through spreadsheet after spreadsheet, studying the numbers until everything ran together in a big blot of red.

It was ten at night before he decided to call his brother. It was late. He hoped they were in bed. He hoped he was interrupting. Unfortunately, Chris sounded wide-awake.

After David finished explaining the apartment situation, he added the single cherry to the top of what felt like a melted ice cream sundae.

"You take the proceeds, Chris. I'm good."

"I don't want your money," his brother explained, while David took his desk magnet and trailed paper clips around in circles.

"Stop being a proud idiot," David told him.

"I'm not saying this because I'm a proud idiot. It's because I won't give you the satisfaction of showing Christine how much money you have and exactly how much money we don't."

"It's the right thing to do," David said, not denying the other remark. It was probably true. Okay, it was true.

"No. We split it up even. Half to you, half to me," Chris insisted.

David set his mouth in a hard line. Chris couldn't see it, but he could sure as hell hear it. "No. I don't need it."

"David, this is insane."

"There're a lot of things that are insane, Chris."

"You're not going to get over this, are you?"

That was the heart of the matter. Exactly the reason he now

hated talking to his brother. "Would you get over this? Would anybody? I'm the guy who's been screwed, Chris. Screwed in the ass. Don't be all martyr because your brother is pissed that you slept with his wife."

Chris was quiet for a long, guilty minute. "I love her."

Like that absolved him of sin. Not in David's world. Not even close. "I loved her, too, asshole."

And of course, Chris picked up on the least important part. "But you don't, anymore?" he asked, and David heard the hope in his voice. Yeah, betraying your own brother did that to you.

"You don't get a free pass because my feelings change. Love can be killed, Chris. Spousal love, brotherly love."

"I miss you, David."

David stopped pushing paper clips around his desk. He didn't want those words to hurt, didn't want his brother to have the luxury of opening one of David's veins and letting the blood flow. It had been four years. David hardened his heart because only a stupid man would get sucker-punched twice.

"Screw you, Chris."

After he hung up, David threw his cell phone across the room. A second later he listened to the tinny ring, ignored it and ran a muddled hand through his hair. He wasn't a phone-thrower. He was an analyst who watched *Star Trek* and read to feel better about his own life. It used to be easy to look around and know his life was the best. Arrogant? Yes. True? Yes. But now...something had changed inside him. His balance was off, the arrogance felt gratuitous, thrown in without anything to back it up. As if he didn't deserve it anymore, and David didn't like it.

Right then his boss stepped into his office. Not Jamie, Andrew. "Bad time?"

"No." David frowned at the phone in the corner. BlackBerry on Berber. Classy. "Sorry."

"I wanted to talk to you about Mercantile Financials."

The bet. "The earnings report came in today. I forgot to look."

"You blew the call."

David stared into Andrew's impassive gaze. Always cool. Not a phone-thrower. "They're up?"

His boss nodded.

A thousand questions sped through his brain like a CNBC crawl. He had been sure about this. Seven down quarters, and then oops. You're back in the black. The numbers had to be wrong.

"The euro's up. They made a killing overseas."

David wanted to stick to his guns, but it was really late on a Friday night. His brother was snug in bed with David's wife. The only woman David wanted to be snug with was eight hundred miles away in Chicago, and he'd blown a call because he'd assumed that nobody could have an up-year in this financial environment. There were no guns in his holsters to stick to.

Yet still he couldn't stop. "Their model's off."

"Sometimes it doesn't have to make sense. It just is."

David's phone began ringing again. Andrew looked in the direction of the BlackBerry. Looked at David.

David stared at his boss impassively. Always Be Cool was a good motto to follow. "I was so sure they were overshooting their projections."

"I was probably just lucky," Andrew said, showing humility for absolutely no good reason except to protect David's ego. David didn't reply.

"You okay?"

"I'm good."

"Jamie said—"

"I'm good," David interrupted because he didn't need sympathy. He didn't want pity. He was fine. He'd be fine.

Andrew looked at him, nodded. "Okay. You're in L.A. on Thursday? McKinsey Partners?"

David checked his desk calendar. "L.A. Then Phoenix. Sigeros Labs."

"You've been logging a lot of miles. Maybe you should take a break."

Which was a nice way of saying his judgment was starting to blow.

David shrugged, choosing to ignore the unspoken directive. "You can take time off. I won't stop you."

"I've got a long weekend scheduled in a couple of weeks, but I can double up the week before."

"You don't have to clear your schedule with me."

"I thought I should say something."

"She's nice?"

"Who?"

"Long-weekend she."

David nodded.

"Good. Not the reason you're throwing the phone?" Andrew picked up the BlackBerry and tossed it back to David.

David stuffed it into the desk drawer. He didn't want to hear the ring if it began again. "No, she's easy, low-maintenance. It's nice." Out of everything, Ashley was the one thing that made him smile.

"Nice is nice."

"Yeah, thanks."

FIVE DAYS LATER, Ashley broke down and called David. She wasn't supposed to, had convinced herself that she was throwing gasoline on an emotional bonfire, which really didn't need to be stoked, but she had thought David would call again. There had been that last conversation when she'd tried to put some much-needed distance between them because apparently eight hundred miles wasn't enough. Silly man, he had listened.

That same silly man sounded stressed when he picked up. "Is something wrong?"

"No, why?"

"You sound mad. I'm not making you mad, am I? I shouldn't have called, should I?"

"Nah. It's stuff with my ex."

Ashley heaved a long sigh of relief. "Sorry." She didn't want to pry. She was dying to pry, but this was a closed subject. Pandora's box.

"You ever talk to Jacob?" he asked, and she was surprised he remembered the name. She didn't know the name of his ex-wife. Ashley thought about lying about her relationship with Jacob, and pretend that she was one of the mature adults who could be close friends with their ex. But David didn't need her to be a mature adult now. He needed a soft shoulder that he could lean on.

"No. It's like it's all an embarrassment to him now. You know, as if we'd both like to forget about it."

"You think that way, too, or is that just him?"

"It used to be just him. But now it's me, too. Marriage is hard. I didn't used to think that. You really have to love somebody—really have to like somebody—to want to invest so much work in it."

Over the line, she heard him quietly swear, and she hated that he still hurt. For now, she'd just call his ex-wife "bitch." It made her feel smugly superior. "David? What's wrong? With your ex, I mean. Do you still love her?"

"No." His voice was flat, emotionless, and she wished he trusted her. "It's nothing."

"I'm sorry. I wish I was there."

"Me, too."

Ashley bit her tongue because she wanted to get on a plane, which was a damned fool idea any way she sliced it.

"If I did, you know, it'd be better than Spanish Fly."

"Are you teasing me, Ashley Larsen?"

"Does it help?"

"Yes."

"Then I'm teasing."

"And if it didn't help, what would you be doing then?"

"Embarrassing myself."

He laughed, just as she intended.

"I wish you were here, Ash."

"Ditto." In the back of the house, she could hear Val's restless padding. Never a good sign. "I should go."

"Miami."

"Yeah, Miami."

9

DAVID'S GYM downtown was a beaten brick warehouse that looked more like an automotive garage than a health club. But this was no ordinary health club. It was a place where the white-collar types fled their desks, pulled on the gloves and proceeded to beat the crap out of each other. And it was all sanctioned by the New York State Sports Authority. White-collar boxing. Yahoo.

The newfound desire for bloodshed had started shortly after the divorce. He was spending too much time alone, too much time wondering how he'd screwed up, and a guy from work had invited him here. David had taped up his hands, pulled on the gloves and ended up with a full set of blisters, a serious dent to his confidence and a walloping punch to the gut. He'd had the time of his life.

Today was no picnic. A few rounds with the heavy bag, and then sparring with Tony DiNapoli, a trader from Goldman still who had a house in the Hamptons and a Lamborghini in his garage that cost more than David's monthly rent.

David narrowly dodged two jabs in the general direction of his chin, and Tony landed a lucky slug to his chest, but in the end, the bout was never in doubt. After they climbed out of the ring, David pulled off his gloves and flexed his fingers. He shouldn't brag. It was a sign of poor moral character.

So, he was a scumbag. He grinned happily. "Money does not buy happiness, nor does it buy stamina and the ability to whip my ass."

Tony was still hunched over, breathing heavily. "Some day, McLean."

"In your dreams," he quipped, pulling the tape off his hands.

"Trish wants you to meet her cousin."

David dumped the tape in the trash and grabbed a towel, heading for the locker room. "No."

"I'm going to tell her you're gay."

"Eat shit, Tony."

"Don't you miss it?" Tony asked, pulling his bag from the locker. "Don't you miss the siren's call of the pudendum? I bet you do. It's why you're walking around all tight-assed all the time. You're just remembering what it was like."

David merely stared blandly. "Why should I miss what I still have?"

"You're seeing somebody?"

Was he seeing Ashley? Did once a month in a hotel room somewhere across the United States count as seeing her? Slowly he smiled. "Yes. Yes, I am."

Tony swore, flipping his towel against the bench. "It's Elena, isn't it? She sits there, watching you in the ring with those exotic eyes, drooling all over herself. You should be ashamed, my friend, taking advantage of a young, nubile twenty-one-year-old with a body that could stop a rocket. I would beat you myself, if only because I am beside myself with jealousy."

"She's only twenty-one, Tony. That's not my speed."

"That's every man's speed."

"Not mine."

"You really got somebody? You're not lying to me?"

"I got somebody." I *think*.

"Now you've got me tied up in knots thinking of Elena. I'm heading to the showers, and if you hear ragged moans of pleasure, leave a man to his privacy. Next time, McLean. This time, I'm going to pummel you into a thousand tiny pieces."

"Save your bull for your customers, Tony."

"Do you know Transatlantic Pipe? The board's about to kick out the CEO, and bring in a new one. A good one. A very, very good one. I'm telling you, it's a buying opportunity."

"Really? What do you know?"

"Enough. And my friend, only for you."

At Tony's devious smile, David got an idea. "Say, do you know a guy at Chase Investments? Barney something?"

"Barney Thompson or Barney Burdetti?"

"He's probably young. Jerky. Full of himself and likes the ladies."

"That's Burdetti. Definitely Burdetti. You wouldn't believe—"

"Can you invite him for lunch?"

"Got a man crush, David?"

"Nah, doing a favor for a friend."

"The 'somebody' friend?"

"Another friend."

"And suddenly, you got a lot of friends. Do I need to hate you? Are you suddenly having more sex than me?"

This time, David swore. "Sadly, probably not."

"Okay, I won't hate you then. Give me a couple of weeks, and I'll see if I can't wangle him for lunch. I'll tell him your firm is still running double-digit gains. After the big meltdown, everybody's nervous."

"I'll be nice," David offered, lying through his teeth.

MIAMI IN JUNE was golden sunlight, pastel-painted stucco and ocean beaches so white it hurt your eyes.

Or so she'd been told.

Ashley had been in Miami for nearly three hours and all she'd seen was a muddled airport under renovations, the inside of a cab, the luxurious oceanfront room at the Setai hotel and the naked body of one finely made man.

Yes, Miami was a town of many, many things to see and do,

but currently, she was only interested in one, and that was what made her nervous.

She fell back against the plush pillows, this time too tired to roll away from the warm invitation of his body—until her hand reached out and found an answering set of fingers that clasped around hers. Ashley's heart squeezed in a manner that had nothing to do with the sex. She broke free and rolled away before the heart-squeezing got worse.

The room was intensely quiet. Too quiet despite the low thrum of the air conditioning, the rhythmic rush of the ocean lapping on the beach and the silent scream of a woman getting in over her head.

His breathing was slow and steady, in and out, then over again, and she noticed how quickly her lungs matched his in time. Her gaze held fast to the wall, desperately clinging there.

Damn.

He didn't try and touch her, nor speak to her, and she was grateful for that simple courtesy. Yes, David was a perceptive man, and he could tell she was a woman teetering on the edge.

The worst thing was that it had been different this time. Frantic coupling? Check. Heart-ripping pleasure? Check. Exploding orgasm? Check. Check. Check. So what was new?

The way she needed to lock eyes when he was filling her. The way her fingers buried in the thick hair as if they belonged there. The way his body felt covering hers.

This wasn't stranger sex anymore. The excitement and sense of the forbidden was gone, but what it left behind was something more disturbing.

So, what's the big deal? Hop a flight to New York every now and again. You know this affair is nothing but compatible sex and working off a little stress.

You don't know anything, Val.

I know more than you.

The hotel walls were dark brown, the color of the earth, the color of his eyes when he was spilling himself inside her.

Ashley buried herself farther under the sheets. Unfortunately, they smelled like her, like him...like them, but still her nose stayed there, her mind memorizing the scent.

His finger stroked down her back, following the arc of her spine. Ashley smiled at the wall, but kept firmly to her side of the bed.

"You make me feel cheap," he finally said, no trace of hurt in his voice, and she was grateful for that small courtesy as well.

David continued to talk, one benign finger coaxing her closer and closer.

"I know you're only here to use and abuse me, but I have needs, too."

At that, Ashley rolled over and stared at him suspiciously, but his face was as benign as that single finger that was tracking her skin.

"You think of me as just a fast-action pump and drill, variable speed settings and excellent torque, but I have feelings and when you turn away from me..." He looked at her, hazel eyes dancing, and sniffed.

All completely benign.

"What do you want?" she asked cautiously.

He shrugged. "I don't know. But I need to feel you respect me."

Ashley scooched closer. "I respect you."

He sniffed again. "I need you to like me for my mind, not just the awesome sex."

His eyes were still dancing, a smile playing on his mouth. As long as everything was casual, Ashley could play, too.

She scooched even closer, and curled into the safe crook of his arm, ignoring the warning voices in her head.

"You have a very nice mind. Sharp. Almost—dare I say—quick, for such a brawny stud such as yourself."

Slowly his hand slid over her shoulder, not nearly as casual as the smile on his face, or the easy look in his eyes.

"Thank you for noticing."

Content at last, Ashley smiled. For the first time she took a good look at their surroundings, at the steely gray ocean rushing back and forth outside the wall of windows.

He had picked the hotel this time because "the color red gave him a headache." Ashley was curious to see what he would do. It wasn't the stiff elegance of the Ritz, nor the lust tropics of the Biltmore, instead it was understated beauty.

"Nice room," she said. "I approve."

Beyond the windows, ominous afternoon clouds started to draw down on the Atlantic and announced the late-day storm you could set a clock by. Ashley watched as the clouds grew darker.

"The view's great," she added. He was so quiet that she turned her head, daring to look, but there was nothing to be afraid of.

"So, who's our target this time?" he asked.

Ah, business. That was safe.

"Mariah D'Angelo. Twenty-seven. Got written up in *WWD*, and she's starting to attract the attention of some of the big guns."

He quirked a brow. "Big guns of the fashion industry?"

"You know—the usual suspects in trendy poof."

"Trendy poof? You're going to have to tutor me on the fashion lingo."

She gave him a studious look. "I think you'll do fine."

The rain began, a quiet patter, starting slow, then quickly growing in intensity.

"You like the rain?" she asked him, enjoying this easy camaraderie. It was like being friends, with benefits.

"Rain in New York is a bitch. Streets flood, subways are late, cabs are scarce and there's always an umbrella to jam you up."

"Sounds charming."

"However…when I'm not outside…for example, if I'm sleeping late or watching TV, or reading, I don't mind it. I like it then."

Her cheek rubbed against his chest, ostensibly because she felt restless and needed to move. This wasn't easy camaraderie. This was "I miss you and I want to lay with you."

And what's wrong with that?

I can't go to New York.
Okay, you win with that one.
No, I lose.

"You actually read?" she asked, back to snarky-snark because mundane chatter wasn't mundane enough anymore.

"Shocking, I know."

"I bet you read work stuff." She needed it to be work stuff because any other answer indicated depth of character, and a seriousness that she didn't want to think about. He was already too close to ideal. She needed to find flaws. Serious character flaws that she could sink her teeth into.

"Some of it's for work," he answered, so she hedged her bets.

"Comic books the rest of the time, right? Sci-fi, big trolls eating up Hobbit civilizations?"

"Comics, Steinbeck, Tolkien, Harlan Coben and Edgar Allan Poe. A veritable smorgasbord of literary taste."

Ashley looked at him, shocked. "Poe? Nobody does that."

"I do," he protested, looking slightly hurt. "I'm very cerebral."

She studied the hard swell of his arms, biceps that had never hefted the pages of Poe. No, David McLean just knew how to play a good game of mind-screw. "Cerebral, my ass."

His free hand slid lower and lingered. "Your ass is many things. Cerebral is not one of them."

And they'd moved full circle back to sex. Outside the rain was bearing down, isolating her from the rest of the world, isolating them.

She rose up on his chest, inviting his eyes to wander over her bare skin. This, sex, she could handle.

"I like the rain," she whispered.

The amusement fell from his face, leaving behind lust…and something not so easy.

He pulled her closer, took her face, took her mouth, and it was far from easy. His kiss wasn't hot passion or casual sex or mind-screwing play.

Without thinking, Ashley found herself sinking into this

new kiss. The storm rolled across the Atlantic. She loved the rain, loved the feel of his body under hers, feeling his cock stir with carnal intent. But his heartbeat was firm, sure. Those powerful arms were tight, secure. He wasn't letting her go.

Ashley lifted her head, stared into eyes that were not so simple, not so casual.

"Don't think, Ash. Just go with it," he urged.

He wanted her to step in the airplane, push away from everything she knew was smart, rational and logical.

And he called himself an analyst? Shameful.

However, smart, rational and logical weren't currently invading her head. The storm outside, the storm in her head had drowned them out.

Her mouth hovered lower, her eyes not so simple, not so casual.

Just go with it? She would.

IT WAS ALMOST SEVEN when they met with Mariah, just as the woman was closing up her studio. The place was blazing with psychedelic colors and a chaotic mix of fabric and textures that defied description.

Very chichi with a head rush.

The clothes were arranged in disordered, yet strategic piles. It was organized anarchy, which suited the owner, because Mariah D'Angelo was as intimidating as leg warmers, circa 1983. Her hair hung in a long, kinked black braid down her back, and she wore blue jeans, an artistically ripped black T-shirt, her feet sporting polka-dot high-tops.

Hard to believe, yet true.

David took up an innocent bystander stance against the far wall while Ashley launched into her spiel without a sweat. "I want you to add your designs to the event. I'll do two challenges. Casual and cocktail, and look, I'm even telling, so it'll be easy. You know what they are. Just give me your best stuff, and we let the customers decide. No secrets. I don't have a big operation. Only four stores, and they're not even…"

David coughed once, soft yet effective. Uplifting, not downtrodden, was the mantra of the night.

"But we get a lot of traffic and the media coverage has already started." It was true, *Chicago Fashion Weekly* had put two paragraphs in the September calendar. "It's a golden opportunity."

"What about my expenses?" asked Mariah, cutting to the heart of the matter.

"All covered," promised David, who had no idea of the balance on the Ashley's Closet credit card.

Mariah looked at David, then Ashley, then shrugged in a completely naive, trusting manner. "I'm in."

Ashley hugged her, until Mariah—not that trusting—pulled away.

"I'm sorry," Ashley apologized. "I'm working to recharge my…"

Another cough from David.

"Revolutionize the stores. Transform the fashion design landscape in Chicago," she finished, flashing David a relieved grin. There. That wasn't so hard after all.

The best part was that Mariah looked excited. "Do you want to check out the studio?"

Ashley examined the day-glo colors, the cottony soft fabrics, and sighed. "I think it's my destiny."

In the end, Ashley walked out wearing a newly purchased bijou pink bandeau top, with a matching sarong skirt with the sheerest of chiffon layers that danced around her thighs. To complete the frivolous ensemble—très Miami—she wore a white hat with a big, floppy brim. *Beach Blanket Bingo* meets Jackie Onassis.

She and David strolled through the open-air plaza, the summer breeze rippling through the skirt. She felt dramatic, alive, confident. She was the Ashley that she'd always dreamed of being.

"Can you believe it? She was entranced, like I was, you know, fabulous."

"You were good," he told her, and this time she didn't mind

the warm light in his eyes. She was even holding his hand, a daring move rife with untoward possibilities, but tonight she was walking on ocean air, with a salsa beat accompanying the marcato of her blood.

Couples cruised the square, doing nothing but enjoying life—what a concept.

"I had her eating from the palm of my hand."

"Especially after you bought the clothes."

"Oh, fine, burst my bubble, you big lug. Whining to me about how you're all sensitive. You've got all the sensitivity of a razor blade."

"Look at you. Giving back, a jab, jab, cross, and then wham, the body blow."

Ashley stopped and stared. "Boxing!"

He shot her a confused look. "What?"

Ashley patiently explained to him the significance. "You box."

He nodded, still not grasping the genius of her analytical skills.

"I bet you want to know how I figured it out. Don't you? You are dying to know."

Obviously sensing—finally!—the importance of this moment, he nodded again. Smart man. "Go ahead. Share."

"Your arms," she told him, her fingers trailing over his bicep in a brazenly uninhibited move.

"My arms?"

"It now makes perfect sense. Your biceps are too big for swimming, you don't have runners' legs, your thighs are too thick, runners' are like matchsticks. But boxing…it fits."

"You've been studying my body in some detail, haven't you?" he asked, stroking his chin, very Sherlock Holmes.

"Embarrassed when a woman expresses admiration for your physiology?"

"Not at all. I thought it was my awe-inspiring sexual prowess that drew you, but this, too? My ego is growing by leaps, bounds…inches."

Ashley knocked at his arm. "Pervert."

He didn't even try and deny it. "Busted."

She studied his face and grinned. "I did great, didn't I?"

"You were great."

"It's going to work, isn't it?"

"It is," he answered with complete confidence.

With one finger she flicked back the brim of her hat, pulled him close. "That was the exact, correct answer."

His hand slid over the bare skin of her back, gliding underneath the thin material of her top. "I really like this. Very practical. Accessible. Sexy."

"You think?"

"I think."

"We should go back," she suggested.

"We should," he replied, giving her a long kiss. Then he took her hand and they walked briskly to the hotel.

"I have to be honest. I cannot lie," she confessed. "It really is your sexual prowess."

"Now who's the pervert?"

"Busted," she said, tucking nicely under his arm.

David only laughed.

IT WAS THREE in the morning, but outside the hotel it didn't matter. The beach was still alive with Friday-night noise. The moon was full and golden, a brilliant orb that cast the room in its magical embrace. Inside the bed, it was warm and comfortable, a secret place.

"Tell me about your wife," asked Ashley, daring to venture to secret subjects.

David propped up one elbow, and even in the faint light she could see the requisite jaw-clench. "There's not a lot to say. We were married out of college. She's a perfectionist."

Ashley smiled and David, being overly sensitive, glared. "Why is that funny?"

She tried to keep a straight face and failed. "You can be a little stilted when you're not happy. I can't imagine two of you."

"I'm not stilted," he insisted.

"You're not relaxed," she pointed out, avoiding mention of the locked shoulders or the fisted hands.

"I'm relaxed." His jaw clenched even more.

"Do you truly believe that?"

He winced and fell back in bed. "No."

She thought to carry on, now that she had wandered into the deep end. "I think you have suppressed anger issues." After dealing with her sister, understanding the ins and outs of the human condition, such as it was, she had learned to spot the signs.

"I don't."

"It's because of her, isn't it? You can't forgive her. Not that I can blame you, but it still eats at you."

He propped back up on his elbow. "Don't analyze me."

Obviously David didn't take to psychobabble as easily as Val. Still, Ashley was curious about his marriage, the marriage he didn't want to talk about, and curious about the bitch. Ashley couldn't help her feelings. Whoever had worked over David, well, the word *bitch* fit, and Ashley was nothing if not accurate.

"I don't want you to hurt," she told him, and the deep truth in those words surprised her. She didn't like him locked-jawed and locked-mind. She understood that sometimes he needed to be that way, but she didn't have to like it.

He leaned closer, and the locked jaw disappeared. She reached up a hand to tame his hair, and inadvertently her body curved into his.

"You're too soft, Ashley Larsen." David looked at her, then looked away, staring intently at the same wall that Ashley had studied only hours before. Sometimes studying a wall was easier than studying the mess of your own life.

"I'm sorry she hurt you," she said, pressing a kiss over his heart, her fingers tracing initials there. Her initials.

David caught her hand. "Are you trying to heal me with the magic sex energy?"

So, he wanted to make a joke now? At least he wasn't

looking at the wall anymore. Okay, she'd wait. "Very perceptive. My vagina is a powerful thing—full of ancient medicine."

At that, David moved over her, pushed deep inside her, and his eyes locked with hers. Her breathing changed, slowed, and her hands clutched at his back to hold him there. This time, there was no frantic coupling, no pounding rain, no mundane chatter, no jokes. There was only this unshakable thread between them. An odd connection that she once believed must be the pull of hormones, and the feel of his thick cock filling her. Ashley had assumed that this void that he filled was the one between her legs. She was wrong.

The void he filled was the one in her heart.

All her life, especially when reading fairy tales, she had believed in love the old-fashioned way—you had to earn it. But this felt like a gift. Some shimmering chalice that the gods had handed her on a misguided whim. All she had to do was drink from it. All she had to do was swallow the taste of this. All she had to do was accept the gift that she had been given.

Without hesitation, David knotted their fingers together like pieces of a puzzle locking into place. Each time he pushed deeper, she rose up to follow without question. There was no choice, not here, not now. Later, she would think. Right now, slow pleasure built inside her, each wave of sensation larger than before, growing outward, farther, seeping into places far removed from the apex of her thighs. It was so much easier when it was nothing but lust, but now her feelings were muddled, woven into a knot that she had no desire to untangle. Not now.

This man, the one who overturned the world without thinking twice, pulled at her.

The candles hissed, their glow falling to dark. His seductive mouth grazed her lips, her neck, and she gasped at each gentle touch. A trail of unshakable dreams followed in the wake of his kiss, a trail of purposeful hunger followed in the wake of each insistent thrust.

"Ashley," he whispered, and her heart skittered in fear.

He wanted to ruin this perfection. Words, once said, could never be unsaid. Deeds, once done, could never be undone. Ashley loved this drive within him, the need to push harder and higher, but not here. Not yet. She wanted to drink it in, sip at the taste. But to think about it, worry about it, was to ruin it.

Fears could be conquered, not easily, but it could be done. Worries could be dismissed, put off for another day. But loyalties and responsibilities—those pieces of herself that made her who she was—could not be so easily set aside.

"Ashley..."

Her lips pressed against his to trap his words, her thighs clenched tightly around him.

"Don't think about it," she murmured. "Just go with it."

David, being the smart man that he was, didn't say another word.

AT 7:00 A.M., THE PHONE RANG. Ashley's cell.

She untwisted herself from David, and reached to the nightstand.

"Hello?"

"Ashley? It's your mother."

"Mom?" Her mother's voice was shaky and afraid. Instantly, Ashley knew.

"It's Val. I don't know what to do. Last night..."

Ashley's heart stopped because this wasn't fair. She had reconciled herself to her own happy ending. She wanted to believe, she wanted to hope.

Her mother's words rushed out in one frantic sentence. *"Shedidn'tcomehome."*

10

ASHLEY DIDN'T BOTHER to shower. It would have taken too much time. She threw her clothes in her carry-on, stuffing the floppy hat on her head.

David sat up. His eyes were full of concern. "What's wrong?"

Ashley jammed her toiletries into the side pocket of her carry-on. "Nothing. Nothing is wrong. I have to get home."

"Is something wrong with your mom?"

"No." She glanced down, realizing that she wasn't dressed. God. Furiously she unzipped the carry-on and pulled out some shorts and a shirt. She had worn them before, and they would be wrinkled. Screw the wrinkles.

"Is it your niece?"

"No."

He stood and calmly pulled on his jeans, as if he knew exactly what to do. No panicking. No caring about wrinkles. "Your sister?"

She didn't bother to answer. She was too close to tears.

"Ashley."

She looked up. "I just need to be home. Okay? Where's my feet?"

His eyes darkened with pain, and she didn't want to be the cause of it, but right now, that wasn't her concern. Tomorrow it would be. But not today.

"Feet?" he asked, all pain gone, the careful mask back in place.

"Slippers. I need my slippers." She saw the pink fur bulging from the side pocket. There. She was ready.

David pulled a shirt over his head. "I'll drive you to the airport."

"Don't worry about it. Get some sleep. I'll catch a cab."

"I want to drive you to the airport," he said again, being a gentleman, being stubborn, being David.

"I don't need your help," she nearly shouted. She knew she could handle this. She always handled this, always taken charge when Val disappeared—for days, weeks, months at a time. Today was different. She couldn't juggle David and Val at the same time, they were both too demanding, and she wasn't that good.

David merely stared, and this time there was no pain, only the icy coolness of a man who knows that unfeeling is wiser.

Ashley looked away, found the brown walls, the gutted remains of the candles. "I have to leave."

His eyes raked over the room, the rumpled bed, and then he looked away as well. "Sure. I had a great time. Loads of fun. Call me."

HER PLANE LANDED at O'Hare at one in the afternoon, and the first person she saw when she entered her house was Val. Apparently, she was no longer missing.

Ashley, nonviolent, marshmallow Ashley, threw her carry-on across the room.

"What the hell did you do?"

Val's face crumpled because Ashley never yelled, never cursed and never got mad. No, Ashley let people beat on her over and over again.

"I was helping someone from AA. She called last night. I'm her sponsor. She needed help, Ashley. I could help her."

Ashley pulled a hand through her tangled hair. "Why didn't you call Mom and tell her? Val, you know what Mom will think if you disappeared. You know what I would think if you disappeared."

"My phone wasn't charged. I forgot." It was typical Val. Life with a recovering alcoholic was like having another child. No, that was an overstatement. Brianna was easier.

Ashley swore. "Where's Mom?"

"I don't know. I guess she took Brianna to school this morning and then left for work."

"Does she know you're okay?"

"Not yet."

"Don't you think you should tell her, Val?"

Val scuffed at the floor with her bare foot. "She'll be mad."

"No, Val, she won't get mad at you." *Not like I'm mad at you.*

Reluctantly Val called their mother, and there were quiet murmurs as Val reassured her. Now that the crisis was over, now that Ashley knew that her sister hadn't been drinking, she collapsed, exhausted, into a chair. Her hand covered her face, partly because her eyes hurt, and partly because she didn't want to look at Val right now. Her family had always been her first concern, and Jacob hadn't minded. No, that was part of the problem in their marriage. Honestly, he hadn't even noticed. But David noticed. David cared. He wasn't a man who liked being left alone in a Miami hotel room. Divorce did that to you—made you see everything as a betrayal.

Ashley understood.

"Ashley?" There was Val. Though she wasn't looking at her, Ashley could imagine the neediness on her face. Val wanted to know that everything was all right, but it wasn't all right.

After years of thinking Val would be okay, and instead Ashley rescuing her over and over again, gullibility had transformed into a protective sort of paranoia, mostly for cause. However, Val needed to know that disappearing all night was not acceptable behavior. She had to teach Val to be responsible.

Her hand fell from her face, and Ashley let Val see years of anger in all its rawness. Val flinched. Ashley barreled on. "You couldn't borrow a phone? Didn't you think we'd worry?"

"I didn't think. You're mad at me, aren't you?" Val socked her fist into the couch. "Even when I'm doing something right I still screw it up."

Ashley sighed, resigned to the unteachable. "You're not screwing up. We didn't know. We worried."

"You don't trust me. Thirteen months sober, and you still don't trust me. I have worked my ass off to get you and Mom to stop looking at me like I'm going to raid your wallet, or wreck the car, or call from jail, but it's never gonna stop, is it?"

Brianna would be home soon. Their mother would be home soon. Ashley was still wearing the bunny slippers and the smell of David. She couldn't fight this battle. Not now.

"Val..."

Val socked the couch again. This time, a lot harder. "Shut up, Ashley." Val stalked off and Ashley, resigned to having hurt the entire world, turned on the television. Her eyes processed a new method for making homemade pierogi on the Food Channel, her mind blessedly blank, until she heard Val's footfalls on the wooden floor.

Softer footfalls, not nearly as mad.

Ashley immediately noticed the tear stains, the swollen eyes that looked full of hurt, and she wished the medical community had some pill, some shot that could take away Val's pain and give her confidence.

"I'm sorry," muttered Val. "Of course you're not going to trust me."

"I trusted you."

Val laughed with heavy scorn, and no humor at all. "You flew home because you thought everything was fine? No, you flew home because you thought I was out drunk, throwing up vodka at some shithole bar, and you knew Mom couldn't handle it by herself."

"I didn't think that, Val." Actually, she had thought it, but she wanted to be wrong. That should count for something.

All her life Val had been searching for strength. Sadly, the only place Val found strength was in her sister. "You shouldn't have to put up with this. I'm sorry. I don't want to let you down, Ash."

Ashley closed her eyes. She was tired and hungry, and now she wanted a hot, cleansing shower, so that the tangles from her hair would disappear, so that she wouldn't smell David on her skin. She had left Miami for nothing. The wanting was still there, a painful ache, and she didn't need those wants, nor those aches. Well, at least now, she, David and Val could all be miserable at once.

Slowly she uncurled from her chair and accepted the world she had, not the world she wanted. She noted Val's tortured eyes and her patience snapped. Self-misery didn't set well with her.

"You don't want to let me down? Then don't!"

THE FLOPPY HAT stayed hopelessly slung on the chipped, wooden four-poster. The bunny slippers stayed neatly lined up in the closet, breathlessly awaiting their next outing.

Ashley's days were spent coaching Sophie on the ins and outs of the radically diverse Lakeview clientele, which was a talent unto itself. The women of north Chicago weren't Gold Coast socialites, needing the latest from Nordstrom. No, they wanted retro and ripped. And if a man wanted to buy himself a dress, you didn't blink twice, and told him his hips definitely did not look too fat in that skirt.

At the Wicker Park store, Scarlett was going great guns. When Ashley had first goggled at the graffiti window display, Scarlett had brandished her spray-paint can proudly, not sensing the property-insurance-rate-hike fear in Ashley's risk-management heart. However, to give the woman her due, instead of looking trashed, the place now had an urban feel that actually mixed well with the street's other businesses.

Alas, sales at the Naperville store were down three-point-seven percent. Probably the latest in nonwrinkle fabric that Ashley had embarrassingly gone overboard with. Altogether her bottom line was slowly sinking into the red.

Each day, after she got home, she punched the numbers into her computer, and her spirits fell a little further, so much so that she almost stopped doing it, but David had taught her to follow the numbers—no matter how bad.

If the numbers were bad, the nights were the worst. Sitting up in her bed, cell phone in hand, willing it to ring. He didn't call. No surprise there.

She had seen the damage in his eyes when she left the hotel room, and she knew he didn't like to hurt. Honestly, who did? He'd show the pain for a flash of a second, and then it would disappear behind that brick wall of stubbornness, as if he wanted to be somehow impenetrable to pain.

Hence, no call.

It took her seven days to call him, which sounded like a long time, but she had to carefully plot out what she wanted to say. David deserved to know about Val. He deserved to know about Val's issues, but Ashley had never liked discussing her sister. Val's skeletons were firmly wedged deep in the Larsen closet right next to Ashley's slippers.

Talking about Val's problems felt vaguely traitorous, like laughing at someone else's bad haircut or discussing a fashion-don't behind a friend's back. But she knew she had to tell David the truth. Their relationship was no longer causal, something more than stranger sex. She didn't know exactly what, but whereas she had a certain loyalty to her family, now she had a certain loyalty to him as well.

He picked up on the fourth ring. Either he was in a meeting, or else he was upset. Considering it was a Friday night, 9:00 p.m. on the east coast, she was betting on the latter.

"Hello?"

"It's Ashley."

Silence.

Okay, he was angry. He didn't know her problems because she had not shared with him. And if she had shared her problems, he wouldn't be mad.

"Why are you mad?" she asked. It didn't seem right to blurt out, "My sister is an alcoholic." Some things needed buildup.

"I'm not mad," he answered, which was nice because it helped to provide the necessary buildup.

"You're mad."

"I'm mad," he said. Look how easy they fell into the same rhythms, the same arguments, the same routine. The consistency only made her sad. Seeing her hat, she took it off the bed post and perched it on her head. It made her feel better.

"I had a family emergency," she told him, still working on the buildup.

"I get that, Ashley. I understand that. But don't you think you can tell me why you left? I was worried, I was thinking, why won't she tell me? Is it because it's awful, or because it's nothing? For all I know, your sister had a hangnail and that's why you ran."

"It wasn't a hangnail."

"Then what was it?"

Ashley gathered her courage and prepared to tell her sister's worst-kept secret. Slowly the tongue got it together, the lips formed the right sounds and the words haltingly emerged. "She drinks. Drinks too much. She used to drink. She doesn't anymore. But it hasn't been very long."

"How long?"

"Thirteen months, seven days. It wasn't fun."

For a moment, he was quiet. "Why did you leave Miami?" he asked, as if she hadn't just told him that her sister was a recovering alcoholic, and still wasn't in a good place.

"My mother called. Val was missing. She's found now."

"Sober?" he asked crisply, as if they were checking off boxes on a survey.

"Sober. She'd just left her phone off. No big deal," she said. "Now do you understand?" With restless fingers, she played with the brim of the hat. Letting it droop down in her eyes, pushing it off to the side. Nothing seemed right.

"How old is your sister?"

"Thirty." And they were back to the survey questions. "She has a daughter. Eight years old. There was no one to take care of Brianna, that's my niece, except for Mom, and she's, oh, I don't know, but it's not a good idea. I had to be here." Ashley stared at herself in the mirror, and the floppy hat didn't seem so jazzy anymore.

"Does she do this a lot?"

Ashley didn't know what to say. Over the past thirteen months, life had been fairly quiet, especially compared to Val's bender that had lasted through most of Brianna's second year. That had been followed by three years of sobriety. But then Val had tried to go to community college, and instead spent most of her afternoons skipping class and sitting in the pub. Neither Ashley nor their Mom had known about that lost semester until the grades showed up in the mail. "It comes and goes."

"You shouldn't put up with it. She's an adult. She's capable. She is, right?"

"She's my sister, David," she whispered, in case anyone could hear.

I can hear fine.

"And that means she's not capable?"

"No, she is."

"You're not tough enough, Ashley. You have to be strong, and say, not my problem. They own that problem. And if they make stupid decisions, you can't let it ruin your life."

"She's not ruining my life."

"All right. Rephrase. You can't let it hurt you, you can't let it affect you."

"She's family."

"Trust me, that's not an excuse. Your family can hurt you most of all."

"David—"

"Stop. I'll drop it. You have to do what you think is right. I'm only the innocent bystander, not my concern. Who's the last designer gonna be?" he said, and obviously they were finished talking about Val and her problems. Business was easier for both of them.

"I'll stick to Chicago. There's a guy in Wicker Park. I need to give one to the home team."

"You want me there?" he asked, a completely stupid question for such a smart man.

"Of course. I want you. In Chicago."

"I can't," he said, his voice hoarse. Ashley stopped playing with her hat, frowned at the phone.

"I didn't say when," she said to let him know that she could see through his little denial tactic. "You don't want to come here, do you? You're still mad."

"It's not you."

"It's my *family?*" she asked incredulously.

"It's something else, Ashley."

"Like what?" He was so clever about keeping his secrets. Now, he wanted to know every detail about her life, and like a gullible idiot, she had told him, but when it came to opening up, he was a clam. A tongueless, noiseless, speechless clam. Ashley hated clams.

"I don't want to say anything," the clam answered.

Furiously, Ashley jumped up from the bed, and began to pace. David needed to hear this. Oh, he needed to hear every word.

"That doesn't work for me, and let me tell you why. I just spent seven days beating myself up because I didn't want to tell you about my sister. It's not an easy subject to talk about, and it's not my story to tell, so I have issues with saying anything about it. Big issues. But I knew I had to tell you because it wasn't right to leave like that. It's not me. And because I knew I had to tell you, I stopped beating myself up, practiced my words—several times, mind you—and I called and I told you the truth. So I don't want to hear, 'I don't want to say anything.' I have laid bare my soul here, so you can suck it up, and bare yours as well. What the hell is the matter with Chicago?"

There was a long silence and she stopped pacing, afraid she'd been too rough. Sure. From the closet, her slippers were busting a bunny-gut. But at least she'd done what needed to be done. Or at least, she'd thought she'd done what needed to be done.

What if she'd been wrong? What if she had moved this relationship up a level, and he hadn't? What if they were still having stranger sex and she didn't know it?

What if she had betrayed Val's secrets to a man not worthy of knowing them?

Gee, thanks, sis.

No, I don't believe that.

Ha.

She waited, feeling uncertain, not even sure if he was still on the line.

Finally, he spoke. "My ex-wife lives in Chicago."

That was it? Ashley began to pace again. She had assumed it was something bad. Something heart-twistingly awful. "I'm wanted for a felony there." "I was once mugged on the South Side—the memories get to me at night." Or even, "I have a love child roaming the streets, I can't bear the guilt."

This was it? She stopped her pacing and sighed loud enough that he could hear.

"It's a big city, David. The third largest city in the United States. I guarantee you won't see her."

"I know. It's weird."

"You *should* see her. Confront your fears head on."

"That's a really bad idea."

"Only because you're terrified."

"I'm not terrified."

"Liar."

This time, he sighed, a frustrated sigh tinged with overtones of "you don't get it"—much like hers had sounded. "Ashley, it's complicated."

Ashley wasn't deterred. "How long since you've seen her?"

Silence.

"You haven't seen her, have you?" she asked, and it killed her that he was still so busted up over his ex. Studies had shown that men had a much harder time than women. Ashley had never believed it—until now.

"There's no reason for me to see her. She's married. She's got a new life."

"And so do you," she reminded him softly. Ashley was some part of that new life, she knew that without a doubt.

"Then you come with me."

Come with me. It was definitely moving their relationship into a level beyond stranger sex. Meet the ex-wife. And she wanted to be there for him. She wanted to meet the bitch in person, possibly glare at her when no one was looking.

But then what the heck would they talk about? And what about the questions?

Sure, come with him, meet his ex, explain that yes, they met on a plane and live half a nation apart, but their relationship transcends such obstacles. Oh, God. This was a bad idea. They'd have to lie.

"I don't know," she told him, staring at herself in the jazzy white hat. She looked like a woman who tackled the world head-on. Hats could do that to you. Fool you into being something you aren't.

"Terrified?"

"Yes," she answered truthfully.

"Would you do it for me?" he asked. It was a terrifically cheap shot because there was guilt involved in this equation, since she had left him stranded in Miami alone *and* there were few things she wouldn't do for David. The list was growing smaller daily. He was not the world's most perfect man, he was not the world's easiest man, but he was constant and loyal and he cared about her dreams when sometimes she ignored them. He got big bonus points for that. Dreams were very fragile things.

"When?"

"I'll set it up. Two weeks from now, last week in June. Christine's schedule is flexible."

Christine. His ex-wife was named Christine. It was a nice

name, an elegant name. Not as elegant as say, Ashley, for instance, but a name was only a set of letters arranged in some arbitrary order.

"You're sure this is a good idea?" he asked.

It's an awful idea. A god-awful idea, Ash.

"You want to borrow my bunny slippers?"

"Only if you're still attached. Preferably naked."

She plopped onto the bed, smiling for the first time in days. Seven days to be exact. "I could be naked now."

"Jeez, Ashley, do not tease. Fourteen days is killer…. Are you really naked?"

Her smile shifted into a grin. She shed her Hello Kitty sleep shirt, slid her panties down her legs and looked in the mirror. Something was missing. She pulled the brim low, low over her eyes. Trampy, vampy. Better. This was the way a woman should look when she's talking to her lover.

"Now I'm naked. Except for the hat."

"You're wearing a hat?"

"The white one we got in Miami. It makes me daring."

"How daring?" he asked, the words sounding wonderfully strangled.

She merely laughed, then fell back against the pillows. The cell was at one ear, her free hand sliding over her breasts, taking a short moment to get to know her ever-tightening nipples on a close, personal basis. She'd never been much for self-exploration, either the physical or mental kind, but honestly, it did have advantages. Being eight hundred miles away from sex could make you creative.

"Ashley, what are you doing?"

"Touching my breasts," she told him in a hushed voice. "I have very sensitive nipples, did you know that? Little buds that perk up at the slightest hint of a cool breeze, or a playful finger, or a hungry tongue."

"Oh, jeez."

"I wish you were here to see."

"I do, too. I didn't know my imagination was this vivid, but gawd, you wouldn't believe the stuff in my brain. I didn't even know I had this stuff in my brain until now."

"Do you like my breasts, David?"

"They're perfect. Soft and plump. I love the way they fill my hands."

She checked her breasts and smiled. "You have nice hands," she whispered, sliding her fingers down her body in a little dance. "I like when you touch me between my legs."

"You're touching yourself, aren't you? I'm a dead man. Tell me you're touching yourself. No, don't tell me." He coughed, his voice deeper, huskier, and she felt an answering shiver skim across her breasts, her skin. "Go ahead, I can take it."

"Now I'm touching myself. It's so nice and warm and comfortable. Taking all the time in the world." It was the hat, she kept telling herself. It was the hat that made her voice sound different, sensual, aroused...turning her on even more.

Her old quilted bedspread was soft against her bare skin, but it felt odd to be lying here in her room, naked, pleasuring herself. She'd always kept her love life, her sex life, separate from the house, spending the night out if she needed, but this felt forbidden.

David's voice urged her on, and her body responded as if he were there, as if they were his hands on her, not her own. Between her thighs, she was wet and swollen.

"I want you here. In Chicago. Touching me. Tasting me. Filling me."

"A plane... I could get on a plane...now."

"But then what would I do? That'd be...hours. No, I think you're going to have to talk me through this one."

To please her, he talked about her body, how he loved to plunge inside her. He told her that her skin was soft, the taste of honey against his tongue. As he spoke, her fingers danced with more talent than before. When he talked of her breasts, she heard awe. *Awe.* His words stroked over her, as surely as his hands, and her eyes drifted shut because she no longer wanted to stare at four walls. She wanted him in her head, taking her body.

His voice grew more ragged, his whispers more intimate, and when he took himself in hand, he told her, her fingers stroked even faster. Over the phone line, he couldn't see her blushing skin, or the way her feet dug into the covers, needing a place to hide.

There she lay, on her old bed, her fingers buried between her thighs. Her heart skipped forward, the beat of her blood matching each slide of her hand. He asked her to show him this when they were together, and she wondered whether she had the courage. She thought for a moment, smiled, and said yes. It was a stranger's voice that was talking, and her hand moved faster.

"I need to come, David," she breathed, and her hips rose, higher and higher, until she felt as if she were flying. Her hand tightened on the phone, and she could hear David, she could feel David.

At last.

"David?" she asked, because he had gotten so quiet.

"I think I died."

"I'm sorry," she said, apologizing for more than this.

"You shouldn't apologize so easily. I was a bastard." His voice was soft and warm, softer and warmer than her hand, softer and warmer than her old quilt, and she wished the sound of it wasn't quite so appealing. It made all the wants return, and as valiant as her hand was, as familiar as her quilt was, they were a poor imitation, and she knew it.

"Spoken like a man who just got his rocks off," she joked, because it would be two weeks—at least—before she saw him again.

"I'll call you when I set up the dinner," he continued, still in that same appealing tone. Ashley sighed as the wants returned.

"I miss you," she told him reluctantly.

"I miss you, too," he said. "I'll call tomorrow night."

Ashley hung up the phone and stood up to stare at the naked

woman in the mirror, wearing the floppy white hat and her heart on her sleeve.

This was the woman who hadn't drawn a paycheck in four years. This was the woman who was going to lure some of the brightest designers in the country to her boutique, as if it were some great privilege. And this was the woman who was going to have to introduce David to her family. More specifically, Val.

Ashley frowned because she hadn't wanted to go there yet. Val wouldn't like David. Ashley knew it. Actually, Val would be fine with him until she learned he lived all the way in New York City. Then she would hate him. And proceed to tell Ashley about it in many detailed lectures. Telling Ashley how he wasn't good enough for her, that she should hold out for someone better.

I wouldn't do that.
Yes, you would.
Only because it's true.
Sometimes families sucked.

11

DAVID WAS HAPPY now that he knew about Ashley's sister. Not happy, as in, he was glad her sister is an alcoholic, but that was a better option than the thought of some man—Jacob?—calling her back to Chicago, and putting the wariness in her eyes. Ashley didn't realize that he couldn't stand to see her hurt. He wanted to protect her, to keep the wolves away, but he was too far away to do a great job of that. So, he had to trust her, to believe that she could manage on her own.

Still, that wasn't always enough, and sometimes he found himself calling her just to hear her voice, just to make sure. When he heard her breathy, nervous rambles, he would get instantly hard, feeling the insistent urge to plunge his cock inside her over and over again, while watching her face, that reckless mouth. She had no idea how much he thought about her, embedded between her thighs; if she did, it would probably scare her. Hell, it scared him, and he was a guy.

They didn't have phone sex again. He didn't ask, and she didn't ask, and since he wasn't sure if he would survive another night like that again, he was almost glad. Almost.

The ache in his cock, the tightness in his balls, kept him from thinking about Chris and Christine. Ashley did that. She made some of the hurt go away. The trip to Chicago was a few days from now, and he was excited, aroused and ready to punch his brother's face, all at the same time.

He would land in DC on Monday, then fly through

Oklahoma City on the trip back, but before he got to Chicago, he had one thing on his calendar. Lunch with Martina's ex, Barney Burdetti.

THEY MET AT Raw, a sushi place near Church. On a normal day, David wasn't a big fan of sushi, but today, it wasn't about sushi, it was about pretending to be Martina's perfect man. It wasn't that he wanted to be Martina's perfect man, it was merely that he wanted to teach the jackass that had cheated on her a lesson.

Martina's actual perfect man wasn't hugely tall, a couple of inches shorter than David, and his face had that pinched-fox look, that some women might have considered attractive. Whatever. And as he listened to Barney drone on about his accomplishments, talk about the multitudes of women in his life, David came to the realization that Barney was more clueless than most men.

They discussed the markets. Barney and David's friend Tony bitched about the slowdown, while David smiled, perhaps more arrogantly than he should, but hey, what the hell. And when Barney began to talk about how much he loved books, how he used to sleep with a hot little editor from midtown, David saw the opportunity he'd been waiting for.

"No, kidding, I've been seeing a lady in the book biz. I've always had a weakness for cool blondes. Tiny, with crystal blue eyes. God…" He wiped his brow. "Sorry, I just start thinking."

Tony nearly cracked up. "David works a little too hard. Sex does a number on his brain. He'll be cruising along at the gym, and then, boom, you can knock him out. I ask, what happened? He shrugs. Getting laid though, he gets more excited than most."

"She's good, huh?" asked the weasel.

"I don't like to talk about that."

Tony busted out laughing. "Since when?"

David glared.

Barney was intrigued. "You're among friends. You don't need to be shy."

"Nah, she's different," he said. "I mean, don't get me wrong, she definitely keeps me up at nights. All night, sometimes. Gawd, just the other night…" David trailed off meaningfully, sipped at his martini, and smiled as any well-satisfied man would.

Tony shook his head. "I think it's getting serious."

David nodded. "Right, she wants to settle down. She's only twenty-four, I told her that she was too young to think about that sort of thing, but her sister just had a kid, and now she's an aunt, and she goes on and on about little Jameson. Who names a kid after Irish whiskey? Apparently, in her family, they do."

David knew the exact moment that Barney started putting the pieces together. It was like watching gears click into place. He nodded slowly. "Sounds like she's thinking about marriage."

"Maybe," answered David, shrugging in a perfectly casual manner. "I don't know. I'm not ready. I got divorced a few years back, and I want to relax, sow some wild oats, plough some fields…"

The man leaned forward, waving his chopsticks like a drunken samurai. "You can't lead her on like that. What if she gets hurts? You can't hurt her," protested the guy who had slid a knife right through her heart. David frowned, and studied Barney more carefully, the pinched lines in his forehead, the anger in his eyes. When he'd first met this guy, he'd wanted to punch him in the face, but now…not so much. Did the man have a living, beating heart after all?

"I don't want to cause any problems," David began, watching Barney's face as he talked. Testing the waters. "Honestly, she hasn't said anything, so I'm probably assuming. But you know, a guy can't be too careful." He put an extra dose of jackass in his laughter just to see what Barney would do.

"She's probably just jumping into another relationship too fast. You know, I've seen women who break up with a guy, get their heart broken, and then boom, they stick to the next guy like glue."

"That could explain it."

"Has she said anything about this other guy?"

"What other guy," asked David innocently.

"The guy she just broke up with. I bet she's still hung up on him."

"I don't know."

"Well, what did she say?"

"Geez, Barney, don't get yourself so worked up here. David's a nice guy. He's not some shark among women," Tony said.

"Seems like an asshole to me."

David looked at him, hurt. This shouldn't be so much fun. "Hey, I don't know how I've offended you here. Let's change the subject."

"I want to know what she said."

"She's never mentioned another guy, okay. Why should you care?"

At that moment, Barney took a long sip of his drink and started lying his ass off. "It's happened to me before. I was seeing this woman who was talking about how special we were, and how things were so perfect, and I was thinking, hmm, maybe, and then suddenly, she mentions the guy she used to be in love with, the asshole she's still in love with, and before I know it, I show up at her apartment, and who's there?"

"The asshole," answered Tony.

"It's happened to you, too?"

"Nah, I just figured it out."

"So she really loved that guy? She went back to him?"

Barney nodded once.

"He must have loved her, too. In that asshole way of his," said David.

Tony laughed, and David shot him a look. Tony stopped laughing and shrugged. "I thought it was a joke. It was funny."

Lunch broke up shortly after that, Barney leaving with a thoughtful look in his eyes. As for David, he felt strangely…touched. Maybe the bastard loved her after all. Maybe next time the man wouldn't cheat. Maybe pigs would fly. But Martina seemed to have a thing for him, so who was he to judge?

He'd have to tell Ashley about this one. She would laugh, and maybe, she'd think a little better of him. She'd seen a lot of his bad sides, and not too many of the good.

"So, who's the babe?" asked Tony, as they headed toward the gym.

"Ashley," he answered.

"She's a book editor?"

David shook his head. "She owns clothing stores."

"You're doing a book editor, too?"

Tony was such a novice about some things. David rolled his eyes. "Nah, I made all that up."

Tony slapped him on the back. "You had me going. I was nearly hating you."

"We spar. I beat you. You can hate me again."

"You are one-hundred-percent triple-A asshole."

David grinned. "I know."

DAVID'S PLANE TO Chicago touched down six hours before they were supposed to have dinner with his ex-wife. Ashley was anxious to see him. To calm her nerves, instead of sitting bogged in traffic, she took the train to the airport and met him outside at the arrivals area. The sunglasses were to keep her eyes from giving away too much, but the hat gave away more than her eyes ever could. He saw her, grinned, and she started to laugh.

It felt so marvelous to laugh.

He flicked at the brim, took off her sunglasses and nodded once. "I will never look at this hat the same way again." Then he was kissing her, and she was kissing him back, and she wanted to laugh again. He did that. Made her happy inside. His mouth tasted like airplane coffee and too many lonely nights, and she could feel the hunger growing inside her. Fourteen days shouldn't have been that long for a woman who once had a dry spell last a year and a half. Now fourteen days was more than a lifetime. *And fourteen nights.* What she would give for fourteen nights with this man. Against her thigh, he was thick and more than ready, and she rubbed—only once because she wasn't that cruel. David groaned nicely.

"Where's your hotel?" she asked, because she wasn't that cruel, either.

He gestured toward the shuttle bus.

Ashley looked up, surprised. "Here? *Our* hotel? You got a room at O'Hare?"

He shrugged, a flush on his face. "I know. It's goofy. You don't need to remind me."

Something inside her melted to goo. She would have wagered he didn't have a romantic bone in his body. She would have lost. "I don't think it's goofy. I think it's cute."

"Cute? Oh, God. I don't want to be cute," he said, but his eyes held a dark liquid green that warmed her.

The shuttle was slow, the airport was packed, and the waiting was interminable. His hand crept out, his fingers curled around hers, and she didn't mind. The shuttle driver wanted to chat. He thought they were on a layover, headed to some tropical vacation spot for honeymooners.

"It was the hat," the driver told Ashley. "And you have that look."

She blushed, not wanting to blush, but doing it anyway. David was different. She was different. The world was different. Ashley told herself that it was a rehearsal for meeting Christine the bitch, when she would need to act the part of devoted lover, right now, though, there wasn't any acting involved.

When they got to the hotel, it was different, too. Oh, sure, they didn't get that far into the room, but this time, David lifted her, the hat falling helplessly to the ground. With his hips, he pinned her against the door, and she wrapped her legs around him like the hussy she was. One hand fisted with hers, holding it there between them. The other hand grabbed tight at her waist like an anchor. His mouth locked with hers, kissing her as if it'd been a lifetime since they'd been together. For three heartbeats he held her there, hands joined, mouths joined, and then she could feel the length of him, thick and hard between her thighs, and she wanted to be joined there as well.

"Hurry," she murmured against his mouth, her hips already starting to grind because she knew the fast rhythms of their sex. It was the rhythm of her blood, her heart.

David raised his head, stared into her eyes, and her body stilled. This was different.

His eyes were raw with passion and something far more damning. Today she could see herself reflected in his eyes. The way he saw her. The tenderness, the love simmering there. Today he was changing things. Since Miami, he had waited, but he wasn't a patient man, and she knew it. He wouldn't wait anymore. Truly, he didn't need to. The world was shifting, tilting, and it seemed appropriate that she wasn't standing on solid ground. No, her entire being was balanced solely on him.

Her blood bubbled with it, forgot the worries, forgot the doubts.

Ashley smiled.

Gently he feathered a kiss against the side of her mouth, pressed another to her lips, and then the hand at her waist slid down, lower, pulling her panties to one side, until there was a line of cotton cutting along her already overstimulated sex. The pain was exquisite, and she whimpered, pleading for him. At this moment, she was at his mercy.

Thankfully, he didn't make her wait long. His thrust was slow, stretching her, filling her, until she didn't dare move, didn't dare breathe, and she didn't dare look away from the insistent demand in his eyes. She worried that he was going to be the death of her, this stubborn man laying claim to her heart, but she was more worried that he was also going to be her life.

He was waiting, waiting for an answer. Slowly she pressed a single kiss to his mouth, it was the only answer she could give, and only then did he begin to move.

It wasn't supposed to turn out like this. Today he was so sure, so gentle, so far removed from their usual overheated matings. She'd never seen this side to him, he'd kept it too well hidden, or maybe she hadn't wanted to see. Against her skin she could feel the burn of his body. Strong thighs that would never let her fall. Strong arms that held her easily.

Outside, the planes were taking off, roaring overhead, defying gravity. Inside, the world was spinning out of control, defying gravity as well. It wasn't supposed to turn out like this.

The shadows of the sun cast a dark flush on his skin, a drop of sweat beading against his neck, and she licked it away, tasting his salt, tasting him.

"I missed you," he whispered. The simple words pulled at her heart.

"You make up for it nicely," she answered back, her body moving so perfectly with his. There wasn't any humor in the words. She had tried, she had failed.

His mouth nipped at the side of her mouth, once, twice, and then he was kissing her again, and Ashley was lost. It was so perfect it hurt.

Her free hand curled tighter around his neck, bringing him close, bringing him deeper inside her. It was supposed to be a long-distance affair. It was supposed to be hot and torrid. They were supposed to have lost this passion once the newness wore off, once she got to know him better. Oh, God, she liked him even more.

David touched the corner of her eye with his mouth. "Don't cry. I would never hurt you."

"I know."

He unlocked their hands, held her and took her to bed. Then he bent and began to undress her. "I'm not going to take you against the door," he said, and her shaking hands moved to the buttons on his shirt, the fly of his pants, until he was bare. Thick arms, a hard chest and a cock that jutted out impatiently. All hers.

He lifted her shirt over her head, slid her skirt down her

legs, exposing the thin gossamer of her bra and panties to his hungry gaze.

She expected a bold compliment, a lusty remark, but he didn't say a word, only the jerk of his sex betraying anything at all. Silently he moved over her, his mouth covering her breast through the thin silk. His lips pulled slow and hard, and her head fell back, her mind too drowsy with the feel of him, the scent of him, the touch of him.

Sure fingers tossed her bra aside before his mouth returned to hers. He used his tongue, his teeth, all to leisurely drive her insane. This intoxicating new rhythm was killing her. Her legs spread wide, wantonly wide, slid up and down the length of his and the fine curve of his ass, which only seemed to increase the heavy pressure of his lips.

Only once did he look at her. Her hand reached out, smoothed his hair, and she knew he was going to destroy her carefully ordered life.

Their eyes met, and then he lowered his head, proceeding to do just that.

It was a thorough seduction, coaxing her hands to wrap around his back, his waist. Eventually his mouth tarried lower, playing with the hollows of her belly, his fingers taking the band of her panties, pulling them down her legs, her skin burning, her nerves frayed.

His mouth followed, dallied too long between her thighs, and she whimpered, and then moaned, and fisted her hands in the blankets, dragging the covers apart.

In her entire life, Ashley had never been so thoroughly adored. There was no other word for it. He demanded so much from her, but he gave infinitely more. Now he knew her so well. He knew where to touch, where to tease, his hands soothing her hips, as he loved her so carefully.

The hotel room felt like magic this day. The orange covers shimmered to gold, the late afternoon sunlight glistened against the walls like pearl. The thundering jets outside were only matched by the silent thundering of her heart. He took her hand, joined it with his and brought her entwined hand to his mouth. Then he slipped inside her, and quietly she gasped.

I love you.

She didn't want to say the words, but they tumbled out before she could stop them.

"Good," he whispered, and took her mouth once more.

Afterwards, when he had decimated the last of the feeble denials in her heart, he pulled her to him, and she stayed curled there. When she was this close, she could smell the crisp musk of his cologne, so slight, so subtle, mixed with the heady scent of David. Her nose tickled with the scent, with the crisp hair on his chest, and she wanted to stay here all day. To watch the moon play silver on his dark hair, to watch the sun bloom across his skin, to watch the rise of his breath as he slept. She'd never watched him sleep. They never had the chance. Tonight she would watch him sleep.

Under her hand, his heart was steady and strong. He didn't speak, and she was glad there were no probing questions, no insistent pushes. Not now, not today. Maybe he knew he had already won, and she had never clued in they were locked in a battle. It was the way of her life. Too much awareness, one day too late.

So they both lay there, not speaking to each other, not looking at each, not bearing to be too far apart. The minutes ticked past, until his watch beeped once.

"We need to go," he told her. "The train leaves in half an hour."

Ashley nodded, and slipped on her clothes. "David?" she asked. The room was heavy with so much left unsaid. Normally, it wasn't her way to ask; normally, it was his way to tell, and these new rules muddled her head.

He buttoned his shirt, and came to her side, not touching her, but his eyes were the softest shade of green. "Let's get through this. We'll figure it out. I'm a smart man, did you know that? You should know that."

She smiled, slipped her hand in his, and nodded once.

12

THEY TOOK THE Northwest line to Norwood Park. Not one of the most monied neighborhoods in Chicago, but a nice one with trees and tidy lawns. One for blue-collar families who shopped at Sears, not at boutiques, and Ashley wondered about Christine's new life. This wasn't tony Manhattan. Not by a long shot. Ashley dropped the bitch label, only because now she felt a tiny bit sorry for Christine.

As the train rumbled along the tracks, and the clock ticked closer to six, David grew more and more still. The locked jaw was back, the shoulders were so straight she swore he'd grown five inches, and his eyes had turned to ice. He wore a jacket and tie, as if this were business, rather than personal, but as a woman who donned bunny slippers and floppy hats in order to buck up her courage, she understood.

"It'll be fine," she told him, with an encouraging smile.

The smile he gave her was tight, and not so fine, as he vacantly stared out the window.

He's a coward. I knew it. Can't take facing a little woman. What sort of man is that?

Shut up, Val. You're not going to do this to me.

He's still hung up on her. That's the problem. Get over him, Ash.

Ashley wished that David would talk, if only so she wouldn't have to listen to Val's voice in her head. It was a few blocks from the station to the house, but Ashley didn't mind. The warm summer air was cool, and she made one-sided small talk, trying to ignore the pebble that was fast turning into a boulder in the pit of her stomach.

The house was in a long line of homes that sat behind Kennedy Expressway. The noise of the cars was constant. There was a neat yard, lined with bright yellow and pink flowers, and a Subaru parked in the drive. As they approached the door, it opened, and a lady walked out. Tall, elegant, dressed in jeans and a sweater that was the pure vibrancy of Carolina Herrera. Possibly secondhand, but still jazzy. This woman was exactly what the name Christine implied, but she was smiling and waved happily, as if this were old home week. Whatever.

What was odd was David's reaction to her. His smile grew less cold, his shoulders relaxed and while the greetings were still somewhat stilted, it wasn't nearly as bad as what Ashley had anticipated. Apparently, it wasn't nearly as bad as what he had anticipated, either.

"Come inside. Chris is out back, working on the lawnmower. It breaks down weekly."

And she left David for a man who drove a Subaru, and whose lawnmower broke down weekly? Okay, Christine was just flat-out stupid, thought Ashley, because there was judgmental and then there was factually correct.

The house was tiny, a living room with dark paneling, a kitchen that was tidy, but locked back in the '70s. However, Christine had left a mark. The artwork was top-notch, and there were fresh flowers in every room. In fact it was so nice that Ashley began to relax, David began to relax. Everything was fine until the man walked in through the back door, and then the locked jaw returned, the shoulders tensed, and David's smile was gone like the wind. He didn't even try to pretend to be polite. Ashley stared, confused.

"David," the man said.

"Chris," David answered with a tight nod. Then he seemed to remember his manners. "This is Ashley. Ashley, David, Christine."

Chris was nearly as tall as David, with dark hair and hazel eyes. Obviously Christine stayed to a certain physical type. "My brother hasn't said anything about you," Chris said, taking Ashley's hand, shaking it in a gentlemanly way. Exactly like David.

His brother? Ashley froze, removing all traces of anything from her face.

Christine, exquisite hostess that she was, broke the silence. "Let's go to the living room. Ashley, would you like something to drink?"

"I'd love one, thanks."

"What do you drink?"

"Whatever you have." Tonight wasn't the night to be picky.

The inside of the house was tastefully shabby. The furniture wasn't new, no Ethan Allen here, but it was obvious that Christine had a good eye. Apparently two. *Oh, God.*

Ashley finally dared to look at David. He should have told her this. He should have prepared her, but unfortunately, David was too preoccupied with not looking at his brother.

Oh, God.

Ashley took a seat on the couch, David followed, and she grabbed his hand, her fingers digging into his flesh, not as much in anger as panic. They would get through this, they would get through this. If she repeated it often enough, it would be true.

Christine, bless her, started to talk, and it took a moment for Ashley to register that she was talking to her.

"So, how long have you and David been seeing each other? I mean, coming all the way from New York. That sounds fun, honestly. But serious, too." Then she shot David a relieved look. "I'm glad to see it."

So Christine assumed that Ashley lived in New York, near David. It would be easier if Christine thought that, rather than trying to explain that Ashley didn't live in New York. The whole plane thing. The whole travel thing. Ashley opened her mouth.

"Ashley lives here. We met on a plane." David obviously didn't intend to keep things simple.

"You met on a plane to Chicago? Today?" Christine looked shocked, and Ashley started to explain, but David got there first.

"No, it was a while back. It works for us," David said curtly, and that was one way to end that conversation.

Chris sat silently, sipping his beer. Christine, still polite, bless her heart, was not deterred. "So, what do you do, Ashley?"

"I own some boutiques in town. Ashley's Closet. Naperville, State Street, Wicker Park, Lakeview. I'm in fashion," she added stupidly.

"I haven't heard of it, but I love to shop," said Christine, completely unnecessarily.

"You should visit," answered Ashley, completely unnecessarily.

"I will," Christine replied, and Ashley prayed she was only being polite.

Meanwhile, David and Chris hadn't said a word. Ashley glanced at David and then smiled at Christine. "Do you mind if I go outside for a minute? I get a little claustrophobic sometimes. I have so many phobias, sometimes I can't keep track. David, can you come with me?"

He flew off the couch, and they walked briskly outside, down the three steps to stand under the lone elm tree in the yard.

"You're claustrophobic?"

"No," she said, leaning back against the hard, stabilizing bark of the tree. She needed support right at that moment.

"I'm sorry," he blurted, and while she had been ready to give him a large piece of her mind for dumping her in this unprepared, the apology stopped it at once.

She pulled once at his tie. "I'll live. Will you?"

David nodded once, but his eyes still hurt, and now she knew why. It wasn't Christine that had sliced him in two. It was his brother. She couldn't imagine the betrayal, but the pain she understood all too well. With a husband or a wife, you could sign a paper, and they were no more. With a brother, or a sister, the pain cut deeper, the anger more cold. It was blood.

Ashley didn't like to think about the years that Val had drank herself into oblivion. It was so much easier to pretend it had never happened. Apparently David dealt with his pain the same way.

Not caring who was watching, Ashley slid her hands around his neck, and kissed him. His broad arms wrapped around her like a lifeline, and she liked being needed. He'd bailed her out a few times, for once, she could return the favor. He rested his forehead against her own. "I'm sorry," he repeated.

"You have nothing to be sorry about. We'll get through it." Then she would chop his brother into small pieces, but that would be left for another day. And honestly, she did like Christine. The woman was back to being a bitch, albeit a stupid bitch, because she had picked the wrong brother, but Ashley wasn't about to complain.

"Are you okay?" she asked.

"I'm fine."

"Should I kill him for you?"

He laughed, a rough, awkward sound, but it tugged at Ashley's heart just the same. "You'd commit capital murder for me?"

"In a heartbeat."

"I love you, Ash."

She grabbed his hand and squeezed, and they went back to confront the evil bitch of an ex-wife and David's back-stabbing son-of-a-bitch brother.

He's calling you Ash? That's my nickname. I don't like him, Ash. I don't trust him.

Ashley smiled at David, pushing the voice aside for now. Sometimes procrastination could be a very useful thing.

FOR DAVID, it was four hours in the bowels of hell, but he survived, and actually by the end of the night, he had talked with Chris about the apartment, and they agreed to split the proceeds in half. David didn't feel the need to be petty anymore. Ashley did that to him—kept him from being juvenile and vindictive.

The anger was still there, the rage, but it didn't burn so hot anymore.

In the last four years, Chris had changed some. There was a cut of gray in his hair that hadn't been there before, and there were neat lines bracketing his mouth, but when Chris looked at Christine, there was something in his eyes that should have made David hurt, but didn't. Maybe he should have visited here earlier, he wasn't sure, but he was here now.

Okay, they would never be as close as they had been, but maybe...

As the evening went on, Ashley stuck to him like glue. Almost—dare he say it?—flagrantly possessive. It surprised him, that protective streak within her. He'd never seen it before, except maybe once, when she took off from Miami to find her sister. It was just one more reason that he loved her. Every time he was with her, he found new reasons to love her. New things about her that pleased him, comforted him. He'd never thought about needing someone. In a lot of ways, he hadn't needed Christine, but at that time, David didn't need anyone. He was so sure that he owned the world.

Now he knew better. Now he knew that he could need.

With Ashley, things would be different. Ashley loved David. David loved Ashley, and he was going to do everything in his power to make this permanent. She'd love it in New York. All he had to do was convince her to move with whatever means necessary, and David was nothing if not creative.

He found her eyes, Christine was showing her the latest in art deco vases, and Ashley moved across the room, coming to sit on the arm of his chair. "You about ready to go?" he asked, because he'd done his duty, he'd made his peace. All he wanted to do now was get back to the hotel, bury himself deep inside Ashley and make up for fourteen days lost.

She loved him.

Her smile was slow and wicked, and made him catch his breath. Suddenly, he couldn't wait to leave.

"Let's call a cab," he suggested.

"You don't want to take the train back?" she asked, and obviously people in Chicago weren't as efficient about their transportation as New York.

David leaned closer, pitched his voice low, but he didn't care who heard, he was more interested in tasting the side of Ashley's neck. Right below her ear, where the skin felt like silk. "We're not far. The cab will be faster."

Ashley, his wonderful Ashley, jumped up from her seat and clapped her hands together. "All right. I bet you guys have to get up early tomorrow. I know I do." She took Christine's hand, pumped once. "Great to meet you. Come by the store." Then she looked at David, her smile falling a few points. "It was nice to meet some of David's family. I can see the resemblance. You're lucky to have him."

Chris stared at the carpet, and after one phone call and ten minutes of waiting, the cab honked outside, and thank God, that was over.

Christine waved them off as if everyone were the best of friends.

Once Ashley and David were safely in the cab, speeding away from Christine and Chris and Norwood Park, David dove in and took Ashley's lips. She curved into his arms, her mouth opening, her tongue teasing his. He shouldn't be making out in the backseat of a cab, but these were desperate times, and he was a desperate man. Her fingers grabbed his thigh, moved higher to cover the bulge at his fly, and began to move in the most supremely confident way.

Oh, hell, yes. "Tell me you're going back to the hotel with me."

Ashley slapped the seat, not the reaction he wanted. "Crap. I need to call home. They don't know where I am." Quickly she plucked her phone from her purse and punched in a number, and David sat silently willing his cock to be patient.

"Val, hey, it's me. Listen, I got tied up at the store. It's going to be late. I probably won't make it home tonight."

At the store?

"I know, it's a pain. I hate inventory."

He was inventory? It was the middle of June. Who did inventory in the middle of the month? She didn't need to lie about this. And if she was going to lie, she needed a better lie.

"No, no, I don't need your help. I've got the staff here. We'll finish up, and I'll just sack out in the back. No need to worry. How was your day…? Excellent. Give Brianna and Mom a kiss, and I'll see you in the morning."

She clicked off the phone and David told himself it didn't matter. Then he promptly asked her, "Why didn't you tell them?"

Yeah, it mattered.

Carefully she shrugged. "They don't need to know."

There was something strange in her face, something evasive, and it bothered him that she needed to keep their relationship secret, as if there were something wrong with it. There was nothing wrong with it, and everything right with it.

Still, she was an adult, she knew her family better. He should let her handle it the way she needed to handle it.

And still he couldn't shut up. All right, it bothered him. He wanted to be understanding and sensitive, and all those "good" qualities, but he wasn't. She had told him that he didn't like to admit things, so fine, he admitted things. It bothered him. He turned to Ashley and tried to reason. "You're an adult now, so who cares? It's no big deal. If you don't tell them, it makes it a big deal. You should say something, Ashley. Tell her the truth."

"I'll do it when the time is right," she told him, which did nothing to make him feel better. In fact, it only made it worse. "I just wanted to get through tonight…and we did."

"Yeah," he said, and he settled her against his shoulder. "We got through it."

Still she didn't relax. He could feel the tension in her shoulders, her neck. He only wished she would trust him to fix what was wrong with their being together. He could, he knew he could. All he had to do was convince her family he was the perfect man. A challenge? He was up for it. For Ashley, he would do anything.

WHEN THEY GOT BACK to the hotel, Ashley felt oddly unprepared. He loved her, she loved him. Okay, fine, now what were they supposed to do about it? The first second he entered the room, he put away his jacket, and pulled at his tie. Ashley blinked twice, noting what was obviously his evening ritual. How odd; she had never known. Fascinated, she sat in the black leather desk chair, and watched David proceed with his life. He was heading to the bathroom before he noticed.

"What?" he asked.

"This is new."

He thought for a second. "It is. I like it. You like it?"

"I do."

"Good," he said, wandering off to the bathroom.

Eventually he poked his head around the corner of the room. "You didn't bring pajamas, did you?"

And he was nervous. "No."

"Okay. I'm fine with that."

She thought for a second. "David, do you sleep in pajamas?"

"Not since the divorce, but I'm usually alone. I packed some tonight."

"Why?" she asked, because she wanted to understand how his mind worked. It was a mystery all unto itself.

"It seemed rude not to," he explained.

Ashley giggled. "Now you get shy?"

"I'm not shy. It just doesn't seem right. What if you get offended or something? Women and men, they're different. They think about things differently."

She curled her feet up under her. "Yeah?"

"Fine. Laugh at me, but I'm telling you, there're men who aren't so sensitive." He pushed at his hair, and the cowlick reared up in the back. "Do you mind if I check in with the office? I'm expecting an answer on something. It won't take more than two to three minutes."

Ashley shook her head. "I don't mind."

He unbuttoned his shirt and pulled the laptop from his case and settled down to work. While he sat there, she watched him contentedly. She'd never seen him work before. His eyes were always moving, and he was fast on the keys, his fingers flying, which didn't surprise her at all. She'd seen those fingers in action—on her.

He hadn't been kidding about the time. No more than three minutes later, he shut the lid and stowed the computer away. "Thanks. We're in the middle of earnings season. It's a zoo."

Then he held out his hand, sat down on the bed, legs splayed and pulled her between them. "Thank you for staying."

"Well, you're in my town. It's the least I can do."

He kissed her once. "I appreciate it." Then his mouth moved to her neck, tickling her with his stubble. She giggled and he raised his head. "Do you want me to shave? I can shave."

"No, I like it." And she liked this. He was new, too. Strange to see such an arrogant man so unsure about domesticity. Domesticity. She had been worried about it, now it sounded like bliss. She settled in between his thighs. "How was it tonight?" she asked, when his mouth returned to nuzzle her neck.

"Fine."

Ashley sighed, frustration and pleasure mixed together in one disjointed sound. "You don't have to tell me 'fine.' I was there. It was miserable. I want to know how you were feeling."

He raised his head. "Can we not talk about my feelings?"

And now he was ruining all her fantasies of what domestic bliss should entail. "Why don't you want to talk about your feelings? I like talking about your feelings."

Long, efficient fingers worked the buttons on her shirt. "I

think you secretly delight in other people's misery. You're a closet sadist."

"How did you know?"

"It was the beady gleam in your eyes that gave you way, Marquise de Sade," he told her, then he took her blouse and hung it up in the closet, right next to his jacket. David McLean was a tidy man. She liked that. She liked having a man to pick up her socks, not that she would throw down her socks, but it was comforting to know that if she did, he wasn't too proud to pick them up.

She stood, stripping off her pants, a straight-line pair that she had bought from a tiny shop in Galena. They were elegant, looked pricey and wrinkled like the devil. She handed them to him, just to test her theory. "I don't have beady eyes," she told him, watching as he headed for the closet.

Ashley grinned when he returned and his hands lifted her face to the light. "Let me see. Definitely beady. Shifty even."

His fingers unhooked the clasp on her bra, his hands gliding over her breasts, his sigh pure male satisfaction, like a cold beer in August, or a win in extra innings. For a moment, she surrendered to the lovely idea of being the cause of said satisfaction, but there were bigger things to consider. Namely, whether passion and domesticity could be wrapped up in one package. "You know what's on TV tonight?"

"I admit I didn't check." He shucked the last of his clothes, began to put them all away, and as she studied the irrefutable evidence of his arousal, she realized that yes, passion and domesticity could coexist nicely.

"The original *Halloween* is on television. Can we watch it?"

He turned, hanger in hand, wearing only a disconcerted frown. It was truly a lovely picture. "I'm in town for twenty-four hours, and you want to watch television?"

Ashley considered pointing out the three minutes that he had spent working on his computer, but decided that would be small of her. "Stay another day," she offered instead, laying out on the bed, a not-so-virginal sacrifice clad only in a demure scrap of innocent white silk.

David took a long, hard look, considered the offer, scratched the dark stubble at his jaw. "I'd have to juggle things."

"Juggle. You're a good juggler," she told him, watching with a pleased smiled as he climbed into bed. "Besides, we have to talk to Horatio Moore tomorrow. He's the guy in Wicker Park."

"Oh, God. I had forgotten," he said, stretching out next to her.

"Already you've forgotten your mission?" Ashley tsked, her avid gaze wandering over the exquisite easy-to-wear lines of his body. Highlighting the collection were strong, masculine arms that were never too big, never too rough. The broad chest was iconically male, accentuated by two sharply defined whirls of hair that trailed low in a fanciful temptation that drew the eye lower still. The long, lean legs were an eye-pleasing frame to an ass that belonged in a Calvin Klein ad. Completing the look was the bold design of his cock, long and thick with classical styling, the perfect combination of both form and function.

He made her silly with lust. Her nipples perked, her demure scrap of white lace now thoroughly damp. As an analyst who evaluated things daily, David noticed…and caught her wrists, pulling her closer. "My only mission is to pleasure you."

"Then you have to stay another day," she insisted, and he slid the demure scrap down her legs, tossing it over the side of the bed. Obviously there were limits to his orderly nature.

Her mouth grew dry with anticipation. He sat up against the headboard, pulled her back against him, skin to skin, and his hands traced over her breasts, flirting with her thighs. "I'm supposed to be in San Jose tomorrow."

"San Jose?" She blew a raspberry. "They don't deserve you. Chicago deserves you."

"I can be persuaded," he said gallantly, and against her back, the long ridge of his erection bucked in agreement.

With lazy eyes she watched them in the mirror, his body

blocked by hers, except for the warm hands cupping her breasts, the unwavering thumbs at her nipples that stoked a pulse between her legs. "I accept that challenge," she offered, brave words from a woman being steadily seduced into submission.

His mouth played with her neck, her ear, and she cocked her head to one side. "Introduce me to your family," he whispered, and instantly she stiffened.

"Not this time. Maybe next."

"Scared?" he asked, his mouth still against her neck, but his hands were still.

"No."

"Yes?"

"Yes," she admitted, her posture hardening from happily distracted hussy to not quite so stupidly distracted anymore.

David's busy hands resumed their task, and Ashley relaxed again. "You don't have to be. Honestly, I'm not that intimidating."

"It's not you I'm worried about."

"Who are you worried about?" he asked, showing an apparent fascination for the sensitive skin below her ear. Happy sensitive skin.

"It's Val. She won't like you."

In the mirror, she could see the stubborn lock to his jaw. "And why not?" he protested. "Come on, that's ridiculous. I'm nice. I'm polite, even chivalrous at times. I can bring you to orgasm six, seven times a night, and God knows, that should count for something."

"It merely says I'm easy," she told him, opening her glistening thighs to illustrate the point—and perhaps distract him as well.

David wasn't that easily sidetracked. "Why won't she like me, Ash?"

"She's just quirky," she said, pulling away, turning her back on the inviting picture in the mirror, and this time, David didn't seem to object.

"Does she like any of the men you go out with?"

"I haven't dated a lot. The stores have kept me busy. It was just easier that way."

"Is this going to be a problem? If it is, I'd rather know about it."

He talked as if everything was so simple. And if she admitted to him that it was going to be a problem—which she did—what did he expect to happen? What did he think he could do about it? Ashley couldn't fix the problem. David couldn't fix the problem. Only Val could fix the problem, and she was trying. Honestly, she was trying.

"Is this going to be a problem?" he asked again, and she knew it wasn't Val he was asking about. It was more a question of whether Ashley would have a problem if Val had a problem.

"Like the issue with your brother, and how you told me about that one?" she shot back, avoiding the answer nicely.

David ran his hand over his face. "Exactly like that one. Damn, you're going to make me talk, aren't you? Fine. You want to know, I'll tell you. Tonight wasn't so bad. Christine didn't faze me at all. At first, I wanted to hit him, not because of what he did to her, but what he did to me."

After that, he shut his mouth tightly, as if he had fulfilled all obligations of discussing his feelings. Not by a long shot. Ashley was diving in.

She pulled a pillow from the bed, and lay on her stomach, her feet kicking up in the air. "Were you two close? Has he always been in Chicago?"

She could feel his eyes touch on her ass, but he didn't reach for her. Obviously passion and domesticity could exist, but passion and families couldn't. Made perfect sense to her. "They moved here after the divorce. He said they needed a fresh start. He was right."

"He loves her," she said softly.

He gave her a cold look. "I don't care. That's his business."

"Sorry. Tell me what it was like growing up. You never talk about that."

"Well, since all of my memories involved my brother, I didn't want to talk about it."

Past tense. She noticed. "You could now?"

David thought, mulled it over and pulled her back against him. His hands moved over her, not as much to seduce her, as to soothe him. She didn't mind. She liked that she could do that. Soothe him. "I can talk now."

And he did. He told her about the time that Chris had skipped school to go to the Yankees game, and David had lied for him. But then their mother had found out, and they were both grounded for two weeks, which David thought was tremendously unfair since he hadn't skipped school. He told Ashley about the Christmas that their father had taken them camping up at Lake George, and Chris had told David that the shadow creeping in the darkness toward their tent was a bear—not a raccoon. All his life, he and his brother had been together, until one day they weren't. Families shouldn't be split apart like that; it wasn't right. Someone always ended up hurting, and in this case, it was David.

After he finished all that talking, he looked at Ashley and smiled. "You know, I'm sensing a trend. All my life, my brother has given me the crappy end of the stick."

She covered his hands with her own. "Except with Christine. You are so lucky to be rid of her," she told him.

His fingers slid lower, tempting, tempting… "You're jealous, aren't you?"

"Am not." One long finger slid inside her, and Ashley's back arched high in relief.

"I don't mind. I think it's kind of sexy," he said, his thumb finding her most suggestive spot, and circling there, until she forgot about planes, forgot about television, forgot about her sister, and focused on nothing but the insistent torment of his hand.

In the mirror, she saw them together, saw the heavy darkness of his eyes, saw the swollen flush of her body milking his hand, and for the first time in her life, she saw herself come.

Later, her lungs remembered to breathe, and she turned her head to kiss him. When kissing wasn't enough, she turned in his arms and slid over him, her lips tasting the skin of his chest, sampling the taut lines of his abs, and then, with serious intent, she slid lower, her hands sizing his cock.

"What about the movie?" he asked curiously.

"Maybe later," she told him, before her mouth closed over him. There was domesticity, and then there was stupid.

13

EARLY THE NEXT MORNING, before the sun even thought about getting up, the airplanes resumed roaring overhead. David didn't open his eyes. He simply lay there, with Ashley curled up, half on the bed, half on him. It was pretty much the best blanket ever. Airplanes weren't so bad. They had given him this.

For a few minutes he stayed there, not daring to move, sure this was all a dream. Her leg stirred, sliding against his own, and his cock really didn't care if it was a dream or not. Gawd, he was a goat.

Her head was pillowed on his chest, and he pushed back the hair from her face. He had thought she was the weak one, vulnerable, letting everyone walk over her. David was wrong about that. Yesterday, she'd gotten him through the worst dinner in his life. He shouldn't wake her, he should let her sleep, but this was his last day. He never told her how hard it was to leave. He didn't even tell her that he was thinking about moving to Chicago. It wasn't a bad town. They had banks, they had the Chicago Board of Trade. No, it wasn't New York, but Chicago had one very important thing that New York didn't. Ashley Larsen. The woman he loved.

He couldn't help but sigh.

The outside lights filtered in through the sheers, casting the room in a dim glow, and Ashley lifted up on one elbow, sleepy eyes met his own.

"Good morning," she said. "Welcome to O'Hare, the airport that never sleeps."

"Hmm," he answered, kissing her once, pulling her fully on top of him, then burying his face against her hair. He liked the soft smell of it, one more thing New York didn't have. "I'm sorry we didn't get to watch the movie."

"No, I think my movies will always lose out to your sex. I can read the writing on the wall."

He lifted his head to stare at her. "*My* sex?"

"Fine. *Our* sex."

"I like that. Our sex." His head fell back again, and he stroked her arm. The condoms were on the nightstand within reach. If he just stretched...

"You want to go see my stores?"

He lifted his head, squinted. "Now?"

"No, this morning. We meet with Horatio at two. We have lots of time."

David looked at the box of condoms, examined the valley between her bare breasts. Come on, this was important to her. This was her dream, and all he could think about was sex? Hours and hours of sex? That was his dream. But no, this wasn't about David, this was about Ashley.

"Sure," he told her, even managing to smile.

"We don't have to," she said, obviously sensing his hesitation, or perhaps the morning wood that was happily finding its home between her thighs.

"No. I want to," he insisted, now feeling extreme guilt. But she was naked. And her nipples were starting to go dark and pouty, and her eyes were laughing at him.

He watched as she reached for a condom. "We could do both."

"Both?" he asked innocently.

She took the packet in her teeth and ripped. His eyes narrowed. She did that on purpose.

"It won't take long," she answered, busy fingers at work.

"It might," he shot back.

"I'm talking about the stores," she said, and he felt less guilt mainly because she was impaling herself on him and thus, guilt was impossible.

"I want to see them. I really do. I'm here. We should—" she lowered herself in one sharp move "—see them."

David couldn't speak if he tried.

Her arms slid up his chest, curled around his neck, and oh, damn, he was staring down the valley of her breasts once again.

"Later," she said, kissing him, riding him, pleasing him.

THEY ENDED UP sleeping through the morning runway traffic. David knew the right thing to do was wake her up, then they could get dressed and he'd see Ashley's Closet in person. His hands curled over her shoulder and shook her awake. Sleepy eyes looked at him.

He was definitely moving to Chicago.

"We should go."

"Okay," she murmured, and then promptly fell back against his chest.

He propped her up a bit. "I want to see your stores, Ashley. It's important."

"We can sleep."

"We can sleep tonight. You should get up." If she didn't get up now, they weren't leaving, and then he would not be the supportive man he wanted her to see. Last night, he wasn't watching her movies, now they weren't visiting her stores.

"Hmm..."

David flew out of bed before he could change his mind. "I'm going to take a shower," he announced, eyeing the silky skin of her back, the way her ass bumped high in her sleep. That bump was so cute, so curvy, so intensely...inviting. He could just fit into that bump. "I'm going to take a cold shower."

She rolled over, and David froze. The ass was safely stowed away, but now there were breasts. A shadowy triangle of hair beckoned between her thighs. Perfect thighs. He could sense his willpower disappearing. "You're not being fair to me. You know, first the movie, now this. I'm trying to be good. I'm trying to show you I'm not a horndog. You're killing the image, Ashley."

She threw a pillow at his head.

"I'm taking my shower," he stated for the record, turning his eyes away from the bed.

The box on the nightstand torpedoed soon after, condoms flying out like rain.

Obviously Ashley Larsen wasn't a morning person.

David turned on the shower and smiled.

God, he loved her.

THE SOUND OF the shower killed her libido, and Ashley sighed. Oh, fine. She flung her legs over the side of the bed and raked her hand through her tangled hair. When she moved to stand, her legs wobbled—only for a second. But she and David didn't have long. One more day.

Not quite in her happy place, she trudged to the bathroom, ready to hit the bracing spray, and maybe seduce David in the process. Halfway to the door, the phone rang.

It was Val.

"I have a problem."

Ashley sank back on the bed, and clutched a pillow to her chest. "What sort of problem?"

"I'm sorry."

"Don't apologize, Val. Just tell me what's wrong."

"I didn't know."

"You do know. Tell me."

There was a long silence and Ashley waited. "I wrote some hot checks. I thought I had more money in my account, and Brianna needed some new clothes for school, and I knew payday was coming up."

"How much?" she asked.

"About seven hundred dollars."

"You spent seven hundred dollars on clothes for a little girl?" Ashley swallowed. For a sober Val, that was a lot of money.

"I knew you'd be mad," Val whispered, and Ashley could hear the panic in her voice.

"I'm not mad."

"You're mad, Ash."

"I'm not mad."

"Where are you? I called the stores. You lied to me. Why are you lying to me?"

"We don't need to worry about this now. One thing at a time, right? Where's Brianna?"

Ashley looked up, found David leaning against the wall, hair wet, a towel wrapped around his hips. His eyes were waiting to see what she would do. The hard bent in his jaw said he thought she would cave. A test. Ashley hated tests.

"She's at school. Mom's at work. I didn't tell her. She'll worry. You can help me, right?"

"I can't help you now, Valerie." Coolly she met his eyes. *There. See? She could do it.*

"You don't understand, Ash. They called and wanted me to come down. They told me it was a special sale. It was a trap. So here I am at the mall, and they aren't happy with me. They're going to call the cops."

Cops? Oh, God. "They don't call the cops for bad checks."

"They do if there's more than one bad check."

There was no way that Val could get out of this on her own. Ashley looked at David. *No, Val could get out of this on her own.* "Valerie, I'm not going to do this." Her voice was firm, unwavering, as steady as the hard line of his jaw.

"Please."

"No," she answered, her voice not quite so steady.

"You can't leave me hanging like this." Now Val was doing the angry-pleading thing, and Ashley had never responded well to that. She didn't like it when people were mad at her, she didn't like it when she felt guilt. Feeling both at the same time was guaranteed to kick her butt.

"I have some business to take care of," she stated, not letting her butt get kicked.

"You're with somebody, aren't you? You're out fucking some guy, and you don't give a damn about me. I need you."

Slowly Ashley's gaze drifted away from David. "I can't do this right now."

At that, Val hung up.

"Problem?" That was David. Master of the obvious.

"No. No problem," she replied.

Five seconds later, the phone rang again. David looked at the phone, looked at Ashley. Ashley waited, but then eventually jabbed the talk button with a lot of extra force. She was going to tick somebody off here. If it wasn't Val, it'd be David. But David was the tough one. Val, not so much.

"Yes?"

"I'm sorry, Ashley. I don't mean to yell at you. I don't know what to do. I don't have seven hundred dollars."

She couldn't look at him. Not now. When she looked at him, she couldn't focus, couldn't concentrate, and she needed to keep her wits about her. "You get paid on Monday?"

"Yes. I just need a little money until then. And you might need to talk to these people."

"Where are you at?" Ashley asked, defeat in her voice.

"Nordstrom."

Nordstrom. Yes, when it came to her daughter, Val spared no expense. "I'll be there in about an hour."

"Could you get here any sooner than that? You know I don't handle this stuff well."

"It'll be an hour. I need to get my car."

"Thanks, Ash. I'd be dead without you."

When she hung up, she tried to smile at David.

"Are you okay?" he asked.

Anger would be so much better than sympathy. If he was

angry, she could be mad at him for being angry. With sympathy, there wasn't a lot she could do except analyze her own shortcomings, and wonder if she was doing the right thing. The only problem seemed to be that there never was a right or a wrong thing. There was only two wrongs. Ashley sighed. "I'll be fine."

"You're going to go?"

"Yeah." It wasn't the answer he wanted, and she knew it.

"Do you want me to come with you?"

She stared balefully. "I don't think it'd be smart."

"No, probably not. What about Horatio?"

"Who?"

"The designer guy."

"Damn."

"Want me to reschedule for you? Might as well do something useful."

"No. I can make it there by two. Don't worry about it." She met his eyes, wished she could read his mind. "Are you mad at me?"

"No. I could never get mad at you. Sometimes I get mad for you, but that's a different thing."

"Thank you."

"Don't mention it. You should tell your sister about us. She might actually think twice about calling."

"I will. It's just not the right time."

"There won't be a right time, will there?"

There never is, Ash. Never will be.

I don't need to hear this, Val.

That's you, not me. All you, sis.

"I have to go," she told David, and then quietly, efficiently, she got dressed. She'd had enough of that voice in her head. She'd hear the live version later, and that wouldn't be as easy to shut out.

DAVID WAITED FOR Ashley until one-fifty, by which time he decided that she wasn't going to show up for her meeting with the designer. Four times he had called, not wanting to interrupt, not wanting to yell, but merely to know if he should reschedule the damn meeting.

Four times she didn't answer.

Finally, realizing that Ashley wouldn't be there, he made a command decision to see Horatio himself, betting on a large position of negative consequences with absolutely no capital to back it up. In the biz this was appropriately named "naked short."

Maybe she'd be mad, maybe she'd be happy, but at this point, somebody needed to worry about her livelihood, and apparently it wasn't her.

Hell.

It wasn't that he was angry at her. He wanted to help her, make her life easier, fix things. When he got frustrated, anger seemed to be the emotion du jour, and in this case there was no one to receive that anger, except for one poor client from the vinyl flooring company, and honestly, if it had been some other company, he wouldn't have lashed out, but today, he didn't have the patience for anything.

He took a cab to Wicker Park, finding the shop on a well-trod street of one-named shops and understated bars. There was money here. It was there in the window displays and the polished signage. But the neighborhood was not built on flashy cosmopolitan dollars. This was "I'm too cool to be rich" money.

David opened the glass door to the shop, and stepped inside, only it wasn't a store, more of a workspace. There were a few long tables piled high with fabric, and a maze of clothes racks on wheels were parked with absolutely no respect for traffic flow. As he stepped around one, a man appeared. A Pillsbury Doughboy type, mid-thirties, with a tape measure in his teeth.

"Horatio Moore?" David asked. Then he pulled out his business card, trying for European fashion flair. Ha. Whatever. Today he'd be lucky to pass for Yankee asshole.

The man pulled the tape measure from his mouth. "Who are you?"

Oh, yes, who was he? International man of fashion. Right.

"We represent Ashley Larsen, she had discussed the...fashion event for her stores? Chicago's Next Big Look. She had selected you to showcase your designs in her boutique. It's a great honor."

Horatio squinted in confusion. "You're from New York?"

"We manage a variety of interests."

"I didn't realize this show was this big."

Using two fingers, David pinched his forehead in what he hoped was egotistical ennui. "Big is not what we want. We want exclusive."

"And you want me?"

"Ashley wants you. We're merely the bank."

"Sure, I'll do it," Horatio said with a nod. Apparently being an overbearing ass was the key to success within this world. There were certain parallels with Wall Street. "What's the plan?"

"In September, over the Labor Day weekend, she'll have a set of two challenges. Cocktails and the everyday sort of clothes."

Horatio laughed. "Cocktails? You mean cocktail wear."

"That's it." Jeez, this was clothing, not the GDP. "You make the designs for the show, and the audience will decide which designer represents the Next Big Look for Chicago."

"Who am I up against? Probably Lorenzo. I hate that prick. You know how many times he's stolen designs from me? More than I can count." He pointed to the striped dress in the window. "See that? Admire the slim cut. Look at the way it moves. Sometimes, I swear, I can only stand in awe."

David looked at the dress, frowned. "I can see that."

"The dress is my masterpiece, my signature. Lorenzo ripped it off, and—oh, God, strike me dead now—he added a belt! It's like putting a moustache on the Mona Lisa. Bastard."

"There's no Lorenzo. There's a lady from Miami, Mariah..." He struggled for the name, and gave up, settling on the singular alone. It made her sound more important. Whatever. "And then there's a guy from New York."

"Out-of-towners? Whoa, that'll be awesome. Hey, you want

to look around? I've got a great brown cashmere that would go so well with those shoulders of yours," he said, sweeping his glance over David in a purely professional manner that still made him nervous. This was so not his world.

David took two steps back. Two steps closer to freedom. "No. I have a call with Milan in five minutes. Another time."

"You're sure? I can do some great things for you."

David waved, fleeing the place. *Fashion.* Captain Kirk would have never been caught dead in a boutique, not even if the entire universe was at stake.

Ashley was going to owe him for this one. Big-time.

It was nearly midnight when Ashley got to the hotel. She thought about calling first, telling him the crisis was over, but sometimes it was easier to duck the bullet, rather than take it straight to the heart. When she slid the key card in the locket, she peeked in, found the lights on and David at work at his computer.

"Hello," she said cautiously, trying to gauge the mood. He was shirtless, in blue jeans, quite casual except for the tense line at his shoulders. And of course, no look of impending emotional eruption would be complete without the severe cut of the jawline. Ashley forced a smile.

"Welcome back."

"I'm sorry," she offered, getting the apology right out there in the open, before the real accusations started to fly.

"Is everything okay?" he asked, his voice concerned, but his eyes bothered her, like Miami before the afternoon storm. Miami was so much easier than Chicago.

She wanted to go to him, touch him, wanted to soothe the rigid shoulders, but that was more ducking. Needing to get this over, she cleared the tension from her throat. "Yes. It was a mess. We had a fight with the bank, had to trudge to ten stores. And you know, they really rip you off on checks. The first one actually would have cleared, but no…they had to put the biggest check through first. Sneaky jerks." Her smile wobbled a bit, but she was steady. She walked over to the desk and leaned against the corner, trying for casual, too.

"I'm glad you got it worked out."

A long silence followed, and she didn't like the silence, so she rambled on to fill it. "How was your day? I'm glad you didn't fly back to New York."

"I thought about it, but I'm booked on the first flight out in the morning."

She knew he would have thought about flying back, was almost surprised that he was still in Chicago. Ashley would have sat in the hotel for days waiting for him. David wasn't her. "I'm sorry I didn't call."

"I assumed you had a reason."

"I couldn't get away," she offered, not a great reason, but partly the truth.

"Here," he said, and handed her a card. *Horatio Moore, Designs by Horatio.* "He's in for the show. You'll have to call him, but he agreed."

Oh. My. God. She stared at the card, stared at him. "You met with him?"

"Somebody had to. I tried to call and see what you wanted, but you weren't answering your phone."

Her smile started to wobble again, and she bit her lip, hard, preferring the pain to the guilt. In her life, her dreams had always been pushed aside to take care of other things. More important things. It wasn't that she was walking away, no, but sometimes you had to do what you had to. While she had been busy cleaning up Val's mess, she hadn't expected him to clean up her own.

"I'm sorry," she repeated. Maybe if she kept saying it, he would believe her. He didn't look as if he believed her. He'd barely lifted his eyes from the screen. "We were talking to the cops," she babbled on. "I didn't think talking on the cell would be smart."

"No, I'm sure it wouldn't have been smart. Polite, yes. Sensitive, yes, thoughtful, yes. Smart. Obviously not."

"You're mad," she stated, then went to sit on the bed, then immediately stood, because she didn't want to argue on this bed. There were too many good memories here. She didn't want to spoil it with bad ones, and there would be bad ones now. She braced herself against the wall, hands behind her back and waited. She didn't have to wait long.

"Hell, yes, I'm mad," he blurted, but his voice was eerily calm. She liked it better when he yelled, but he didn't yell, he only swiveled the chair around toward her. "When you left, I was furious at your sister. At the garbage she was dragging you into. But now, my anger has moved beyond that. You could have told me what to do, could have clued me in a bit. If I had known you wouldn't show until midnight, I would have flown home. I like this hotel room, but not that much."

Yup, the truth hurts, but the cold look in his eyes was worse. Ashley wanted to stay calm because now wasn't the time to fall apart and prove everybody right. "All I needed to do was get Valerie in a better place, talk her down from the ledge and then get back here to you."

Apparently that was the tipping point because finally he stood with his arms folded across his chest. Neatly hidden beneath his arms were twin angry fists.

"Do you hear how you talk about her? You sound like she's a four-year-old, Ashley. She's thirty years old. Let her grow up."

In David's mind everything was so easy. Damn the consequences, just do what you needed to do. Life wasn't like that. Ashley took a lingering glance at those arms, wished he would tug her close, wished his hazel eyes weren't so troubled. But no, they were going to have this out. Damn.

"You don't understand," she started, but she'd never been good at educating herself nor anybody else, yet it was important for him to understand this: that there were no good choices here.

"Why don't you explain it to me, Ashley. Explain why you have to play nursemaid. Explain why you put your shops on hold, why you put me on hold, why you put everything on hold when she calls."

She shot away from the wall and started to pace. It was so easy for him to criticize, to point out how to do everything better. Yes, she was prepared to eat crow for screwing up the day, she should have called, but she wouldn't let him do this to her. This, *this,* she didn't deserve. "You don't know."

David cocked his head, a challenge in his eyes. "Tell me."

She glared, opened her mouth to yell, but then she began to speak, carefully, absolutely, so he could follow her. "As bad as you think this is—with the bounced checks, the needing to find lost permission slips for Brianna, the stupid arguments—it's a cakewalk now. I go to bed at night, and I don't have to take a pill to sleep. I don't have to ask the bail bondsman how his kids are doing. I don't have to check my purse in the morning to make sure all the money is there. I don't have a pit in my stomach when the weekend rolls around and I'm not sure if Brianna's going to see her mother or if Aunt Ash and Grandma are sitting primary. This is easy, David. This is *good.* I've been to hell. I don't want to go back. If babysitting and holding her hand keeps me out of hell, I'm all for it. You don't know. People that don't go through it— they don't know. You're all Mr. Tough Love, throw your brother out, throw your ex out, throw Val out. I'm not you. I can't be you. Sometimes I wish I could be like that, but I can't. I'm sorry if that disappoints you and I'm sorry I didn't call today, and I'm sorry that you don't approve of the way I treat Val, but it's what I'm going to do because it works. You think I'm stupid for putting up with this, but *it works,* and nobody, nobody, can argue with that."

He stood there, impassive, a hard wall of stubborn. "You have a right to be happy."

Oh, that was underhanded. He wasn't supposed to be thinking of her. He was supposed to be all mad, and selfish, the manly man who knew it all. That, she could stand up to. This, she wasn't sure. "I am happy," she said, and she wished her voice sounded more certain.

"I want to kill her, Ashley, and I'm not a cop, or a soldier, or somebody that deals with violence on a daily basis. I'm an ordinary guy. I work with *spreadsheets*. Financial models, return on investment, and I want to kill her. I want the problems gone. I want your shops to run in the black, but I can't fix it if you don't want me to. I want you to be happy, and she makes you unhappy. I don't like to see you unhappy. I hate it."

"I'm sorry," she said, apologizing again. She was sorry she hadn't called, she was sorry her sister was a walking reality show, she was sorry that she hadn't been there to meet with Horatio, and most of all, she was sorry because he was flying out early in the morning, and she had wasted a good fourteen hours. Ashley didn't want to waste any more time.

"Are we okay?" she asked him. David looked so frustrated, and she understood, but anger and frustration, those emotions didn't solve anything. She'd gone through that when Val had turned up both drunk and pregnant, an especially awkward situation. From then on, Ashley's decision-making changed forever. It wasn't so easy to be all tough and hard like he wanted her to be. Still, she wished it were easier on him. He was getting a painfully quick lesson on the realities of living with a recovering alcoholic. Yeah, welcome to the club.

His arms dropped to his sides. Helpless. Yes, she knew that look, too. "I want us to be okay," he told her, his voice low. "I want everything fixed, but I don't think everything is fixed."

Of course it wasn't fixed, but Ashley took happy when she got the chance. "Could we pretend? Just until you get on the plane?"

"Until the next crisis?"

"Yeah, until then."

"I'm not very good at pretending, Ashley." She already knew that. She loved that he saw the world so simply, could look at the bad and label it for what it was. When it came to her business, she needed that simplicity, that honesty. She'd learned from it, and was stronger for it.

But the other thing that David had done for her—her aspirations were getting bigger, and they almost seemed obtainable. At one time, she had been ambivalent about doing much more than keeping Val sober. Now, her wish list was longer. She still wanted to keep Val sober, but she also wanted to do right by Ashley's Closet, and most of all she wanted to keep David in her life. It shouldn't be impossible, and if it was, she didn't want anyone to tell her so. Not even him. "Please try. You want me to be happy. Make me happy. We don't have a lot of time, David. I don't want to spend it like this."

David gave her a smile, and she wished it were more certain. Then he came to her, and pulled her close, and for a few moments, his cheek rested on her head and in his arms, she found the very happiness he said she deserved. "I'm very happy now," she whispered. "You make me happy." Surrounded by everything she said she wanted, Ashley smiled to herself, and she wished it were more certain, too.

THE BEDSIDE CLOCK said five-thirty, and outside the sky was turning the first shades of gold. Halfway between 2:00 and 3:00 a.m., David had closed his eyes, but sleep remained out of reach. Theoretically, lying here with Ashley, his fingers skimming through the soft waves of her hair, he should have been one happy man, but something was off. Probably the way she was frowning in her sleep.

Gently he pushed at the twin lines above her eyes, but they wouldn't disappear, no matter how much he willed it. Ashley's frown remained, so David's frown remained as well.

Twenty-four hours ago, he had everything in his life mapped out. He would move here, there would be no more planes, no more tiny hotel shampoo bottles, no more Do Not Disturb signs. Every night he would pull her close, and every morning, she would wake up against him. Like this.

It used to give him hives to think about living in the same city with Chris and Christine. Now, he could even stomach the idea of seeing them—occasionally, and Ashley would have to be with him. That anger he could put aside.

Val? No, that anger wasn't going anywhere as long as she treated Ashley like her own private punching bag.

He shifted, uncomfortable in his skin.

Warily, his free hand fisted, and he increased the pressure until his skin paled white. David was an absolutist. He was paid a decent salary in order to be straight and upfront. He didn't look the other way, he didn't pull his punches—in his job, in the ring, in his life. He never had, and it was probably one of the reasons that Christine had left him.

What Ashley wanted was for him to look the other way. Now, truthfully, there were a lot of things that he would avoid doing to make her happy, but he couldn't stand still and watch her hurt, or watch her frowning in her sleep and then cluelessly pretend that he was okay with this plan.

But that's what she wanted. She put her needs second, her heart second, her life second to someone not nearly as worthy.

And while she was busy saving her sister, she didn't want him to judge. But every day he went out and judged. It was who he was.

Ashley shifted, her warm skin brushed his, her breast pillowed against him. His cock rose, wanting to take her. His heart pumped, wanting to take her. But this time it was his obstinate mind that stood in the way.

He didn't even know how to look the other way. Sure, he could try. David lifted his fists, twisted them in the air, studying the compressed power within. Slowly he released the pressure, wanting to ease the taut burn inside him, but it didn't go away. No, pretending only made it worse.

David's frown deepened, and finally, abandoning all pretense of sleep, he climbed out of bed. His plane took off for New York in a couple of hours. Home. Where was home anymore? He wasn't sure.

Quietly he headed for the shower. After he was dressed,

carry-on packed, he kissed her once on her sleepy, furrowed forehead, trying one last time to make her worries disappear.

"I love you, Ash." His words were whispered and for his ears alone. Then he slipped out of the room before she woke.

14

FRIDAY PASSED and he didn't call. Ashley kept herself busy making plans for the upcoming show, telling herself not to borrow trouble. A reporter from *Chicago News Daily* had promised coverage and the *InStyle* columnist from the *Tribune* was intrigued. In the afternoon, she pulled off the PR hat, donned her manager hat, and smacked some sense into Evelyn, the manager of the Naperville store, who horrendously believed that a midnight blue blouse should be matched with a set of royal purple silk capris.

At first Evelyn was surprised because Ashley wasn't usually such a bossy boss, but Ashley's tolerance level was zero. Eventually Ashley whipped her into shape, giving her a lengthy diatribe on the subtleties of color, how a sophisticated scheme did not let the gradients run into each other like a smash-up on the Kennedy. No, they must flow, and wash together until they are as one. Evelyn was suitably humbled, the purple capris were back with the white blouse where they belonged. Fashion crisis averted.

By the time Ashley pulled into the driveway it was late, she was exhausted and David still hadn't called. Not even an "I'm in New York" call, and she told herself it was not a sign of the end, or even worse, that he was trying to teach her a lesson on phone etiquette, which she didn't mind so much, but David really wasn't the "teach you a lesson" sort of man. So that left her back at "the end" conclusion. Sadly, she was starting to look at the world with harsher eyes which, in a time like this, really stank.

She opened the door to the smells of Val cooking supper, and Ashley smiled at the sign of normalcy. Day one after the great meltdown, and all is well. Yay. She hung her bag on the hall tree just as Brianna barreled forth from her room, and began insistently tugging at her hand.

"You hit the jackpot, Aunt Ash. Come look!"

Sure enough, in the middle of the living room, were three big boxes, and one tiny one. Val looked at her expectantly. "What's going on?"

"I don't know," answered Ashley, completely truthful, but she liked surprises, the good ones, not the bad ones—she wasn't stupid. This looked to be a good surprise, and she hoped against hope that the surprise provider was the one man who hadn't called. If he hadn't called and sent her stuff instead, well, she would be big and forgive him.

"Can I open one?" asked Brianna.

"Sure," Ashley replied, hoping it wasn't anything unsuitable for an eight-year-old, or more likely, something unsuitable that Brianna hadn't seen yet.

Brianna tore into a box and pulled out a small LCD television, then a DVD player, a can of buttered popcorn, and one gift-wrapped box, labeled, Do Not Open Until 11 p.m.

Brianna was entranced. "Who're they from, Ashley?"

Ashley made a goofy face as if this was no big deal, but Ashley was entranced as well. "A friend."

Brianna wasn't swayed, neither was Val. "A TV is always a big deal."

"It's a little TV. Almost tiny."

"Can I have it?" Brianna chirped, in her extra-angelic voice.

"No," Ashley said, clutching the package close, choosing now to impart discipline, mainly because David made her headily selfish.

Brianna scowled, not used to Aunt Ash saying no. "Please?" she asked, blinking her big puppy-dog eyes ever so sweetly.

Ashley stood firm. "Sorry, kid. This is all mine. Someday you'll be grown up, and you can selfishly deny the small children in your life. It's the circle of life. Get used to it now."

Brianna made a face, but she knew she was beat. "Fine." She stomped to her room with extra force. That little bit she had inherited from Val.

Before the really difficult questions began, Ashley gathered her boxes. "I'm going to go try this out," she said, scooting the tower of cardboard down the hallway.

Whistling to herself, she cleared a spot on her dresser for the TV and DVD and stared way too long at the single gift-wrapped package. There was a hesitant knock at the door, and Ashley stowed away the gift, surprised that it was Val, and not Brianna. Hesitant knocks weren't usually her style.

"So, quite a haul there…" Val started, waiting expectantly for Ash to chime in with the answer.

"It's not a big deal. A bet I won a few weeks ago. I had forgotten," Ashley lied like there was no tomorrow. Once the truth about David was out there, there wasn't much she could hide from Val, and for a few more days, a few more weeks, maybe a few more months, she wanted to keep her and David's relationship simple and reduce the chance for failure. Having Val know that David lived in New York increased the failure-quotient possibility by a factor of a gazillion.

"You were never a good liar, Ash."

"I'm not lying."

"Lying, much?"

Ashley stared at the three boxes, and knew that it was the moment that she had dreaded, but it was the moment she couldn't put off any longer. Val should know, and hopefully, if there was a merciful God, it wouldn't be a problem. "It's from a man. I've been seeing him for a while."

Val rolled her eyes. "That's it? Why didn't you say something? I think that's awesome. You need to get out more. Get laid. Relax. I'm very happy for you."

And wow, that was so much easier than she had expected. "Thanks."

"Tell me about him," Val said, pulling up a chair. "What's his name, what does he look like, and most importantly, does he fully understand the nuances of a man's pinnacle role in a woman's sexual fulfillment?"

"David. He's tall, brown hair with a cowlick in the back. Good eyes, smart eyes. Nicely built, and yes."

Val laughed, and it was so nice to hear her laugh. "Sox or Cubs? Which is it? If he goes for the Sox, I'll have to change my mind."

"I know he's not a Sox fan. Not sure about the Cubs, though."

Her sister shrugged it off with a wave of the hand. "Well, I like his taste in presents. Now Brianna can watch cartoons and I can come back here and watch my movies with you."

Oh, peachy. Ashley smiled. "Sounds great."

Val stood up, she knew about David, and all was still right with the world. One day at a time, and today had been a great one. "You don't have to hide these things, or skulk around. Honestly, I'm good, and I'm glad that you're good, too. It's nice we can all be at a good place, together."

"It is nice," she agreed.

"Thanks for the help yesterday, sis. I'm so clueless about these things."

"You're not that clueless, Val. Sometimes you know exactly what you're doing." Her gaze lifted, met her sister's evenly. "You have to start taking charge. I won't always be there to bail you out."

Immediately Val panicked. "What are you saying, Ash? Are you deserting me now? Thirteen months sober and time's up, I'm on my own—"

Ashley held up a hand. "That's not what I'm saying."

"You're giving me a heart attack," Val muttered. "On some days, I think I've got everything under control, and then, it's like the devil whispering to me. You're my role model, you know? I look at you, and think, if I screw up, Ash's going to be mad, and it helps me walk the line. You're my rock."

Ashley withheld her sigh, resigning herself to the role of the rock. "You're doing great." Then, because even rocks needed their alone time, she rubbed her eyes. "How much longer before dinner? Maybe I'll take a nap. I'm beat."

Val was not fooled. "Phone sex with the new dude, right? You don't need to protect me. When do I get to meet him?"

"Soon. I think he'll be here for the show." She hoped.

"Okay, as long as he treats you right."

"So far, so good. Call me when dinner's ready."

"Thanks, Ash. Every night I tell God I don't deserve you, but I'm so very glad you're here."

AT ELEVEN O'CLOCK, her cell rang, just like she knew it would. It was David, mysterious giver of presents.

"Hello," he said, his voice filled with anticipation. He was waiting for her to acknowledge his generosity.

"Hi. How was your day?" It was torment mainly because she liked to know she was keeping him on the edge. David McLean, on the edge, was pretty much the most fun she'd had all day, and today had been a great day.

"I had a good day. Yours?" Now, anticipation was morphing into something more challenging. Avid curiosity. Ashley nearly laughed.

"Good," she told him calmly. "So, anything new?"

"No. You?"

Oh, he was near to breaking. She could hear it. Just one more minute. "How was work? What city are you in?"

"A large metropolis known as Manhattan."

Finally, she stopped, because it seemed cruel to go on. "I got the boxes."

"What happened to soft-hearted Ashley? I miss her, she would never tease me like this. So, did you open them?"

"Only the ones I was supposed to," she answered primly.

"Obedient little minx, aren't you?"

"Not that obedient. Don't get crazy."

"So you opened the little one?"

"No," she admitted, since deep in her heart she was an obedient little minx.

"Ha. You can open it now."

"What's the magic word?"

"Please."

She smiled and tore off the paper, finding her very own copy of a *Halloween* DVD, the original. "That's so sweet. It's not every man that gives a woman a movie about a knife-wielding serial killer."

"That's your bloodthirsty taste, not mine."

"Still, I think it's nice. Thank you."

"Well, go ahead, put it in the player."

"I'm not going to watch it now. I'm going to talk to you."

"No, you can watch it. I owe it to you."

"That's no fun, David."

"No, I bought a copy for me, too. We can do movie by phone. I've never seen this."

"You've never seen *Halloween?* That's un-American."

"I actually purposefully avoided it up until now because I consider myself a sensitive man."

Ashley smothered her giggle. "You're really going to watch it?"

"I am. For you, my darling, anything."

She put the DVD in the player, and pushed the play button. "I want you to know that I told Val about you today. She took it well."

"I told you. You should listen to me more. I'm always right."

Ashley popped the lid on the popcorn as the eerie theme song filtered through the room. "I know. Okay, we're on…." The credits flashed by, and the opening scenes began to show a young couple making love, caught in the throes of forbidden teenage passion. Ashley had forgotten about the opening of the movie, and she coughed twice.

David, of course, was not as discreet. "Oh, now wait a

minute. This is so unfair. I have to sit here and watch someone else get laid? Oh, not the shirt, not the shirt, she's taking off the shirt, Ashley. This is completely unfair. I'm alone here, and while I love my hand, it's to be used only in case of emergencies. This should not be an emergency. I'm doing this for you."

Slowly she lifted a piece of popcorn to her mouth. "Shh... They're about to get whacked."

"Really? Good. There is some justice after all."

One more reason to love David McLean. "You talk during movies, don't you?"

"No, I don't. Not usually. I'll shut up now."

THERE WERE THREE LONG, torturous weeks before she could fly out to New York, in which time she had:

1) Outlined and communicated the show's challenges to Horatio, Mariah and Enrique, who were "stressed," "wowed" and "underwhelmed," in that order.
2) Lined up ongoing coverage from *Chicago Today* and *Chicago This Morning, Chicago Tomorrow* and *Chicago At Night*.
3) Increased sales at the State Street store by an eye-boggling thirty-three percent.
4) Got Val on a budget.
5) Helped Brianna with her school project on global warming and catastrophic climate change—i.e., a tornado in a plastic soda bottle.
6) Watched *Friday the 13th,* parts 1, 2, 3 and 4 remotely with David.
7) Had unsatisfactory phone sex on what was becoming a nightly basis.

David was right. A hand could only go so far. Ashley had upgraded to a vibrator, a turbo-charged device with seven attachments, which did nothing to alleviate said frustration. So by the time she got on the plane to New York her entire female parts were in such twisted misery that she didn't need the bunny slippers. Amazingly, severe sexual frustration and lurid fantasies could kill most phobias, or at least push them aside in favor of bigger, rawer, more stimulating thoughts.

The flight was total misery when she imagined him naked, pounding into her, over and over. If she kept her thighs clenched tight enough, it was almost—*almost*—enough. By the time he picked her up outside the arrivals gate, she was a package of C4 just waiting for the right fuse.

Her hands jerked him close, planted a long one on him, and soon, he *was* getting the vivid picture that her tongue was painting in long, meaningful strokes. She could tell because he was expanding nicely between her thighs. Men could be so shamelessly easy, a completely hypocritical thought, but she was too sexually frustrated to care about being honorable. There was a time for honor, and a time to get laid.

"I need sex, David. I've sat scrunched in that tiny seat, and all I wanted was to have you naked, buried between my legs, hammering inside me, over and over and over and over…."

The very smart man stared, and then took a big, cleansing breath. "I have an idea," he said, grabbed her hand and pulled her down three flights of stairs. Eventually, they were in the long hallway of an international terminal filled with passengers.

"Where are we going?" she needed to ask, not seeing how this was going to help her painful situation. "Isn't there a bathroom or something?"

"Security," he answered. "Trust me."

After passing El Al, Aeroflot, Aer Lingus and some other airline she didn't recognize, they were at the end of the hall, a lone gate proclaiming Pan Pacific. The kiosk was deserted, a high wall keeping the gate partly out of view.

His mouth took hers, and he lifted her on the ticket counter, but Ashley wasn't convinced.

"Are we alone?"

"As good as it's going to get. Pan Pac, they tanked." His hands climbed under her shirt, shoving her bra aside. "Overpriced. Price of fuel killed them," he said, and then his mouth settled on her breast.

"What about cameras? Aren't there cameras here?"

He lifted his head. "I don't know. I don't care. Do you care? Please don't care."

She smiled wickedly and he lowered his head. From that moment on, Ashley closed her eyes, her blood pumping to the even pulls of his mouth, his tongue. Her hips started to clock in rhythm, and he spread her thighs, pressing two fingers inside her.

Oh, yeah.

She grabbed his jaw, pulled his mouth against hers and locked her legs against his waist, pressing, rubbing, doing whatever it took to make her body feel better. He groaned, angling her legs down until she was poised right…right…there.

Magically, efficiently, gloriously he had brought a condom, and with one hard thrust the world turned bright rainbow colors.

"I missed you," she mumbled at one particularly poignant thrust, and David grunted in acknowledgment. Sometimes words weren't necessary. His hands slid beneath her ass, pulling her off the counter, their bodies coming undone, and she moaned until he turned her around, pressed her stomach against the counter, and oh, oh, oh, this was so much better. So perfect. He was hard and thick and she could feel his body hot against hers, his skin slick with sweat. In the distance, the announcer was cancelling someone's flight, but here, Ashley was starting to fly.

His hands slid up, cupping her breasts, squeezing her nipples tight, not gentle. The blunt shove of his hips was not gentle, but the hard bursts of pleasure were killing her in the best way possible.

"There. Faster. Need to do. Faster." Her voice was almost to breaking; Ashley was almost to breaking.

"Faster works," he murmured against her neck, and that was the last rational thought she had. Her hands dug into the smooth plastic of the counter, finding nothing to grip but a hard ledge, and she held on, absorbing the rippling power that was breaking her in two.

Her eyes drifted closed and she could feel his hands, his cock, holding her, filling her, and just as her orgasm was about to…there, she shoved her hips back, forcing him deeper into her womb.

For a minute her body absorbed the shock waves. He covered her with himself, his mouth pressed tiredly beneath her ear. His chest heaved in great waves, and she smiled, exhausted. Marvelously sated, but exhausted.

"We've got to stop meeting like this," he whispered, his breath slowly adjusting to normal. When the last of her climax faded, and her legs could actually support her weight, she turned.

Discreetly, she adjusted her skirt, and tucked her hair behind her ear. David was fixing his clothes, but the shirt, it still wasn't right.

Ashley reached out, tucked in the side, then admired her work. "It was too obvious," she said.

"Men know anyway."

"Really?"

"Trust me. Guys know. Where to?"

"Your apartment," she stated firmly.

"This is new. Sex at the gate, sleeping at my place…" He took her face in his hands. "From bunny slippers to a dominatrix whip. Could be fun."

Ashley wagged a schoolmarm finger at him. "Don't get crazy."

"This isn't my crazy face. This is my optimistic face. So why the change, assuming you don't have peekaboo leather hidden in your carry-on."

"State Street is up thirty-three percent over last month. I'm basking in the glow of my own success. I felt you deserved to bask in my success as well."

"I'm completely unsurprised."

She liked his unsurprisedness, the way he was looking at her with what a less confident woman might consider pride. "Yes, I'm completely unsurprised, too. Let's go home. You can pleasure me more."

LATER IN THE AFTERNOON, they took a cab over to Brooklyn and David watched Ashley work Enrique over with disturbing enthusiasm. There was something new about Ashley today. Something that kept drawing his eye. She was more sure of herself, she didn't have the shell-shocked post-divorced look anymore—one that he suspected he still carried around inside. Even Enrique was sucking up to her, and when she told the designer about the deadlines and shipping arrangements for the show, Enrique began talking about his newest idea, a liquid jersey dress with a keyhole twisted-bodice, whatever the hell that was.

When Ashley nodded and smiled, Enrique sighed.

Yeah, David knew how he felt.

After they left the store, Ashley's fingers curled over his.

"He's eating out of your palm. If your top had been cut half an inch lower, you could have turned him sexually."

"Are you jealous of a gay man? That's so sweet."

David gritted his teeth. "It's not jealousy. I understand how the male brain thinks, what its priorities are."

"Even the homosexual male brain?"

"They have a dick, they have sperm. Some truths are universal. And don't call me sweet."

She didn't call him sweet, but her smile said it. Honestly, he didn't mind. "We going to walk across the bridge, or take a cab home?" Home. He liked the way the word rolled off his tongue.

"No walking. We're cabbing it, today."

"Feeling wimpy?"

"Nope. Just happy."

IT WAS SOMEWHERE long after midnight, and they were still awake. The Ring DVD was playing, but David didn't really care who got killed or how much blood was spilled. There was no sight that could be better than the one before his eyes. Ashley Larsen in his bed. He liked the feel of her there, the new scents that came with her. She was leaving on Sunday, but the pictures in his mind, the memories in his brain, would stay.

Her legs curled into his, silk into rough, her hands stroked his chest, soft and small, her hair fell over his shoulder, and this time, she didn't brush it away. He loved the feel of her hair, her hands on his shoulders, her bare skin against his.

He wasn't a man who stayed for days in bed, but here, with her…he could stay in bed for a lifetime.

When she was here, when they were together, sleeping, talking, making love, everything was at peace. Everything slowed down, and the world felt like such a safe, marvelous place. He liked the peace, he liked the way the anger disappeared, the way happiness stirred.

Ashley was not a woman you doubted. When she loved, he knew it, the world knew it. It was there in her face, her movements, the way she touched him, the way she loved him. It wasn't that David had gone seeking that sort of love, it wasn't that he even thought he required it, but there was something so easy about it.

So simple, so peaceful.

Come to New York. Stay here.

She turned her head and he stroked her lips with a gentle finger. "Come to New York. Stay in New York, Ashley."

Her smile was everything he needed. The light in her dark eyes gave him hope. "It sounds like a lot of fun. And think of all that flying I wouldn't have to do."

Already his mind was jumping to the next part of the plan. "We'd set you up with a boutique in…I don't know, Brooklyn or the Lower East Side, maybe. Soho or the Village, the rent would be nuts, so I wouldn't do four. Start small, work your way out."

"You've thought about this?" she asked.

"Yeah." And he had. It had been bubbling in the back of his mind. He had their life completely mapped out. This could work.

"What about Ashley's Closet?"

"Sell 'em."

She rolled her eyes. "After all this work? Are you crazy?"

"I guess so." He wasn't crazy. He was happy. He was in love.

"You're not crazy. If things were better, I would do it," she said, curling toward him. He could feel the warm weight of her breasts, the gentle slide of her thigh against his own, almost distracting him from his perfect idea, but not quite.

"You would?"

"I would," she told him.

That was all he needed to hear. "So do it. Now that you say it, it doesn't sound so crazy."

"I can't leave Chicago. You come there."

Chicago? "I did sort of consider it, but I live in New York, the financial and fashion capital of the world, home to the New York Yankees, which you could eventually grow to love. It's like God planting a sign. David and Ashley belong here. I don't believe in signs, but Ashley, sometimes it's stupid not to see the obvious."

"Don't do this to me, David." Her smile dimmed and she shifted, not much, but enough that their bodies were no longer touching.

This time he didn't try and pull her back. There were fights he could win, and some that he couldn't. "How long do we stay like this? Forever?"

"No."

"Then what do we do? What are we supposed to do?"

"Come to Chicago."

He gave her a hard look. "Do you think that's a good idea?"

"No. I'll figure out something," she said, and it disappointed him that she couldn't see the truth in the matter. She wanted the world to be one way, and it wasn't. The world didn't bend to you; you had to bend the world.

"No, you won't," he told her, wishing that just once he could be smart enough to keep his mouth shut.

"What's that supposed to mean? I'm not smart enough?"

Frustrated, he rubbed his eyes, not liking the hurt in her own. "You can't leave your sister. She's thirty years old. You can't mother her your entire life."

"I don't want to," she whispered, and her voice was so sad, so sorrowful that this time he did pull her close.

"I know. I'm sorry. I just want you here with me. All of the time. Or even most of the time. I'm tired of sleeping alone. I'm tired of eating alone. I now hate my cell phone because the reception is never good enough to touch, and thankfully jacking off doesn't cause blindness because I'd be pulling disability if it did. I love you, Ash. I thought I could do this. I didn't think I'd fall in love."

Her mouth pressed against his. "I know."

"Come live with me and be my love," he whispered. It was his last, best shot.

"Let me think about it," she said, and then he covered her, sliding into sex, and he loved her as if this was forever. But it wasn't. It was only one night.

In the morning, the sun rose, the alarm clocked blared and Ashley took off on a plane for Chicago. After she was gone, David looked up at the bright golden sky, and wondered how one night could seem so damn short.

15

Labor Day weekend was the ultimate shopping holiday in the fashion business. Friday, the fun and breezy spring fashions reigned supreme. Come Monday, the darker, more somber styles of the fall season had taken over. Ashley hated Labor Day, hated all the rigid rules that dominated a business that proclaimed in a very cosmopolitan accent that it was free of rules and lovingly dwelled in organic chaos.

Never trust a fashionista.

However, it was the number one weekend for people to peruse the racks, the number one weekend for people to consider what the new world of style should look like, and ergo, it was the perfect weekend for the Next Big Look for Chicago.

The night before, she hadn't slept, spending the hours alternately stressing between whether anyone would show up—or even care—and then praying that David's plane wouldn't be late, since today of all days, she didn't want him to be late.

There had been a live segment on *Chicago This Morning—Friday Edition,* in which Ashley was interviewed before the entire hypercritical Chicago metropolis, or at least that's what it felt like. It had gone well, except for the one moment when she fumbled with an extra "err," the ultimate media don't, but she had recovered nicely.

Val had been a trooper, possibly—probably—feeling guilty, but whatever the motivation, Ashley welcomed the help. Even their Mom and Brianna had been there, shoving banquet tables right and then left, then back to right. Three generations of Larsen women doing what they did best—undeciding.

The designers were there at the State Street location of Ashley's Closet. Enrique in a Haight-Ashbury, clubbish look of black leather paired with a silver paisley vest. Mariah had chosen a beautiful rose-organza skirt and Christian Louboutin heels that made her tower over most everyone, and Horatio had chosen a staid black tux, with dark tortoiseshell nerd glasses, complete with a cigar that he used like a conductor's wand, pointing and directing and condemning at will.

Now *this* was organized chaos.

Ashley, on the other hand, was a disorganized mess.

At 10:00 a.m., Christine McLean McLean, aka the bitch, showed up. Sadly, she wasn't there to gloat, she was only being sweet and supportive, which only made Ashley—who was a wreck—hate her more.

Ashley dodged the caterers who were setting up the warming trays, and casually, carefully introduced Christine to Val, which was like introducing Bonnie to Clyde, Thelma to Louise, and Leopold to Loeb.

Brianna, the little traitor, was entranced by Christine's matching hair barrettes and shoes. "That is awesome. Are they fuchsia?"

Christine preened. "Why, yes, what a clever child," she said with a mother-to-be stroke of her still skinny—hate you, hate you—womb.

"You're expecting?" asked Val, and suddenly there were the likes of Thelma and Louise discussing the ins and outs of morning sickness, at which point, Ashley left for the storeroom where she threw back a couple of antacid tablets to calm her stomach.

She was there for half an hour when Val arrived and sat down on a stack of boxes. "So, that's David's ex, eh?"

Ashley held up the tag gun and smiled. "Yes."

"You should have told me, Ash."

There were so many sins of omission that Ashley had failed to mention that she wasn't sure exactly what Val was referring to. "Yes, I'm sure I should have," she said, pricing with nervy restraint.

"He's not Chicago stock. What are you doing?"

Ah, yes. The big sin of omission. Ashley put down her tag gun and pulled out a box of sweaters. Quickly she folded them, face down, arms across, one side to the middle, other side to the middle, and voila, everything meets happily in the middle. "I'm not doing anything, Val. Everything is fine. Don't worry."

"She's his ex?"

"Yeah."

"Divorced men. There's gotta be something wrong."

"I'm divorced, Val."

"I rest my case." And then she grinned, no harm, no foul. "You know I'm kidding. But seriously, I mean, how well do you know this guy. Just met him, and he's sending you TVs and stuff."

Ashley took a deep, calming breathing, feeling the bubble-gum taste of the medicine coat and soothe her stomach. She picked up her tagging gun once again. There was nothing left to price, but she needed the feel of it in her hands nonetheless. "I've been seeing him for a while," she told her sister with easy casualness that she couldn't believe she'd managed to pull off.

Val's eyes sharpened because Ashley's sister was no fool. Yes, they loved to live in denial, but deep inside, nothing got past them. "How long's that?"

"Since April. We don't get to see each other that often, but we meet up. Chicago, Miami, sometimes New York. It works."

"But you can't build a permanent relationship like that. You're thirty-two, Ash. Now, that's not old, but let's say you stick with him for another four years, because you know that women stay in these relationships that aren't good for them for a long, long time. Then, after four years, he runs off and marries his hot, twentysomething secretary. There you are, now thirty-six, and officially S.O.L. Statistically, do you know what your chances are? Go out and get hit by lightning, why don't you?"

Ashley put the gun down and chose her words carefully. "Val, don't." Short, but effective.

"Look. I love you. You're my big sis, and you're the smart one. Usually. But this time... Seriously, it's a recipe for disaster, and I say that as someone who has written many disasters all her own."

"Don't make a big deal out of this, Val. Not today. Not now."

Val sighed, and not in a good way. "Okay. Go ahead, wet your proverbial whistle, have a fun time. I'll be there when you need me, Ash. And you will need me."

Ashley managed a pained smile. "I know."

THE SHOW WAS scheduled to start at two, it was noon, the store was starting to fill, and there was still no sign of David. It was official. Ashley was panicked. Christine, bless her heart, was greeting everyone. Enrique and Horatio were stalking around each other's still boxed-up clothes with a disdainful sneer.

Ashley had hired four models for the day, and they swooshed in with both style, grace and those huge dark sunglasses that were perfect for covering up last night's excesses. Not that she was being catty—oh, God, she was being catty—but honestly, where was David?

In the back, Ashley had marked off a curtained area where each designer could work with their models in secrecy—Horatio had insisted, Ashley didn't care. As each went to their respective corner, Ashley went back into the tiny storeroom and tried to find the voting ballots where each customer could pick their favorite within the categories. She pulled out empty box after empty box, when she felt a familiar, bold, yet comforting hand on her rear.

She knew that hand, she knew that smell, she knew that man.

David.

Ashley turned and clung to him with all the neediness of a woman who had officially given up a lot of phobias in the last four months, but was still, in the deepest parts of her heart, terrified.

His arms came round her, his mouth found hers, and she forgot about the scary parts. After a good, blood-pumping interval, she pulled up to breathe.

Man, he looked good. Edible. He'd ditched his khakis and Brooks Brothers shirt for something a little...dare she say it? Dashing? The jacket was a slouchy, soft, tweedy brown-green that perfectly brought out the earthy tones in his eyes. Underneath he had picked a sexy ivory fitted poet shirt sans collar that was unbuttoned casually low, displaying an eye-catching hint of chest, a finger-tempting splash of chest hair. It was entirely too sexy, entirely too strategically packaged, and she knew without a doubt that someone else had picked it out for him. But the pièce d'résistance? The traditional David McLean jeans—well fitted, well-worn, well filled.

"Someone went shopping."

"You don't like it, do you? It's too artsy, isn't it? I told the guy, give me a suit, something nice, but he said that nobody went to a fashion show in a suit. I told him he was wrong."

"He wasn't wrong, David. You look awesome. Tasty, even, and I'm saying that not only as the woman who wants to bed you, but a fashion professional as well."

He grinned, glanced over her deceptively simple little black dress with its come-hither neckline and heels to match. "Listen to you, sexy shop owner. And did you see all the people out there?"

All those people. Hungry people. Thirsty people. "Have the caterers started to serve yet? It's a mess. The press is pouring through the door, and I have no champagne. Do you know what a show is without champagne? It's a dry heave, that's what it is. It's worse than a dry heave. Gawd, this is going to be a bust."

He rubbed her icy-cold hands with his. "Hello, Ashley. You're going to do fine."

"I'm glad you're here. I didn't think I'd be this nervous."

"You can show me exactly how glad, unless I'm interrupting your regularly scheduled crisis already in progress?"

Temptation was never easy to resist. Ashley didn't even try.

She tugged at his jacket and ran her fingers up over the tweed, loving the texture of fabric and well-muscled man. Then his mouth was on hers, the taste of mint and coffee and lust...much lust. Much unslaked lust. Her hands lowered to his waist, finding the back pockets of his jeans. Digging her fingers in his pockets, she felt the muscles clench under her hands.

"Oh, damn, Ash. Don't seduce me now."

"It's the nerves," she whispered against his mouth.

He pulled free. "Oh, honey, I love your nerves. I love your breasts...." She ground her hips against him, and he stopped fighting the inevitable. His hands searched under her skirt. "Wow, you are soaked. Two minutes. That's all we need."

He pushed a finger inside her and her heart nearly exploded.

"And you must be David. Nice to meet you."

At Val's voice, Ashley's heart did explode. She jumped back, David jumped back, and there stood Val, eyeing him curiously.

Okay, maybe this wasn't going to be so bad. "David, this is my sister. Val."

Politely he held out his hand, shook hers and look at that... It was like nothing. "Nice to meet you," he said.

"Sorry to interrupt, but the champagne is here. They need to know whether to open it now, or wait until the winners are announced."

Damn. Ashley stared at Val. "Are you okay?"

Val waved a hand. "I'm fine. You're the one who looks like she's falling apart."

Ashley smoothed her hair, and glanced at David.

"What do you want me to do?" he asked.

Val smiled at him. "We've got it under control. Kick back. Look pretty."

Ashley shot David another look because sometimes Val didn't say exactly the right thing, but then, sometimes David didn't say exactly the right thing, either. Maybe he didn't notice.

His smile turned a little tighter, and his jaw clenched.

It was going to be a long, long day.

"LADIES AND GENTLEMEN," Ashley paused for dramatic effect. "The winner of Chicago's Next Big Look is...Horatio Moore."

Horatio whooped and Enrique glowered, and Mariah's face fell a little, as the cameras flashed and captured the moment for all eternity. Poor girl, but Ashley wasn't worried for Mariah. She'd seen the offers to manufacture all three of the designers' entries, and today there were no losers.

Nope. Not a one. She examined the store, noted the packed crowd, noted the continuous tap of the cash register and grinned happily.

"Ladies, can you bring those gorgeous looks out one last time?" And the models appeared wearing the cocktail dresses. Personally, Ashley loved Mariah's the best, a neon-blue silk with a fitted waist and a pouf flounce at the knee. But as much as she loved the blue silk, she could see why Horatio won.

The black dress had beautiful beadwork not seen since the '20s. It didn't have the sleek lines of Mariah's, instead it was a graceful drape that forgave many flaws and made every woman look beautiful. In short, it was the perfect dress for the not-so-confident woman.

As for Enrique, he had designed a hideous concoction of red poppies gracing yellow fabric, and it looked more like a two-year-olds' crayon drawing than a dress you wanted to wear for a night on the town, but still there were people wanting to buy from the New York designer. Somehow, between the three, she had found the exact perfect mix.

She, Ashley Larsen.

After two hours of hand-shaking and smiling, and photo ops and answering questions, and another fifteen minutes of soothing Enrique and bolstering Mariah, the sun began to set, the store cleared out, the caterers cleaned up, and Ashley congratulated her four managers on a job well done.

It was over.

Now all she had to do was keep peace between her mother,

her niece, her sister, and the man she loved. Her fingernails dug into her palms. Ha. A piece of cake.

IT WASN'T SO AWFUL, David thought to himself. Ashley's sister seemed much nicer than he had imagined. She looked like a more sharply cast version of Ashley. The same dark hair, the same nose and the mouth, but the eyes were a study in contrasts. David had seen eyes like Val's—the hard-boiled cynics' on Wall Street for instance.

Their mother was another story. Completely different from what his own mother had been like when she was alive. And as he watched Ashley's mother peering out at the dark streets, her hands clamping nervously on Brianna's shoulders, he could see exactly where Ashley got it from.

As for Ashley, she looked exhausted. There were shadows under her eyes that weren't usually there, and strands were starting to escape from the bun. All he wanted to do was get her home, tuck her in bed, not even needing to jump her, which was testament to how tired she looked. He walked over to her, running a hand over her neck, feeling the tense muscles there. "How much do you have to do tonight?"

Her gaze moved across the store. "That's enough. I think I want to celebrate."

Val stood. "Great idea. You deserve it. I didn't think you could do it, Ash, but hell, you did. I'm proud of you, sis. We can hit Paradise Pup. Brianna loves the burgers, don't you, sweetie?"

Brianna, hearing her name, broke into the conversation. "I'm all for that plan."

It wasn't exactly what David had planned, but okay, he was the guest. Ashley needed to decide this one.

She stared at him, and he wished she wouldn't stare at him like that—as if she didn't want to go to dinner with her family because she knew that he knew she was going to cave, and then he'd be disappointed with her, and today of all days, he didn't want to be disappointed with her, and then...

"I don't think I want to go," she was saying. "You take Mom and Brianna if you want to eat there. I'm going to go with David."

Hell had just frozen over. He knew it. David was so shocked that he forgot to smile, and he wanted to smile. Val frowned ominously. "I thought you wanted to celebrate."

Immediately, Ashley realized her mistake. It was there in the wariness in her eyes. "Actually, you know, I don't want to celebrate. I want to go…somewhere quiet."

Val's heavy sigh could be heard in Wisconsin, and her gaze cut to David, death in her sights. "You know, Ash, you're always there to celebrate my special days—the anniversaries, the birthdays, and tonight, I wanted to return the favor because you've done a great thing, but okay, if you feel that way…go away, do your little thing."

Carefully, David studied the pink necklaces in the display case because as much as he wanted to open his mouth, he knew that'd be a mistake.

"Thanks for understanding, Val."

"No problem. Listen, I got this letter from the district attorney this afternoon, and it made me nervous. Can you take a look tonight when you get home?"

Ah, so the battle wasn't over yet. Val was much more effective than he gave her credit for.

"I won't be home tonight, Val."

Holy shit. David's hands nearly drove through the glass. Not only was Ashley holding her own in the ring, she was going for the knockout. Ashley was turning into a fighter. He'd never been more proud.

"Where'll you be, Aunt Ash?"

Ah, the voice of innocence.

"You're too young to know about this," answered Val. "Mom, can you take Brianna out to the car. There's one other thing that I need to talk to Ash about, and then we'll take off. And yes, Brianna, we'll get the burgers."

After they left, David gave Ashley a weak, yet hopefully encouraging smile. She was doing great, just one more round, and then victory was hers. Immediately Ashley took the offensive. "Leave it alone, Val."

"You don't even know what I'm going to say."

"I know exactly what you're going to say. You're going to tell me how I'm making a mistake, and this is a time for family, and how the only people you can depend on are your family, and then you're going to remind me how Jacob was such a mistake, and you think David is a mistake, too, because he lives in New York, and you can't see me in New York, and why even waste my time and his, and now that you've met his ex-wife and seen what a total bitch she is, you can't think he's that smart, and he's probably just using me, or even worse, he's got some squeeze back in New York, and how would I know since I live in another town, because honestly, how can I trust any man. Did I get it all?"

"Very good. Although you missed the important part. Do you love him, Ash?"

"Yes."

"Are you moving? Are you leaving this town and haven't said a word?"

The room got dangerously quiet. David perked up his head, watching Ashley with interest.

"Maybe."

Val looked at David, then looked at Ashley. "I'm wasting my time here, aren't I? Do what you need to do, Ash. Have a nice life." Then she stalked out the room, the bell at the door jingling behind her.

Ashley turned to David, and her face crumpled a bit. "I think that went well."

David gathered her close, but Ashley not only looked exhausted, now she looked beaten. "One day at a time, Ashley. She'll come around."

He hoped.

IT TOOK EXACTLY seven hours for the full effects of the crisis to be known. David and Ashley were both fast asleep in the hotel room when Ashley's cell rang.

Ashley opened one eye, stared at the clock. 4:37 a.m. She didn't want to answer the phone. For the first time in her life she actually considered letting the goddamned phone ring, but she didn't.

"Ash, I need you to come get me." It was Val, stumbling through her words without a care in the world.

"Where are you at, Val?" The words came out of her mouth by rote. She knew the routine. She knew her part.

"How the hell should I know?"

"O'Malleys on Addison?"

"No."

Ashley rubbed her eyes, praying this was a bad dream, but she knew it wasn't a bad dream. Or if it was, she was stuck in it—the same bad dream, over and over and over and over. "Ask the bartender for an address."

Val started to laugh. Vodka did that to people. Made everything funny.

"He's not the bartender, he's the police."

16

DAVID KNEW the answer to his question before he asked it. "I have to go," she told him, already sliding out of bed, turning on the light, pushing her hair from her face. All the excitement of yesterday was gone.

"You don't have to leave."

Mechanically she pulled on clothes—a yellow skirt, a red-flowered shirt and a beaded blue necklace because apparently bright happy apparel was the best way to pretend you weren't dying inside. The dark hollows in her eyes gave proof of the lies.

Those hollow eyes shot him a desperate glance. "Don't do this now," she pleaded.

"I'm sorry, but look at you, Ashley. What are you going to do? What are you supposed to do to help?"

"My sister is drunk at the Cook County jail. I'm going to go, post bail, take her home, throw her in the shower, try and keep the shit from Brianna and Mom, and carry on. That's what I'm going to do."

David rubbed his eyes, feeling the helpless anger burn inside him. He'd never liked helpless. "Do you want me to go?"

This time, she pulled her hair back into a ponytail and didn't even bother to answer, instead she focused on packing to leave.

David grabbed his jeans and shoved his legs into them. While she stuffed her toiletries in the case, he pulled her clothes out of the closet, realized what he was doing, and shoved them back on the hangers that jingled like bells. *No.*

He had tried to stay silent, tried to let her do this, but he couldn't. He could not sit this one out. "When will you stop? When is she going to call, and you say, 'not today?'"

"Not today." Her smile was sad, and David swore, and then her smile got a little more sad. "Do you know what I love about you, David? We have known each other for a few months, but you encourage me to do things, encourage me to take risks, and I do it. Do you know why?"

"Why?"

"I feel safe with you. I know that if I'm with you, no matter what I do, you'll always be there to catch me if I fall. Is that true?"

David didn't like having his motives twisted, his emotions twisted, his heart twisted, and he wanted to lie to her, but in the end, he couldn't. "Yes."

"And I love my sister," she told him, shutting her suitcase, zipping it firmly closed, "and I want her to feel safe with me, David. I want her to know that as long as I'm alive, I will always be there to catch her if she falls. Is that wrong of me? Is it wrong of you?"

"It's not the same thing. What you're doing...with your business and all, that's the good stuff. That's positive. With Val, it's not healthy, Ashley. Sometimes you have to let people make their own mistakes and learn from them."

"You think that if I bail out Val, I'm making a mistake?"

"Yes."

"What are you going to do, David?" she asked him, as if she was absolutely sure she was right. As if there was only one way to deal with the people you love.

There it was. Put up or shut up time.

Furiously David began grabbing his clothes from the closet, not caring how he did it because he wanted the world the way he wanted it. He wanted Ashley to be harder. But it seemed it didn't matter what he wanted. In the end, it was Ashley who got the 4:00 a.m. wake-up calls, Ashley who patiently paid the fees for NSF checks, Ashley who did it all. There was a pattern here, and she didn't mind the pattern. David did. She had worked so hard, and it was all for nothing because she would never get anything *she* wanted, and he'd have to stand there with his thumb up his ass, seeing her sad smile, and seeing the glow fade from her eyes.

No.

"I can't watch this, Ashley. I can't watch you handing her your heart and watching it burn. You sound like you're going out to pick up her laundry, but it's four-thirty in the morning after one of the best days of your life, and you're going to a police station. Doesn't this hurt you? What about you, Ashley?"

"I can handle it. I can help her."

"This is not help."

She pulled her shoes from the closet, then sat down in the chair, seeming oddly composed. She was going to go. Oh, man, she would need a cab. David picked up the phone and dialed the front desk, ready to get her a cab.

There was a knowing smile on her face as she watched.

Before the operator answered, David hung up.

Ashley slid her feet into her yellow heels. It wasn't even 5:00 a.m., and she was wearing yellow heels. The world was not a nice place. "Do you know what pushed her off the ledge, David?" she asked, and deep in his soul he had known that they were going to reach this point eventually.

His hands flexed, then fisted until the knuckles glowed white. "Oh, no. She might want you to believe that our relationship killed her sobriety, but the only person who pushed her off the ledge was Val."

"Action, reaction. Thirteen months she's been sober, David." She stood, smoothed her skirt. Then she met his eyes. "Are you going to be here when I get back?"

She wanted to know what he was going to do. This moment was more than calling her a cab, more than packing her clothes. *Of course I'll be here,* he thought to himself. *I could never leave you.*

His breathing stopped, his lungs not sure what they were supposed to do. He hated this. He hated his goddamned principles. He hated that he couldn't be like her. His eyes drifted shut because he didn't like that sad, knowing smile. When had Ashley gotten so very smart?

Carefully he exhaled, opened his eyes.

"I don't think I should stay. I think I would get very mad, and I would yell at you, and you don't need me to yell at you. You need me to be supportive and say you're doing the right thing, and that's not even close to who I am."

She nodded once, a tiny jerk of the head, and that was the end.

A MAN DIDN'T NEED to be in an empty hotel room. He found the shirt she had left behind and he neatly packed it into his carry-on because he couldn't stay here, and he couldn't simply leave her stuff out there for the maid.

It was five in the morning, the planes were just starting to take off, and David sat on the bed. He had never imagined this moment. He'd never even contemplated it. From the first second on that airplane ride to nowhere, he'd known he'd never met someone that he felt so comfortable with—someone that made him lust, someone that made him laugh.

No point in laughing now.

His case sat on the bed, staring at him, telling him to go home, but David wasn't ready to go home. There wasn't anyone there, and he didn't want to be alone. He picked up his cell and made a call.

CHRIS DIDN'T ACT surprised or weird. He acted as if this were no big deal, and for that, David loved his brother even more.

They ended up sitting on the back deck, drinking a beer and watching the sun come up. As he looked out over the fenced yard, the old picnic table, the flowers beneath the kitchen window, it occurred to David that his brother had created the house their father had always wanted.

"What did you expect her to do, David? You know it's so easy for you to cut people off and never speak to them again, but most of us aren't like that." Chris rested in the lounge chair because this was his home turf. This was his domain, his castle. Here, David was the outsider.

"You picked love over family, why couldn't she do it?"

That was the hard part. David expected the ultimate sacrifice. There was pride involved here. Ashley had a choice. Once again, David had lost.

"I didn't pick love over family."

David drained the last of his beer. Reached for another. "You want to make it sound prettier, Chris? You fucked my wife."

"I loved your wife," Chris answered, sounding hurt that David was mad.

"Geez."

"Don't do that. I loved her more than you ever did. Christine was an ornament to you. You never talked with her, you never even knew what she wanted."

David thought over some of the conversations he'd had with Christine. "She wanted matching clothes and a maid."

Chris shook his head. "She wanted a home. She wanted a kid. She wanted a husband who came home at five and listened to her whine about the day."

It all sounded neat and domestic, and not a thing like the marriage that David and Christine had had. "And that's you?"

"It is. It was never you." His brother looked at him as if David were the alien. As if he were the one who was being a fool, as if the world had swapped sides, and somehow he was stuck alone.

"What am I supposed to do, Chris? Do I have to start going to see a therapist to figure out how I'm supposed to be a man? Do I stock up on self-help books?"

"I don't think so, David. I don't think Ashley thinks so, either."

"She's wrong about this, Chris. I know I think I'm right all the time, and a lot of the time—but not all the time—I'm right. But this time, I'm right."

Thankfully, his brother nodded. "I think so, too."

"Do you really? You're not just saying that because my life sucks at the moment?"

"No, I think you're right. Maybe she'll realize it, too."

David remembered Ashley's smile. She knew David was right. She knew she was doing the wrong thing, but she couldn't help herself. "I don't think so." He stood, tossed the beer can in the garbage that was right behind the grill. Their father had a grill exactly like that. "Why don't you take all the money on the old apartment, Chris. I don't need it."

Chris's jaw shifted into a hard line. "No. We go half. You keep thinking there's something wrong with my financial choices, David, but there's not. I don't need what you need."

At that, David sighed. He'd tried, he failed. "Fifty-fifty it is. I should go."

"You could stay. Christine could make pancakes."

"That's too much. Maybe you could come out to New York some time and we could be brothers for the weekend. I think I'd like that. That, I think I can do."

Chris nodded. "I could do that, too."

17

"HELLO, MY NAME is Valerie, and I'm an alcoholic."

The room was half full. It was an old Lithuanian church with long wooden pews, and the October sunlight pooling in through stained glass. The scent of pine cleaner filled the air, nearly obscuring the scent of humility. This was where people came to wipe out the darkest stains inside themselves.

At this meeting, there were no businessmen in well-cut suits, or women with two-thousand-dollar bags. That was Lincoln Park or Lakeview, not here.

Here was what families left behind, what the nightly news left behind, what the world left behind. Ashley had never liked sitting in these meetings. When Val was outside this place, she was hard and tough and ready to face the world on her own terms. Inside her group's circle, Val's eyes lost the hard edge. Here they were filled with fear. Seeing that fear always reminded Ashley of her own weaknesses.

After everyone had gotten up to speak, after the last of the stale coffee was gone, Ashley waited for the room to empty, because this was the perfect place to talk.

"I'm proud of you, Val." And she was. She knew her sister battled dragons that she would never understand, and she also knew this wasn't easy.

"Thanks. Thirty days isn't long." Nervously Val's hands slid up and down her jeans, her nails short, bitten to the quick.

Ashley smoothly folded her arms, covering her own polished

nails in the process. "Thirty days is a step. A good step. And every day, you take another step."

"I'm glad you're here," her sister said, and the hand-sliding stilled.

"I am, too, but this is it, Val. I won't do this again."

"Do what again? Come to a meeting with me?"

Ashley smiled gently. "The next time I'm not going to answer the phone. The next time you bounce a check, you're in charge."

"I'm not going to do that again."

"Then that makes it much more easier for you."

"What's got into you?"

"I'm kicking ass and taking names. The biz is doing great, but I'm going to sell it. I hope I'm going to New York." Ashley put the statement out there. She wasn't going to dodge anything anymore.

"You're deserting me?" The fear was back in her sister's eyes, and Ashley felt the familiar urge to reassure her, to tell her that she wasn't deserting her, that she would always be there, but David had been right.

"No. This is what you need."

Val grabbed her hand, her fingers digging into Ashley's skin, but Val didn't know what she was doing. That was always the problem. "I can't work this without you."

"That may be, but you're not working it with me very well, so I'm not sure it makes a difference."

Val stood and started to pace. There were certain similarities with David. She'd never tell him, but it was probably a lot of the reason it was so easy to fall in love. These two people whom she loved most of all. These two people who needed her most of all.

"These aren't your words. You've been talking to him, haven't you?"

"No, I haven't talked to David since he left, but he's right. I've been there every time you've had a crisis. Always ready to prop you back up, and when that happens, you don't think you can prop yourself back up, and you have to know that. You have to know that you can do this. I'm your bunny slippers, Val. Sometimes you have to fly without them."

"You can't do this to me." Her sister's voice was louder now. Her hands were on her hips.

Ashley looked away. "I have to."

"What about Brianna?"

This time, Ashley turned back because this was Val the manipulator speaking. This time, Ashley would fight back. Her voice was low and calm, but for nearly two weeks she'd practiced these words in her head. "Ah, yes, your daughter. Think about her, Val. Think about your daughter. Next time, Aunt Ash won't be there. Grandma will, but I wouldn't count on Grandma. You need to count on Val." It was hard talk for Ashley. The tone and words felt foreign to her, but it was time.

"I can't do this."

"Yes, you can. You've told yourself that you can't for so long that you believe it. Go to your meetings. Go to your job. Take care of your daughter. You'll learn something. You'll learn that you can."

Val stared at her, expecting Ashley to give in because Ashley always gave in, but this time Ashley wasn't, and eventually Val figured it out. "You're leaving?"

"Yeah."

"When?"

"I'm getting on a plane tomorrow. I don't know what'll happen, but I have to try. I love him. I'm going to be with him. I'm going to be happy. That's my dream. I want my dream, and you're not going to take it away."

Val's face paled and she took a step back. "I'm sorry. I didn't mean to do that to you."

"I know. But you did. And we're fixing it."

"LADIES AND GENTS, it's bad weather in New York. The fog on the east coast is killing visibility, and we're waiting on the plane to get here. It's in the air, and should be here within half an hour. I apologize for the delay, and appreciate the patience. Sit tight, and I promise we'll be boarding within the hour."

With a cautious eye, Ashley surveyed the family across the gate area. The toddler looked especially deadly with the sugar-infused, "I haven't had my nap" laughter. If there were justice in the world, Ashley would be on aisle seven and the family would be on aisle thirty-seven. It wasn't that she hated kids—some day she would probably want them—but squishy hormones didn't automatically translate to the apocalyptical desire to spend more time in the terror-filled skies.

She leaned her head against the back of the hard chair and closed her eyes, blocking out the noise and chaos that was O'Hare. Today's hellish air travel conditions seemed the price she was going to have to pay for being too cowardly to call. But how did you pick up the phone and explain this new, tougher Ashley? It seemed...wimpy and undetermined. This was a conversation she needed to have in person. She wanted to look in his eyes, watch them melt to an earthy green or freeze to an icy black and then she would know where they stood.

"Ladies and gents, the flight is in. We'll let the New York passengers depart, and then we'll send in the maintenance crew, and before you know it, you'll be on your way."

At last. The doors opened and the passengers streamed out. Ashley watched them emerge: one woman in a clever royal-blue shirt dress with great lines, a teenager in a leather jacket, boot-cut jeans tucked into boots, a woman in a suit, circa 1940, totally *Casablanca,* with a cinched jacket that would be killer uncomfortable. While she pondered whether style should trump comfort, she nearly missed the next passenger, but her heart knew, her mind knew, and her eyes widened at the man in khakis and a blue button-down shirt.

There was a lined crease in the khakis because it took a seriously neat man to iron his khakis. The soft brown hair was longer than before, badly in need of a trim, and that cowlick on the back...her fingers ached to soothe it.

His gaze met hers, dark brows arched in surprise, but he didn't smile, and she wished he would smile. Her heart pinched with something easily identified as fear, but now there was something new. Hope. David was here. Surely that had to count for something.

He took the seat across from her, legs splayed, his hands hard on his thighs. "You're arriving or departing?" he asked, still not smiling, and there was an intensity in his face that gave her a nervous chill.

She licked her lips, his eyes followed the movement, her body lit like a match, and she wished they could simply fall into bed. Everything was so much easier when it was only passion. When this had first started, passion was her only purpose. It was fun, pleasurable, and she didn't have to worry about getting hurt. Somewhere along the way, her heart had started taking risks again. Following the lead of her brave heart, Ashley took a deep breath. This was it, do or die. "I was flying to New York."

"For business?" he asked, in a voice that indicated he wasn't taking risks yet. Okay, fine.

"No."

"You didn't call."

"I was afraid you wouldn't talk to me, that you would think that I wasn't serious. I thought if I got on a plane, and left my life here, you would know I was serious."

"That's what you're doing?"

Still he was forcing her farther out on the ledge. Ashley raised her chin. "I have a broker who's looking for a buyer for the stores."

"Wow."

He didn't look happy, only shocked. She didn't need shock, she needed agreement, concurrence, some sort of sign that she had not just jumped out of the airplane without a chute.

"You were right," she told him, and that caught his attention in a way that store-selling and Ashley's potential relocation plans had not.

"About what?" he asked, his eyes curious, and maybe, hopefully, thawing just a little.

"I told Val that I was moving because I thought I was holding her back. As long as I was there to protect her, she wouldn't trust herself, and she needs to learn to trust herself. To know that she's strong enough solo."

"You told her that?" He was surprised. She could hear it, and she was inordinately pleased that she had surprised him. He didn't know how much he had taught her.

"I did."

"How'd she take it?"

"Better than most anyone could have imagined," she said, glancing down at his carry-on. The same tidy black hard-sided Samsonite that she knew by sight. She'd been so caught up in her own worries that she'd neglected the obvious. "Why are you here?"

For a second he hesitated, his eyes reluctant. "I thought you might need me," he said, his voice low, nervous. So, Ashley wasn't the only one who didn't like standing on the ledge.

"Even though you thought I was making a mistake?" Perhaps there was some cockiness in her tone.

He nodded. "I stayed away as long as I could, but I need you, Ashley." As he talked, the words ran faster. "You should know that I'm a very responsible man, but can be stubborn when I know I'm right. Yes, I have taken defensive driving, but sometimes, a lot of times, sensitivity escapes me, and I have only picked up strange women in airports once, and it was the best day of my entire life." When he looked at her with pleading eyes, everything fell into place. David was terrified.

Her mouth twitched into almost a smile because honestly, standing out on a ledge was so much nicer when you had someone to share it with. "Twice."

"What?"

"You have only picked up strange women in airports twice."

"Are you toying with me, Ashley Larsen?"

"I am."

His chest heaved with a visible sigh. "I brought you a present."

"I love your presents."

"I know," he said, holding out a small box wrapped in gold.

She ripped off the paper to reveal… "*Aliens.* Look at you."

"It's horror, yet sci-fi as well. I felt it was symbolic." He was blushing. She loved that he blushed. He was so strong, and so arrogant, and so stubborn…and yet, then he did these foolish things that pulled at her heart.

"How many copies did you buy?" she asked, not wanting to admit that her heart could be bought with such a trivial gift as classic-horror DVDs.

"Only one," he answered, his voice amused.

"I like the sound of that. No more long-distance television co-watching."

"Nope. If I want to grab you, I have that right."

At that moment, she wanted to touch him, but some invisible hand held her back. Always before they had jumped to the physical first, but this time there were things that needed to be said.

"I love you. You should know that there's baggage in my family and it will probably always be there."

He took her hand, stroking his thumb over her palm. "I love you, too, Ash, and we'll work through it with Val."

"Maybe, but for now, I want to see how she does."

"Maybe she'll do fine."

"I don't know, but I haven't tried moving away before. Maybe it'll do good."

She could feel his strength flowing through her, into her. Someday she would tell him how very desperately she needed him, but not today.

"I found a place for you," he offered, and she was immediately insulted.

"I thought I could live with you. What was all that, 'come live with me and be my love'? No, buddy, once those words were out, you were tied to me for life in ways you could not imagine."

"Not an apartment. A shop. It's in Brooklyn, not far from Enrique because I think your sartorial sign is very Park Slope. All new moms and a more sophisticated palette. Chelsea, Soho? That's not you."

"I could be Chelsea," she told him because she didn't want to be Brooklyn. She wanted to be *über*Chelsea, the cutting edge of style and aesthetic.

David launched a defense of his own position. "I don't know, Ashley. Chelsea? Do you know what happens there? It's pencil skirts and stilettos and red-lined capes and finger-cut opera gloves that come up to the neck, and lots of gold chains. Very avant-garde. It's not your signature. Your style is very traditional. Never argue with your style."

Ashley looked down at the trademarked Ashley Larsen flounce skirt, now pleasingly paired with boots—albeit classical ones—and a V-neck buttercup sweater that was best defined as "traditional."

She gazed at him, he gazed back with his trademark "I'm right" eyebrow-quirk, and at that moment, all was perfect in her world.

"Flight ten-eighty-seven to New York is now boarding. First class, or passengers with small children are now invited to board."

Ashley perked up at the announcement. "That's my flight."

Instantly David frowned. "You don't want to go on this flight. Did you see the sadistic gleam in that kid's eyes? He's going to scream the whole way, and I swear those were Cheerios in his hands that he was firing like missiles. You'll end up with a splitting headache that no aspirin can cure, and who wants to start off in New York with a splitting headache and cleavage full of breakfast cereal?"

"You have a better idea?" she asked, surprised. She had suspected that he would want to depart Chicago as fast as he could.

"Oh, yeah. Here's the deal, you miss the flight, and the airline will honor the ticket later, possibly charge you a change fee, but if you have the right connections, they'll even waive that."

"And you have the right connections?"

"I can be persuasive. I know, it's hard to believe, but yes, the airlines love me."

"You want to go with me back to the house?"

David looked at her with horror. "Are you kidding? No way." He picked up her carry-on, slung it over his shoulder. "I know this room. Honestly. It's great. There's some noise from the planes, but you get used to it really fast."

She got up, left the crowded gate area and began to follow him. She was going to follow him anywhere. "Twice. This is definitely twice."

He glanced over, his eyes were earnest. "So this is working?"

"Like a charm." They passed the newsstand, and familiar memories came rushing back, but this time, there wasn't any nervous reaction, no worries. This was right. This was fate. "Do we need to stop for supplies?"

He turned to stare, disappointment covering his face. "Do I look like a man who comes unprepared?"

"No."

"You keep underestimating me, Ash."

"You are so full of yourself, David," she said, catching his hand.

He bent low, whispered into her ear. "I want you full of myself."

"Pervert," she whispered back.

"I'm a guy. Sue me."

"I love you, David."

"Love you, too, Ash."

And from somewhere behind them, the passengers boarded the plane, departing Chicago for New York. Tomorrow Ashley would worry about the flight. Right now, she only needed one thing, and she had him.

David.

Epilogue

IT WAS A SNOWY Chicago day in January, the very first day to be exact, and there was a small rental truck parked outside the Larsen house. The truck was loaded with boxes, mostly containing an assortment of shoes, skirts, sweaters, shirts and hats. These were Ashley's belongings, and she was torn between needing to organize both her old life and her new one all at the same time.

"Prudence Mayhew was telling me about Saks," Brianna chirped, trailing behind her aunt, while Ashley shuttled boxes from her bedroom to the front hallway. "I want to shop Saks. I could get some new boots, like yours, Aunt Ash. Those are killer boots."

Val shook her head ruefully. "Those are your genes, Ash. Not mine."

Every now and then, Ashley would stop and study her sister, waiting for her to crack or fall apart, but she never did. Val was holding up fine. Maybe this would work after all.

From the living room, David hefted a box on his shoulder. As the muscles rippled in his arms and his back, Ashley found herself feeling a little flushed.

Val sighed. "Nothing like watching a strong man do good physical work."

"Play your cards right, little sister, and you, too, could win one for your very own."

Their mother stepped into the room, carrying one of Ashley's old photo albums and handing it over. "Let's not put the cart before the horse. Val has a lot of work to do—"

"Which she will," Ashley assured her sister.

"—before she's ready to tackle a man."

Wisely, David ignored the women and kept hauling boxes back and forth. This took longer than it should due to the fact that Ashley's mother kept finding old boxes of Ashley memorabilia tucked throughout the house.

While her mother went to retrieve another of Ashley's boxes, Ashley took the time to go over her final instructions.

"Brianna, you have the folders all organized for your mom?"

"Bills, reminders, school junk and important papers."

Ashley nodded. "Very good. Now, Val, if you need to find something, ask Brianna, and she'll know where to start looking."

David came back into the house, snow dusting his hair and the shoulders of his coat. "Last box," he said, and Ashley noticed the look that passed between him and Val. There was a truce, although Val still had issues with him, but David had been...dare she say it? Sensitive.

Of course, Val had been on her best behavior, making a meeting every day, showing up for work early and keeping Brianna up-to-date on school to-dos.

Feeling brave enough to leave them alone, Ashley pulled Brianna back into her bedroom, which looked sadly bereft without her pictures, her collection of hats and the pile of magazines strewn by her bed. She ducked into the closet and pulled out a shoe box.

Solemnly, she put a hand over the lid before Brianna could lift it.

"This is a very, very important secret, Brianna. I'm going to make you give me the world's best promise that you will keep it."

"I'm very bad at secrets, Aunt Ash. I open my mouth and the truth flies out."

Ashley's mouth quirked at the corners. "Yes, I know, we all have our weaknesses, but you have to promise. It's for your mother."

At that, Brianna nodded once. "I swear. What am I swearing for?"

Ashley patted the box. "Sometimes your mother might have problems. You know, big problems, and her voice will get extra screechy, and when that happens, and she's using a lot of really bad words and you're worried about her, I want you to come in my room, grab the box and give it to her."

"Like a present?"

"Exactly."

"What's in the box?"

"You can keep it quiet?"

Brianna considered the question, chewed her lip, then finally nodded. "I can do it."

Ashley lifted the lid.

Brianna gasped. "Those are your bunny slippers. You're giving them to Mom?"

"She might need them. Bunny slippers are a magical thing. When you slip on the power of these puppies, there's not a lot you can't overcome. When Val gets upset, you make her wear these, and tell her that Aunt Ash is watching, and she's right there. Can you remember all that?"

"I think so."

"Are you scared, Brianna?"

"Nah. Not as long as you promise to take me shopping at Saks. Prudence would really kill to shop there, she told me."

"Not only courageous, but mercenary as well. I don't know where you got those genes, Brianna, but treasure them. They will get you far."

David poked his head in the room. "The snow's really starting to pick up. We should leave."

Ashley's niece studied him with somber brown eyes. "We're going to miss her."

David smile was apologetic. "I know. I'm sorry."

Eventually Brianna shrugged, because to an eight-year-old, the world was a simple place. "We'll be okay."

Ashley gave Brianna a quick hug. "I think so, too."

It was another hour before all the goodbyes were said, and finally Ashley was taking a step off the curb.

New York.

She was moving to New York. She swallowed hard, took a good long look at David. She loved him, she trusted him, she knew him, but this was huge, this was…

Ash, he's not a serial killer. I will never ever say this aloud, but he's good for you. He's holding your dreams safe. That's worth bonus points.

Ashley stared hard at her sister, who was waving, managing a smile, all while blinking furiously.

You're right, Val.

I know I'm right.

The snow began to fall faster, the ground turning from icy brown to pristine white, and Brianna picked up a patch of snow and threw it at her grandmother. Ashley smiled. They would be fine.

David opened the door, watching her closely. "You're sure?"

She gave him her hand and climbed in the cab. "Positive."

Outside was cold, the wind starting to pick up, but the heater was running on high, and here she was warm, safe…. Fearless. She waved out the window, hoping her mother would remember to keep the oil changed, hoping that Brianna would keep up with her homework, and hoping Val would stay strong.

"She's going to be okay. Those Larsen women, honestly, they don't know their own strength." David gave her shoulder a comforting squeeze before starting up the engine and pulling away from the curb.

"You're right, David."

"I know I'm right."

Ashley leaned over and surprised him with a kiss.

"What was that for?"

"For letting my family fly out to visit over spring break." The darling man didn't even looked shocked. "I think they'll really enjoy seeing the city, and Brianna, she's got a great eye for fashion. So are you shaking with fear at the prospect?" she asked, eyeing him carefully.

"Not even a quiver."

Ashley's smile was slow, but sure. "I'm feeling a quiver. Do you want to know where?"

"Seven hundred and ninety-two miles, and you're going to torture me the entire way?"

"It's the new me."

"Don't make me stop this car."

Ashley laughed and rested her head on his shoulder, no bunny slippers necessary. Yes, indeed, everything was going to be just fine.

*Celebrate Harlequin's 60th anniversary with
Harlequin® Superromance®
and the DIAMOND LEGACY miniseries!*

*Follow the stories of four cousins as they come to terms with
the complications of love and what it means to be a family.
Discover with them the sixty-year-old secret that rocks not
one but two families in…
A DAUGHTER'S TRUST by Tara Taylor Quinn.*

*Available in September 2009 from
Harlequin® Superromance®*

RICK'S APPOINTMENT with his attorney early Wednesday morning went only moderately better than his meeting with social services the day before. The prognosis wasn't great—but at least his attorney was going to file a motion for DNA testing. Just so Rick could petition to see the child...his sister's baby. The sister he didn't know he had until it was too late.

The rest of what his attorney said had been downhill from there.

Cell phone in hand before he'd even reached his Nitro, Rick punched in the speed dial number he'd programmed the day before.

Maybe foster parent Sue Bookman hadn't received his message. Or had lost his number. Maybe she didn't want to talk to him. At this point he didn't much care what she wanted.

"Hello?" She answered before the first ring was complete. And sounded breathless.

Young and breathless.

"Ms. Bookman?"

"Yes. This is Rick Kraynick, right?"

"Yes, ma'am."

"I recognized your number on caller ID," she said, her voice uneven, as though she was still engaged in whatever physical activity had her so breathless to begin with. "I'm sorry I didn't get back to you. I've been a little...distracted."

The words came in more disjointed spurts. Was she jogging?

"No problem," he said, when, in fact, he'd spent the better

part of the night before watching his phone. And fretting. "Did I get you at a bad time?"

"No worse than usual," she said, adding, "Better than some. So, how can I help?"

God, if only this could be so easy. He'd ask. She'd help. And life could go well. At least for one little person in his family.

It would be a first.

"Mr. Kraynick?"

"Yes. Sorry. I was…are you sure there isn't a better time to call?"

"I'm bouncing a baby, Mr. Kraynick. It's what I do."

"Is it Carrie?" he asked quickly, his pulse racing.

"How do you know Carrie?" She sounded defensive, which wouldn't do him any good.

"I'm her uncle," he explained, "her mother's—Christy's—older brother, and I know you have her."

"I can neither confirm nor deny your allegations, Mr. Kraynick. Please call social services." She rattled off the number.

"Wait!" he said, unable to hide his urgency. "Please," he said more calmly. "Just hear me out."

"How did you find me?"

"A friend of Christy's."

"I'm sorry I can't help you, Mr. Kraynick," she said softly. "This conversation is over."

"I grew up in foster care," he said, as though that gave him some special privilege. Some insider's edge.

"Then you know you shouldn't be calling me at all."

"Yes… But Carrie is my niece," he said. "I need to see her. To know that she's okay."

"You'll have to go through social services to arrange that."

"I'm sure you know it's not as easy as it sounds. I'm a single man with no real ties and I've no intention of petitioning for custody. They aren't real eager to give me the time of day. I never even knew Carrie's mother. For all intents and purposes, our mother didn't raise either one of us. All I have going for me is half a set of genes. My lawyer's on it, but it could be weeks—months—before this is sorted out. Carrie could be adopted by then. Which would be fine, great for her, but then I'd have lost my chance. I don't want to take her. I won't hurt her. I just have to see her."

"I'm sorry, Mr. Kraynick, but…"

* * * * *

*Find out if Rick Kraynick will ever have a chance to meet his niece.
Look for A DAUGHTER'S TRUST by Tara Taylor Quinn, available in September 2009.*

Copyright © 2009 by Tara Taylor Quinn

HARLEQUIN 60 YEARS of pure reading pleasure

We'll be spotlighting a different series every month throughout 2009 to celebrate our 60th anniversary.

Look for Harlequin® Superromance® in September!

Celebrate with The Diamond Legacy miniseries!

Follow the stories of four cousins as they come to terms with the complications of love and what it means to be a family. Discover with them the sixty-year-old secret that rocks not one but two families.

A DAUGHTER'S TRUST by *Tara Taylor Quinn*
September

FOR THE LOVE OF FAMILY by *Kathleen O'Brien*
October

LIKE FATHER, LIKE SON by *Karina Bliss*
November

A MOTHER'S SECRET by *Janice Kay Johnson*
December

Available wherever books are sold.

---

www.eHarlequin.com

HSRBPA09

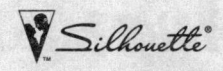

SPECIAL EDITION

FROM *NEW YORK TIMES* BESTSELLING AUTHOR

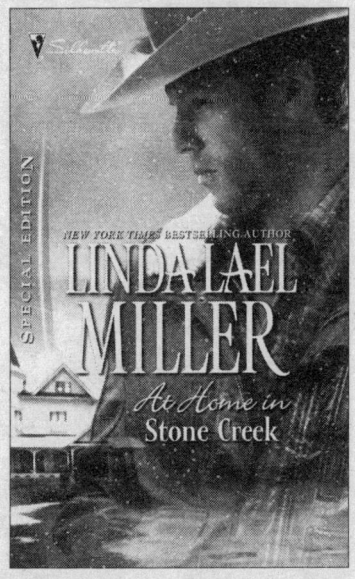

Ashley O'Ballivan had her heart broken by a man years ago—and now he's mysteriously back. Jack McCall *isn't* the person she thinks he is. For her sake, he must keep his distance, but his feelings for her are powerful. To protect her—from his enemies and himself—he has to leave...vowing to fight his way home to her and Stone Creek forever.

Available in November wherever books are sold.

Visit Silhouette Books at www.eHarlequin.com

REQUEST YOUR FREE BOOKS!

2 FREE NOVELS PLUS 2 FREE GIFTS!

HARLEQUIN® *Blaze*™
Red-hot reads!

YES! Please send me 2 FREE Harlequin® Blaze™ novels and my 2 FREE gifts (gifts are worth about $10). After receiving them, if I don't wish to receive any more books, I can return the shipping statement marked "cancel". If I don't cancel, I will receive 6 brand-new novels every month and be billed just $4.24 per book in the U.S. or $4.71 per book in Canada. That's a savings of 15% off the cover price. It's quite a bargain. Shipping and handling is just 50¢ per book.* I understand that accepting the 2 free books and gifts places me under no obligation to buy anything. I can always return a shipment and cancel at any time. Even if I never buy another book, the two free books and gifts are mine to keep forever.

151 HDN EYS2 351 HDN EYTE

Name	(PLEASE PRINT)	
Address		Apt. #
City	State/Prov.	Zip/Postal Code

Signature (if under 18, a parent or guardian must sign)

Mail to the Harlequin Reader Service:
IN U.S.A.: P.O. Box 1867, Buffalo, NY 14240-1867
IN CANADA: P.O. Box 609, Fort Erie, Ontario L2A 5X3

Not valid to current subscribers of Harlequin Blaze books.

Want to try two free books from another line?
Call 1-800-873-8635 or visit www.morefreebooks.com.

* Terms and prices subject to change without notice. Prices do not include applicable taxes. N.Y. residents add applicable sales tax. Canadian residents will be charged applicable provincial taxes and GST. Offer not valid in Quebec. This offer is limited to one order per household. All orders subject to approval. Credit or debit balances in a customer's account(s) may be offset by any other outstanding balance owed by or to the customer. Please allow 4 to 6 weeks for delivery. Offer available while quantities last.

Your Privacy: Harlequin Books is committed to protecting your privacy. Our Privacy Policy is available online at www.eHarlequin.com or upon request from the Reader Service. From time to time we make our lists of customers available to reputable third parties who may have a product or service of interest to you. If you would prefer we not share your name and address, please check here. ☐

You're invited to join our Tell Harlequin Reader Panel!

By joining our new reader panel you will:

- Receive Harlequin® books—they are FREE and yours to keep with no obligation to purchase anything!
- Participate in fun online surveys
- Exchange opinions and ideas with women just like you
- Have a say in our new book ideas and help us publish the best in women's fiction

In addition, you will have a chance to win great prizes and receive special gifts! See Web site for details. Some conditions apply. Space is limited.

To join, visit us at
www.TellHarlequin.com.

Tell
HARLEQUIN

HARLEQUIN Blaze

COMING NEXT MONTH
Available August 25, 2009

#489 GETTING PHYSICAL Jade Lee
For American student/waitress Zoe Lewis, Tantric sex—sex as a spiritual experience—is a totally foreign concept. Strange, yet irresistible. Then she's partnered with Tantric master Stephen Chiu…and discovers just how far great sex can take a girl!

#490 MADE YOU LOOK Jamie Sobrato
Forbidden Fantasies
She spies with her little eye… From the privacy of her living room Arianna Day has a front-row seat for her neighbor Noah Quinn's sex forays. And she knows he's the perfect man to end her bout of celibacy. Now to come up with the right plan to make him look…

#491 TEXAS HEAT Debbi Rawlins
Encounters
Four college girlfriends arrive at the Sugarloaf ranch to celebrate an engagement announcement. With all the tasty cowboys around, each will have a reunion weekend she'll never forget!

#492 FEELS LIKE THE FIRST TIME Tawny Weber
Dressed to Thrill
Zoe Gaston hated high school. So the thought of going back for her reunion doesn't exactly thrill her. Little does she guess that there's a really hot guy who's been waiting ten long years to do just that!

#493 HER LAST LINE OF DEFENSE Marie Donovan
Uniformly Hot!
Instructing a debutante in survival training is not how Green Beret Luc Boudreau planned to spend his temporary leave. Problem is, he kind of likes this feisty fish out of water and it turns out the feeling's mutual. But will they find any common ground other than their shared bedroll…?

#494 ONE GOOD MAN Alison Kent
American Heroes: The Texas Rangers
Jamie Danby needs a hero—badly. As the only witness to a brutal shooting, she's been flying below the radar for years. Now her cover's blown and she needs a sexy Texas Ranger around 24/7 to make her feel safe. The best sex of her life is just a bonus!

www.eHarlequin.com